PRAISE FOR M J TROW & MARYANNE COLEMAN

'Trow makes the political intrigue of the time palpable.'
Publishers Weekly

'Trow's style is subtle and often humorous'
mysteryfile.com

'Among the charms of Trow's Lestrade novels…are tight historical detail, an unusual mix of slapstick and literate humor, and unpredictable plots'
Publishers Weekly

Also by M J Trow & Maryanne Coleman

The Kit Marlowe Series
Grand & Bachelor Mysteries
The Maxwell Series
The Lestrade Series
Goblin Market
Pandemonium

The Year of the Snake

M J TROW & MARYANNE COLEMAN

LUME BOOKS

LUME BOOKS

First published in 2018 by Lume Books
30 Great Guildford St,
London, SE1 0HS

ISBN 978-1-83901-173-3

www.lumebooks.co.uk

About the authors

Mei (M.J.) and **Carol (Maryanne Coleman) Trow** have been married for forty-five years and have been writing together for roughly seven. Mei was a teacher for thirty-six years, retiring in 2008, and Carol was a biomedical scientist for almost thirty years, with a brief break when their son, Taliesin, was born. Writing as Maryanne, Carol has written two books of a fantasy trilogy, *Goblin Market* and *Pandemonium*. Mei has written almost one hundred books altogether, fiction and non-fiction which includes military, historical biography, true crime and some acclaimed 'ghosting' projects, including the number one bestseller *Survivor*. They live on the Isle of Wight in a wing of a Victorian vicarage and don't have much time for hobbies, though if they did, they would include illustration, militaria collecting, reading and gardening. Their grandson Arthur is their favourite hobby, however, and one for which they can always find time.

I

The dead man lay propped on his pillow in the tablinum, surrounded by the scrolls of his books. Those that weren't written in elegant Greek were by writers of the old school – Cicero, Cato the Censor, Terentius Afer. He had had no time for the scurrilous poets of his boyhood and had once flogged Calidus for reading the filthy passages of Ovid.

It was Calidus who knelt at his side now, as the single candle flame flickered in the cool night air. All his life he had known this man, ridden with him on the hunt, followed his litter bearers through the teeming streets of Rome, talked with him in the dying embers of the day. Calidus looked up, to the wall beyond the makeshift bed and saw the letters glittering there, their planished bronze sending back the guttering light – *SPQR*, the Senate and the People of Rome. The slave knew perfectly well that this was the last time he would have the old man to himself, to enjoy the companionship of his silence as he had so often. Soon, the women would come to wash the body and smother it in oil. They would wrap him in his best toga, the one he had hated wearing, with its hundred folds and its purple edge, and then he would begin his last journey with Charon, the ferryman, across the Styx. And he would become a public thing, an object of devotion or derision, depending on the men who bore his coffin and watched him burn. Tonight, just for a few moments, the old man belonged to his slave alone. To the slave who was his steward, his book-keeper, his companion of a mile.

'Well, well,' Calidus could already hear men say, as they reached over to say their farewells, 'old Nerva, eh? I thought he was dead already. End of an era. The Esquiline won't be the same. Thank the gods for that – now we can all have some peace. Jupiter Highest and Best; I thought he'd never die.'

Calidus smiled. He could see them all now, old Nerva's fellow senators, the proconsuls and governors who had quaked before him, the fishmongers who served him in the Forum Boarium, the barber Civilis who trimmed his hair and shaved him daily. Some would be crying. Some would be laughing. One who was crying, Calidus thought of now. His Paula had loved the old man, as all his people did. She had been there earlier today, at Flavia's side as the widow had kissed her husband for the last time, tears splashing down her cheeks and landing like kisses from her very soul on the old man's face, swept smooth of the cares of life by the hand of death. Then the women had gone, and the house on the Esquiline had fallen silent.

Calidus had bent to whisper his own farewell when something stopped him. The old man's tunic was stained yellow at the front, just below the scrawny neck. This wasn't right. 'Peacefully in his sleep,' the messenger had said, riding hard through the night out of the Flaminian Gate for the villa at Tibur; the face itself was peaceful enough, but the vomit ...

'Papirius!' the slave shouted, crossing the study in two strides and hauling the curtain aside. 'Papirius, are you there?'

'Yes, yes,' Papirius shuffled to his feet. His gout was killing him, and it *was* the middle of the night. 'What?'

'What's this?' Calidus pointed to the stains on the tunic.

Papirius Longinus had been the family doctor forever. He had brought all three of old Nerva's sons into the world and had, one by one, pronounced them dead. He didn't usually bother himself with slaves, but Calidus was different – how different, he might never know. Papirius had lifted him, too, struggling and wriggling, from between his mother's straining thighs, but not in this house, and not on the Esquiline. He had attended Calidus' wedding, smiling benignly as Paula placed her offering on the altar of the household gods, the dolls of her childhood, the rattle of her earliest years. And like the mother hen he was, he had clucked and fussed over their child, the flame-haired Paulina, when she had first come into the world on a wild night in November, just over a year ago.

'Vomit.' Papirius turned to go back to his couch; standing was something he tried to avoid when he could, especially in the middle of the night, and besides, it hardly took a man of medicine to identify that.

Calidus' face said it all. 'They told me he went peacefully.'

The doctor looked down at his old friend. 'Nobody goes peacefully, Calidus,' he said. 'That's just something you tell loved ones, for their peace of mind. When they called me, he was rambling, incoherent. He was lying here. Clearly, he'd been trying to read, but it was all too much for him. He told me he could hear his heart beating, feel it like a drum in his chest. There was a snake, he said, there,' the doctor pointed, 'in the corner.'

'Hallucinations?'

'Undoubtedly. He wouldn't be quiet, however, until I checked. Needless to say, there was nothing.'

'But the snake ...'

'... is the guardian of the underworld and writhes, hissing, in the hair of the gorgon, yes, I know. On the other hand, it is the animal of choice of Aesculapius, a god I am particularly fond of, as it happens. There's a street vendor near the Basilica Aemilia who sings to the slithery buggers, plays the flute for them and they dance. Sometimes, a snake is just a snake. And sometimes it's just something in an old man's head as he dies.'

'Even so ...'

Papirius chuckled, an odd sound in the middle of the night in that room of death. 'You slaves,' he shook his head. 'This is the third year of the reign of little Nero, may all his troubles be imperial ones. This is Rome, the navel of the world. See that?' The doctor pointed through the open archway to the altar of the lares, where the household gods flickered eerily by candlelight. 'Ossipago, Genialis, Tellus Mater – all of it claptrap.'

'Papirius ...' Calidus didn't believe in tempting fate like this. You couldn't be too careful.

The doctor leaned towards the slave. 'There's only one God, Calidus, my clever boy – it's called science. Trust me. There was no snake.' He looked down again at his old friend, the face calm in the candlelight, its demons fled and he patted his shoulder. 'Just the ramblings of an old man.'

'All right,' Calidus said. 'Forget the snake. What caused his death, Papirius? What does your god of science tell you about that?'

The doctor looked at him. 'The truth?' he asked.

'Nothing else will do,' Calidus told him.

'He killed himself.'

The silence of the room was almost painful. The hiss and click of the burning candle wicks sounded as loud as thunder.

'What?'

Papirius shrugged. 'What's fine, what's Roman,' he said. 'I don't know whether you've noticed, but there's a lot of it about.'

Calidus was shaking his head. 'He'd have asked me,' he said, 'to help him. His hands were getting shaky, and he didn't have as much power in his grip anymore, but he would have used a sword. *That's* the Roman way.'

'Agreed,' the doctor said. 'But old Nerva was a troubled soul. Believe me.'

'Troubled? Why?'

Papirius took the boy by the arm and led him away from the corpse on the bed. 'How old are you, Cal?' He knew the answer already.

'Twenty-one summers,' the slave told him.

'Twenty-one summers,' the doctor nodded, 'and you haven't finished shitting yellow yet. Oh, you're aptly named – Calidus, the clever one – you're smart, and you learn quickly. And yes, you're steward of the house of Nerva – no mean achievement in one so young. But you're also a child and a child of your class. The day a slave understands the world – the real world, that is – I'll hang up my scalpel and call it a day. Let it go, boy.' Papirius patted Calidus' arm, absent-mindedly comforting him. 'Gaius Lucius Nerva had his demons.' He glanced back to the body of his friend. 'And no doubt you'd say they have him now. But …' Papirius stopped for a moment, emotion filling his chest. A horrible thought had just occurred to him, and he needed a moment to close this particular Pandora's box before everything escaped and filled his brain; he was now the oldest man he knew. Not a comfortable thought for one who spent his life battling mortality. He gave himself a shake. 'Now, come on. There's much to be done. Let me get my women to work. And you've got the munera ceremonies to sort out – I doubt Flavia will be able to cope on her own.'

Calidus looked at the body too. He knew that Papirius was right. There was much to be done. Even so, as he crossed the room to call in the women who did these things, he swore he saw a snake slither across the floor.

*

The slave Quinius had accompanied the old man during his last days. Calidus had been at the villa in Tibur, in the beautiful country away from the hells of Rome. Gaius Nerva had read daily, as was his habit, played a little dice, staggered to the baths of Agrippa. He had even accepted a dinner invitation at the Villa Gellius, not that he could stand the man. It was soon after that that the old man had become introverted, strange. Cold, unblinking eyes, he told Quinius, were watching him from the darkness, and a forked tongue was licking his face.

'Make it stop, Quinius,' the old man had pleaded. 'Make it stop.'

II

Flavia looked in the mirror as the candles beside her table wavered and flared. In the bubble surface of polished bronze, she saw … what? A lonely widow with one foot in the grave and the other on the planking of Charon's boat? She allowed herself a smile. No, the girl in her was still there, rattling the abacus beads; wearing the fox skin in the wilderness; wrestling with her brothers, always older, always stronger; standing as a bride at the altar in her saffron shoes and red veil. She had been twelve and terrified of the handsome man who was the youngest senator in Rome. But he had been kindness itself, not just on their wedding night but for all the nights that followed. She had borne him three sons, and the gods had taken them all. They had given her no daughters; Juno had not smiled on her, but Cupid had and Venus and Fortuna, after a fashion. Flavia could not complain.

But what now? Gaius had been her rock; always there, always steady, as the storm of politics had raged around him. There was no rock, now, only the hiss and crash of the waves of life as a widow, throwing spume and sorrow into the air so she could scarcely see. The tears that blinded her eyes rolled, one by one, unheeded down her face, and she tasted salt in her mouth.

Then, someone, tapping at the door, saying her name. Could it be, that after all … she turned from the mirror, hope brightening her eyes. But no, it was not Gaius, not dead after all, laughing and chaffing her for being so sad.

'Calidus,' she said, with as much of a smile as she could muster. 'Come in.'

'It's late, mistress,' he said, bowing his head.

'It's never too late for you,' she said, 'and whatever happened to "Mater Flavia"?'

He smiled too. 'I couldn't presume ...' he began, but her raised hand stopped him.

'I don't think Paula has to bother with the white make-up tomorrow, do you?' She turned to the mirror again. 'I'm pale enough as it is.' Calidus stepped forward and stood next to her, sharing the reflection. She took his hand. 'What will become of us, Calidus?' she asked him.

'We'll carry on, Mater Flavia,' he said, 'as we always have.'

'Will we?' There was pain etched on her still-lovely face, and there was fear there too. 'You know what this is?' She held up a parchment scroll, heavy with wax and ribbons. 'Gaius' will.'

'I wrote it, Mater Flavia,' he said, 'remember?'

'Yes. Yes, of course. How silly of me. You knew he wanted all the ceremonies – the hunt, the games, the oration.'

'He shall have them,' Calidus said. 'I'll start first thing tomorrow.'

'Thank you, Calidus.' She let go of his hand. 'There's one more thing.' She got up and crossed to a box on her bedside table. There was another scroll here, smaller than her husband's will but wrapped in ribbon all the same. She broke the seal, opened it and smiled. Then she passed it to him. 'I don't believe you wrote this.'

Calidus hadn't. It was in Nerva's hand, marked by the slight wobble of an old man's fingers. He read it in astonishment and let the parchment fall. He looked at her uncomprehendingly.

Her eyes creased into a smile. 'It's not all that unusual, Calidus,' she said. 'Many great men free their slaves when they die. You know he loved you like a son?'

Calidus could only nod.

'Then, as of today, you are Gaius Lucius Calidus, and you are a free man.' She stood in front of him, holding both of his hands in hers. 'As my token to you, I am setting Paula free too. The world lies before you, Gaius Lucius Calidus. All you cannot do in this great empire of ours is hold public office. Nothing else is beyond you.'

He wanted to hold the woman, take her in his arms as she had held him so often as a child. But, a moment ago, he was a slave, without rights, without a name, without existence under the law. He couldn't wipe all that away like the tears that trickled down both their cheeks. The clay slave tags still hung around his neck.

'What will you do?' she asked him.

'What I have always done, Mater Flavia,' he said. 'Serve you and the house of Nerva.'

She nodded, biting her lips to stop herself from bursting into helpless weeping. She had shed enough tears already this night; more would break her. 'Look after it, Calidus,' she whispered. 'I won't always be here. Look after the house of Nerva for me, won't you?'

*

'What?' Paula looked into her husband's eyes. This was surely no time for jokes, and yet … 'Free? Both of us?'

Calidus shrugged and smiled properly for the first time since he had heard the news of Nerva's death. 'Yes. I haven't thrashed out all of the details yet, but …'

'And Paulina?'

'That's one of the details.'

'But … where will we live? *How* will we live?' The world of the freedman might be as wide and as bright as the morning sky, but it had clouds on the horizon. Paula had heard too many stories of freed slaves dead of starvation within a year of their release.

'Mater Flavia will still need us,' Calidus told her. 'I will continue as her steward, you as her maid. But, instead of being slaves, we will be paid a salary, we will still have a roof over our heads. But, Paula, think of it!' He pulled her to him and danced her round the room to a wild music only he could hear. 'We will belong to no man.'

She struggled out of his arms. 'Except each other, presumably,' she said, sulkily.

'Always that,' he pulled her back into his arms and kissed the tip of her nose. 'Always that, my love.'

She was looking down at the slave tag around her neck. 'And what does this do to our marriage?' she asked. 'Are we even still married?'

Calidus blinked. He hadn't even considered that that might change. 'Of course,' he said. 'Our marriage was celebrated properly, you know that.'

'But only with Gaius Nerva's consent,' she said, looking mulish. Love her though he did, Calidus had learned to dread that look. 'A contubernia, that's all. Marriage, but not marriage. That's what we've got.' She scowled at him under her eyebrows, and he laughed out loud.

'Well, that's a big word, isn't it?' he said, but he wondered as he spoke why she had even thought of it. 'But does it matter, in the scheme of things?'

'It matters to me,' she said. 'I think …' and she smiled up at him, the pretence of anger too much to keep up, '… I think we should have another wedding, a proper wedding, with knots in my girdle, and veils, and … and …'

'A party, in other words,' Calidus said.

She stamped her foot, but gently. 'I want to tell the world we love each other, Calidus, that I am your wife. If that sounds like a party to you …' she buried her head in his chest, then raised her face, wreathed in smiles, 'then yes, a party. We owe it to Paulina.'

'And we owe it to Gaius Nerva,' Calidus said, solemnly. 'We owe it to him to make him proud of us.'

'He loved you Calidus,' Paula said, tears springing to her eyes as easily as a smile had come to her lips. 'He always did. Mater Flavia said he used to dandle you on his knee when you were a baby. Even your name was his idea. She told me that the master always said he knew as soon as he saw you that you would be the cleverest man in his household. In Rome, why not?'

Calidus smiled at the memory. 'Yes,' he said. 'He used to tell me that story when I was only a boy. He would say that he saw me when I was just a few hours old, and I looked at him with just one eye, but such a piercing look he almost expected me to speak. He named me Calidus on the spot, and my mother and father were so proud.' He looked into the distance and tried to remember the parents he had scarcely known. His father, just a pair of hard hands and a deep voice above his head which were suddenly not there anymore. His mother, a soft voice and a gentle presence, worn out before her time, trying to be all things to all men; she wasn't spoken of much in the house of Gaius Nerva.

'So … we can get married again, can we? Properly?'

Calidus moved over to a couch and dropped down onto it, suddenly tired to his very bones. 'I'll look into it,' he promised. 'And if we can't, then we will have a party, I promise. All of Rome will know you are my wife. But first …' He buried his head in his hands.

Paula knelt at his feet and gently raised his head so he was looking at her. 'I know you have a lot to arrange, Cal. I'm sorry. I should be thinking about the master … I will never think of him as anything else. Is that wrong?'

'No, of course not.' Calidus pulled her closer and rested his cheek on the top of her glossy head. 'I have a lot to arrange, yes, but … something isn't ringing true to me, Paula. Why did he die like that?'

'He was old.' Her voice was muffled by his arms.

'He was, I can't deny that,' he agreed. 'But … old or not, he was *well*, Paula. He could still do everything he wanted; he walked, he read, he … he was *well*. You saw more of him than I did while I have been at Tibur. He *was* well, wasn't he?'

She nodded, as best she could. 'He seemed so,' she told him. She gave a little chuckle. 'In fact, one of the kitchen girls overheard him and Mater Flavia … well, I don't want to gossip.'

He smiled into her hair. Gossip was meat and drink to his Paula, but she was never vicious or prurient with it, not like some of the other slaves. In his head, he corrected himself, leaving out the 'other'.

'So, everything was as it should be?'

'Yes. Until … the last day or so, he had not been sleeping well. He kept Quinius by him all the time. And Quinius … he won't tell us the details, but the master talked of snakes and dark things. Not like him at all.'

Calidus had known an old woman when he was a child, Matidia, who had gone the same way. She had suddenly started shuffling along the streets, her clothing all anyhow, her eyes wild. She muttered and flapped at invisible beasts in the air around her head. And then, one day, she had lost all movement in one side, had dragged herself into the street and, raving, had died there.

'Could he move his arms? His legs?'

'I didn't hear that he couldn't,' she told him. 'He was reading, nearly to the end.'

'He was sick, though. Vomiting.'

She shook her head. 'I didn't hear that. Perhaps ...' she pulled away from him and wagged her head dubiously. 'Perhaps, just at the end. Perhaps that's what people do, when ...' she baulked at the rest of the sentence. She had no experience of death, not yet.

Calidus had not been so lucky. 'Death isn't pretty,' he said. 'All things escape the body when someone dies. Demons, old Matidia always said. But vomit? I've never heard of nor seen that before. Vomit means one thing to me.'

Paula thought of little Paulina. The child had been colicky and hard to rear, though it was difficult to imagine that now, as she raced through all the day and slept like a beautiful putto all night, her dimpled face surrounded by her glowing curls. When she was sick, she would forget about it in a moment, but in adults, Calidus was right; vomiting was not a sign of health and wellbeing, it meant that something was very wrong, that the body wanted to rid itself of something that should not be in there, whether it was a demon or ... 'Poison,' she muttered, her eyes wide. 'Poison.'

Calidus nodded, and they held each other close again, two against the world, as the word flew like an evil insect, buzzing around the room, tarnishing all it touched in its mad progress.

*

'Io, Saturnalia!'

The smile on Licinius Glabrio's face faded as he spoke. He hated this festival. It served no purpose, except to sow discord and stir up the rabble. December, he knew, had thirty-one days, and the nones fell on the fifth day. The day, leaden-skied and chill, had nine hours. The night, bringing bitter winds from the north, had thirteen. Thirteen hours of darkness, thirteen hours of evil, in which the lamiae, the night owls, took men's breath away; as someone had taken the breath of Gaius Lucius Nerva. The sun was in the sign of Sagittarius, the archer, and the solstice was under the protection of Vesta, whose sacred flame burned forever in the Forum.

Wood was cut. Vines were manured. Beans were sown. But always, at the end of December, the Saturnalia.

'Cheer up, Glabrio.' Marcus Maxentius was riding beside his fellow senator on their way to the hunt, their slaves jogging behind them along the army road. 'Don't worry – *somebody* will give you a present.'

'Damn the presents,' Glabrio grunted. 'It's those buggers behind us who worry me. A pleb's as good as his master at this time of year – tradition insists upon it.' He leaned in closer to the man. 'And I don't know if you've noticed, but they outnumber us four to one, these slaves.'

'We've got a she-wolf by the ears, all right,' Maxentius nodded, 'but Spartacus was a long time ago, old friend. Don't tell me you believe those horror stories your old nanny used to tell you?'

'There's mischief in the wind, Maxentius – I can feel it. And with old Nerva gone …'

'I must admit, I thought he'd been dead for years,' Maxentius said.

Glabrio scowled at the man. 'I know you never liked him,' he said, 'but he was a friend of mine, Maxentius; I'd ask you to remember that. Ah, now *he is* dead.'

Maxentius followed Glabrio's pointing finger. Ahead of them, as the army road narrowed and the cedars dipped towards the river, a knot of horsemen sat, exchanging wine cups and laughing. A wizened old man sat with them, his gelding almost as clapped out as he was.

'Ave, Septimus Numidius,' Maxentius called cheerily.

The old man cupped his good ear with his hand and looked puzzled.

'Marcus Maxentius,' the senator reined in and shook the man's hand. It was like clutching a skeleton. He gestured to his friend. 'Licinius Glabrio.'

'Io. Saturnalia,' the old man crowed, proceeding to unbuckle a party hat from his saddlebag.

'Jupiter Highest and Best,' Maxentius muttered. 'Do you think he's come to the right party? I didn't know it was fancy dress.'

Glabrio nudged him and urged his grey nearer to the old man. 'How are you, Septimus?' he asked, slowly and loudly like you had to.

'Yes, I'm Septimus,' the old man grinned toothlessly. 'Septimus Numidius. I used to be a senator, you know.'

'Jupiter Highest and Best.' Maxentius felt he had to say it again.

'Yes,' Glabrio smiled, 'I know. This is a sad day, Septimus.'

'Saturnalia?' the old man frowned. 'No, no. A happy festival, I've always thought. Parties. Presents. Slaves taking the place of masters. Here!' He turned as well as his old bones would let him in his four-pronged saddle. 'You, boy!' A lad who could have been no more than twelve hurried to his side. 'Have my horse.' And he struggled to dismount.

There was a commotion from the other horsemen, as the boy helped the old man down. 'No, no, that's going too far,' someone said, but Numidius was undeterred. 'It's only once a year,' he beamed, 'and I'm drowning in horses. Can you ride, boy?'

'Yes, master,' the lad said, delighted, terrified and embarrassed all at the same time.

'Up you go, then.'

'What about the hunt, Septimus?' Glabrio asked him.

'Hunt?' the old man was steadying his cup as a slave topped up his wine. 'What hunt?'

*

There was still a mist curling over the Tiber's reeds in the early morning. The city rose like a ghost out of the grey, and the seven hills vanished as if they had never been. The river was brown and sluggish at this time of year, but at least in December, the mosquitoes didn't add to the desolation of the place. The sounds of the city were strangely muted this early in the morning, before the street markets opened and the builders went to work.

The huntsmen had gathered, as requested, at the stand of cedars. Calidus would have preferred this part of the munera to be held in the countryside, at Nerva's villa to the north-east, but that was two hours' hard riding, and he was afraid that many of the old man's friends would not make it that far. As it was, old Septimus Numidius had dropped out. The old man was last seen with a strange sunhat on his head, gabbling away amiably to his slaves as they gently helped him along the road. Not many of the friends had accepted the hunt. Most senators, past and present, were city dwellers. If they travelled anywhere beyond Rome's walls, it was to their country villas, and they were taken there in their carriages. In the city itself, where wheeled vehicles were outlawed during the day, they were carried everywhere on litters. These were not Licinius Glabrio's favourite methods of transport. Whenever he turned up, toga-wrapped, for a Senate meeting, he was all too aware that his life lay in the hands of the four slaves who carried him.

'So … er … Calidus, is it?' Publius Varro had dismounted and was selecting his spear for the morning, from a stand carried by his slaves. He wasn't built for riding – too many wine-rich cenae lolling on couches. 'What's old Nerva dreamed up for us, eh? Giraffes? Camels? Not an elephant, I hope. They've got skins like rhinoceroses. Not sure I've got a spear sharp enough.'

'Wolves, sir,' Calidus told him.

'Wolves?' Varro turned to the man. 'Is that what the will said? Wolves?'

'Um …' Maxentius had caught this conversation. 'We do *know*, do we, about the creation of the city? Romulus? Remus? She-wolves?'

Calidus smiled. 'Have no fear, sir,' he said. 'They're all male.'

'All?' Glabrio was weighting his spear, twirling it expectantly with his left hand and then his right. 'How many have you got?'

'Twenty,' Calidus told him.

'Twenty?' three or four of the huntsmen queried in unison.

'Those buggers hunt in packs, steward,' Maxentius scowled.

'So do we, sir,' Calidus said. 'That'll make it an even contest, won't it?'

The huntsmen weren't so sure. But, if it was in old Nerva's will, so be it. And anyway, Saturnalia or not, this hunt leader was a slave. It wouldn't do to lose face in front of a slave.

'They're also grey.' Varro was in the saddle now, narrowing his eyes towards the river bank ahead. Camels and giraffes now, he was happy with that. The stupid animals just ran ahead of a hunt. They had no fight in them, they just loped off with that ungainly stride they both had. True, a camel had spat at him that time, but it was a small price to pay. And he still had the giraffe skin on the floor of his tablinum on the Palatine. He was less happy as he followed the beaters through the mud flats. What had possessed him to wear his best boots? They were already brown with the

Tiber's mud, and his bay was jittery, to say the least. Wasn't the whole point of the hunt at the munera that the kill was easy? Wasn't it supposed to be held in the arena? Wasn't it supposed to represent Rome's total superiority over all the earth, man and beast?

Varro comforted himself with the knowledge that there wasn't a wolf alive that could stand still for the beaters. The slaves carried flaming torches, so that even in the thickest undergrowth they would be safe and would carry all before them. There were shouts and laughter as the men went about their business, drunk on the Saturnalia and the excitement of the hunt, flames flaring in the trees.

The first wolf saw them crashing through the bushes, yelling in their incomprehensible language. He flattened his ears and lifted his nose to catch the scent. There was a fat man riding his way, unsure in the saddle of the bay. The reek of his sweat almost overpowered everything else. The wolf could see the horse's eyes, wild and wary, and he could smell the horse's fear. The animal would feed the whole pack for a week. He padded forward, head low, haunches high, watching the trees for the others. Most of them had broken cover, grey flashes of speed and movement, ahead of the beaters, but three of them, the older, wiser ones, had circled back. The beaters carried fire but no weapons, and not one of them could outrun a wolf. This pack were from the Umbrian mountains to the north, lean and half starving in the wild, mean and kept half-starved in captivity. Calidus had bought them days ago on the orders of Nerva, neither man believing they would be used to mark a man's death.

A man's death. Publius Varro was annoyed with himself. His stupid horse was spooked, and the animal had shied at nothing, whisking him off to the left and away from the others. The damned mist didn't help. It was thicker here, nearer the river, and the shouts of the beaters and the other hunters seemed far away now, muffled and unreal. Varro tugged on his rein, trying to turn the animal away from the mud, ramming his heels into its flanks to drive it on.

Publius Varro didn't see what the horse saw. He didn't smell what the horse smelt. The bay screamed and reared, its hind legs slipping in the mud. Bugger! He'd lost the reins and knelt there like an idiot as the bay bolted, the saddle slipping sideways in a tangle of straps and leather. He was struggling upright when he heard it – a noise he'd never heard before. He sank to his knees again as he took it in. Ahead of him, outlined by the dark of the stand of trees, a large grey wolf was looking at him with small, deadly, yellow eyes. Its tongue lolled near the ground, an unearthly growl rattling in its throat. It was swaying from side to side, weighing up the size and weight of its next kill. The horse had gone; the man would do.

Varro couldn't look away. His right hand was frozen on the spear shaft. And now, he couldn't hear anything except the pounding of his heart, thudding under tunic, skin and ribs. Run! His numbed brain screamed at him. Run, run, you stupid bastard. Do it. Do it now! But whatever his brain was telling him, his legs weren't listening. He sank in on himself, supporting his body weight on the spear. His eyes were locked on those of the wolf. Those eyes that never wavered, never blinked.

'Down, Varro!' He heard a shout behind him. Or was it in front? It hardly mattered; he threw himself face down in the mud, dropping the spear and shielding his head with his arms. Dis Pater, Hades, Cerberus – all the gods and monsters of the underworld flashed before him in a jumble of terror. He expected any second to feel the hot breath of the wolf on his neck, followed by the razor-sharp teeth stabbing through his skin. He thought he would hear his own skull crack and feel the most appalling pain before darkness closed over him forever.

In fact, he heard the hiss of a spear shaft somewhere above him and a yelp as the wolf went down. He brought up his head when he hoped it was safe, looking at the world between his fingers, all dignity gone. A huge grey wolf lay feet from him, its flanks still working as it struggled to breathe. A broad spear was embedded in the fur just behind its right ear. The animal's tongue lashed the ground once, and its eyes rolled up and it was still.

Varro felt strong hands hauling him upright. And a young man stood, looking at him.

'Calidus,' Varro clutched the man's tunic sleeve. 'I owe you my life. Jupiter and Diana, I owe you my life.' He was giggling helplessly, drunk on relief and panic. Tears of hysteria trickled down his cheeks, and he was finding it difficult to breathe. He turned back to look at the wolf that had nearly killed him. 'Good shot,' he whispered, patting Calidus on the shoulder. 'Good shot. Lucky for me you doubled back, eh? Look,' he suddenly remembered who he was and tried to turn the world the right way up again. 'We don't have to make a big thing of this, do we? I mean, couldn't that spear have been mine? I'll make it worth your while, of course.'

'You will, senator,' Calidus smiled, brushing some of the mud off the man. 'You will. And I'll let you know when.'

'What?' Varro frowned. He didn't like the sound of that. After all, this man was a slave, wasn't he? Being a dead man's steward counted for nothing in the scheme of things. Still, he'd let it go. The man *had* done him a service; they *were* gathered to honour a great Roman; and it *was* Saturnalia. He glanced down quickly; all in all, he was grateful that the Tiber's mud disguised the fact that Publius Varro had just pissed himself.

*

Night came to the Esquiline, as it always did in December, sudden and complete. There was no moon tonight, and the clouds hid the stars. Even so, Nerva's people saw the little party making its way up the twisting road that led to the villa, a litter and slaves carrying torches with a scorpion standard flashing in the flames.

Flavia stood on her balcony, the one that jutted out over the fountain playing in the garden. 'Calidus,' she called to her husband's steward, 'who's that? I couldn't bear visitors tonight.'

'That's a Praetorian standard, Mater Flavia,' he told her. 'Who do we know?'

She shook her head. 'I've lost touch with them,' she said. 'You know Gaius didn't approve. Send them away, will you?'

Calidus bowed and hurried down the steps. He stopped to nod to the open door of the tablinum where Nerva's body lay, wrapped in his toga with the coins for Charon the ferryman shining on his closed eyes. Then he swept on, snatching a cloak in the lararium and touching the gods' statues there before shooing the servants away from the atrium and opening the front door.

'Io, Saturnalia!' the torchbearer hailed him as he jogged up the hill. 'Hail to the house of Gaius Lucius Nerva.'

'Ave, traveller,' Calidus threw the greeting back and waited. A large man with dark curls alighted from the litter. He was wearing the white toga of a tribune of the Praetorian Guard, and there was a sword-hilt half hidden in its folds.

'Fabius Quintus,' he announced himself. 'Tribune of the Emperor's Praetorian Guard.'

'Sir.' Calidus bowed.

'Missed the hunt this morning,' Quintus said. 'Wanted to pay my respects.'

'I'm afraid the Lady Flavia isn't receiving this evening, sir.'

'Really?' Quintus clearly had not been expecting that. He *was* a tribune of the Praetorian Guard, when all was said and done. The widow of a dead senator was nobody. 'Well, will you tell the Lady Flavia that I am deeply sorry for her situation?'

Fabius Quintus was a strikingly handsome man, broad-shouldered and tall. He looked every inch a soldier of the emperor.

'I will, sir,' Calidus bowed.

'Calidus?' A female voice called from the litter. 'Calidus – is that you?'

Until now, Calidus hadn't noticed her; yet, there she sat, shrouded in a deep blue stola against the chill of the night. She lowered her veil and sat smiling at him.

'Julia?' He came forward and stood there, staring at her. 'Julia Eusabia?'

'Yes, it's Julia,' she laughed after the awkward silence. 'Tongue-tied, as always.' She shook her head.

'I'm sorry,' he said. 'It has been quite a while.'

He had forgotten her musical laugh, the way she raised an eyebrow, the fullness of her lips. Since Paula, he had forgotten all about her. Or rather, he hadn't. He had *chosen* to forget, if only because the memory of her was so painful.

'Do you two know each other?' Quintus crossed back to the litter.

'We used to,' she said softly. 'Calidus is the cleverest man I've ever met.'

Quintus snorted. '*Was*, dearest,' he said. 'Past tense.'

She didn't take her eyes off Calidus. 'Yes, of course,' she purred. 'Past tense.'

Quintus cleared his throat. 'We were at a banquet with old Nerva only last week, weren't we, Julia?'

'Yes,' she said, only now tearing her gaze away from Calidus. 'That's right; we were.'

'He seemed right as rain then,' the tribune went on. 'Just goes to show. We none of us know when Dis Pater is going to come calling.' Julia was looking at Calidus again and he at her. 'Who are you?' Quintus asked.

'Calidus, sir,' he told him. 'Gaius Lucius Calidus, Nerva's steward.'

Quintus snorted. 'Well, freedman,' he said, 'if I had more time, I'd scrape you off my boot like the shit you are. In the meantime, we'll be at the games tomorrow, to pay our respects properly.'

'Honoured, sir.' Calidus half-bowed.

Quintus climbed onto the litter alongside Julia. 'How many pairs tomorrow?'

'Three, sir,' Calidus told him. 'Thrax, secutor and retiarius.'

The tribune nodded. 'Good,' he said. 'No women, I suppose? Fighters, I mean.'

'Gaius Lucius Nerva didn't approve, sir,' Calidus smiled.

'No,' Quintus sighed. 'No, that sounds right. Just as well – all that grunting and squealing. Might as well mate with a pig.' He produced a vine stick from somewhere and brought it down smartly on the shoulder of the nearest litter bearer. 'Until tomorrow then, freedman.' And the litter bearers turned, carrying their load down the hill and into the night.

As Calidus reached the atrium, he saw Paula reflected in the water of the impluvium. 'Who was that?' she asked.

'An absolute arsehole called Quintus,' Calidus told her. 'He's a tribune of Nero's guard. The rest of us are assorted smells under his nose.'

'I meant her,' she said, watching him carefully.

'Her?' Calidus paused and looked back to where one of his people was locking the doors. 'No one special. Just someone I used to know.'

III

The crowds had thickened around the Navel of Rome by mid-afternoon. Little children were hoisted onto their father's shoulders to say goodbye to a great man they had never heard of. It was the Saturnalia, so the wine flowed with the laughter. Old Nerva's friends had come to shed a tear and they sat in rows in front of the Old Rostrum, each of them wearing a mask like Gaius Lucius Nerva in his heyday, when he had brown hair and all his teeth. A dozen men, swathed in togas on their chairs, all looking identical, terrified at least one little girl. Paulina was just over a year old, and she couldn't understand what was going on. Her mama had told her she must be good, and her mama was standing with her now, letting the little tot lean against her leg because standing in the Forum of the greatest city in the world is an exhausting business, when you are just over a year old.

The body of the old man lay on its catafalque, the wind of the afternoon lifting the hem of his toga. There was a laurel wreath on his chest and a staff of office held in the scrawny, blackening hands, that looked for all the world as if he was still struggling with the toga he hated. The same wind sneaked past him and as it went, lifted the few hairs the gods had left him into his old age. It could have been the hand of Aeolus himself, bestowing a parting blessing.

Flavia sat beside him, alone. She had no siblings to comfort her in her grief, no children to mourn their father. Only Calidus, her husband's steward, his freedman. It was not the custom for widows to speak at funerals and Flavia's calm face was half hidden behind her black veil. There were old friends from the Senate there, the faceless ones who faced her now. One of them might have spoken, *should* have spoken, perhaps; several of them had offered. But they wouldn't do. Glabrio never *really* understood him; Septimus Numidius could barely remember his own name, still less his dead friend's; Marcus Maxentius hated the man's guts; Publius Varro was a waste of space. So, it had to be Calidus. No one else would do.

The steward had pleaded with Mater Flavia. It was not his place. He was a freedman. Only a few days ago, he had been a slave. This wasn't right; not by any tradition that Calidus knew. But Mater Flavia had insisted – 'I want it to be you, Calidus.' And he was a little boy again, quaking in his sandals in case he had displeased the mistress.

Calidus took his place under the bronze beaks of the warships that jutted from their column on the Rostrum, the captured spoils of an ancient war. The crowd fell silent now, which was unusual for Romans at the Saturnalia. The great and the good knew their place and had come to mourn a senator. Those on the fringes were there for the wine and any handouts that might come their way. After all, the Nervae were nobs, weren't they, as patrician as they come? They'd probably be chucking sesterci around rather than have the bother of having to carry their loose change home.

Calidus looked down at his old master for the last time. 'Romans,' he said, in a clear voice that carried to the Basilica Julia and the Temple of Saturn, garlanded now, on the god's feast days. 'Look on the outward form of Gaius Lucius Nerva, my master, my friend.' He waited until the shifting mob was still, and all eyes were focused on the catafalque.

'He's rather good at this,' Licinius Glabrio murmured behind his mask.

'"Friend", though?' Marcus Maxentius murmured back. 'That's pushing it a bit, surely.'

'We knew nothing,' Calidus went on. 'We were his children. And he taught us. If I can read today, it is because Nerva showed me how. If I write my name, it is *his* hand guiding the stylus. When we wanted to play, he played with us.' He remembered leaping over the old man's back and wrestling with him in the long grass, winning most of the time but not always; life was a lesson, and when they wrestled, the lesson was; you don't always win. Not even when you deserve to. Perhaps especially not then. 'When we wanted to hunt, he hunted with us.'

Publius Varro winced behind his mask. His arse still hurt where his horse had thrown him, and he wasn't sure he'd ever remove that dent from his pride.

'When we were sick,' Calidus went on, 'he nursed us.' He could still feel the old man's hands cooling his fever, holding up with gentle hands the lemon drink made cool with ice from the icehouse at the villa in the Tibur, eked out through the summer months but never begrudged a feverish child. He remembered Nerva kicking Papirius hard when that good man confessed that he had no medical answers. 'Sod Aesculapius, you old fraud,' Nerva had growled at him. 'You find something to get this boy back on his feet, or it's the salt mines for you.'

'When we sinned,' Calidus smiled, 'he shook us until our teeth rattled in our heads.' He waited again. Flavia's head was bowed. So was Paula's. Little Paulina was looking up at her mother, wondering why she was crying, her little fingers patting the woman's arm, trying to comfort her and, all unknowing, making her cry all the more. Paula pulled her daughter closer – mortality was singing in the air today, and she wanted to keep her safe, if that could ever be done.

'Say your goodbyes,' Calidus said. 'We shall none of us look on his like again.'

A roar went up from the crowd, and the senators were on their feet, clapping as was the custom. One by one, they mounted the dais and removed their masks, bowing before the dead man. Calidus had stepped aside and was waiting while this part of the observance took place. Soon, he would see his master lifted onto a cart and carried to the country villa where the flames would be lit, and Gaius Lucius Nerva would be lost in the smoke.

Suddenly, he felt a tug at the purse at his hip. It was only slight – it could have been the accidental nudge of a bystander. Calidus' hand snaked out and trapped somebody else's against the leather.

'Well done,' the hand's owner said, almost in Calidus' ear. 'I've seen some fine orations in my time, but that was ... sweet. Short, certainly. But simple. Moving even.' And the hand's owner used his free one to wipe away a tear.

'Do you always congratulate orators by pinching their purses?' Calidus asked, turning round without loosening his grip. The man he had in his power was a typical Roman, squat and dark, wearing the tunic of a pleb under an outsize cloak. He stank of the Tiber and garum, the fish sauce he virtually lived on.

'Come with me,' Calidus snapped. He had not let go of the wayward hand yet, and he dragged the man through the crowd in the direction of the Lapis Niger and swung him round against the black basalt. 'How would you like to be handed over to the vigilis, purse-lifter?'

'Purse-lifter?' The man was outraged. 'Me? There must be some mistake!'

'There is,' Calidus nodded, 'and you made it. You'll have gathered from the oration that I have friends in high places. A magistrate or two, praetors and proconsuls coming out of my arsehole. Any one of them would be only too happy to see you cracking rocks for the rest of your life. Actually, that's all rather long-winded, isn't it? All that paperwork? Let's cut out the middleman.'

Suddenly, there was a knife in Calidus' hand; the thief hadn't seen where it had come from. 'Stealing at a funeral is a pretty shabby crime, friend. Despicable, even. Well worth a hand.' He pressed the sharp blade against the man's wrist.

'Careful!' The thief's voice rose an octave. 'That's my livelihood, that is.'

'Not anymore.' Calidus put the point of the knife in between the tendons on the soft inside of the thief's wrist and prepared to cut. A bead of blood welled on the greasy skin and trickled slowly to earth, landing with a splash at their feet.

'No!' the purse-lifter screamed, oblivious to the people milling around the black stone. 'What do you want?' he said, through clenched teeth. Try as he might, he couldn't break free of Calidus' grip.

'Let's start with your name,' the steward said. The blade hadn't moved, and another drop of blood grew fat and rolled off onto the ground.

'Germanicus,' the man blurted out.

'Your *real* name,' Calidus leaned into him. 'My wrist's beginning to ache. I may have to …' he pressed a little harder and the man yelped.

'Piso,' he sobbed. 'My name's Piso.'

'Piso?' Calidus frowned. 'The fish? Are you having a laugh?'

'No, honest,' the man gabbled. 'Would I lie to you? I can't remember my given name. I've worked on the river all my life. Fisherman.'

He certainly smelt like it, but Calidus was unconvinced. He ripped Piso's cloak aside and saw four purses hanging from his belt. 'Oh, dear, oh, dear. Not many dace here, Piso; not a trout in sight.'

'Look,' Piso managed a grin of sorts. He had stopped pulling away from Calidus, and his hand hung limp as a fish in the steward's grip. 'Can't we talk about this? I mean, I've got a few sesterci here, as you've probably realised.'

'Indeed,' Calidus nodded, 'but I don't want your money. Where do you live?'

'What?'

'Just answer the question, Piso, or this hand joins Cicero's head on the Rostrum over there.'

'Ah, that's an old wives' tale, that is,' Piso gabbled. 'I happen to know …'

'Got it in one, fisher of purses.'

'What?' Piso frowned. 'How do you mean?'

'It's what you know that I'm interested in. Now, once more, for the record – where do you live?'

'Via Flumena,' Piso said. 'Insula IV.' He gasped as Calidus released his pressure on the knife and slid it back into its sheath. Calidus looked at the man. 'I'll trust you,' he said, 'although for the life of me, I don't know why I should. I may have need of you in a day or two.'

'What for?'

'To give you a fighting chance to keep that hand of yours,' Calidus told him. 'And if I find you *don't* live along the Via Flumena, Insula IV, then rest assured I will come and look elsewhere. And,' he patted the man's cheek, 'I never forget a face.'

The horns blasted out over the Forum, which Calidus knew was the signal for the funeral cortege to move on. The crowd was cheering, throwing ribbons and rattles into the air, waving their Saturnalia caps. There was nothing like a funeral for bringing out the best in people. As for Piso, he had long gone, vanished into the gridded jungle that was Rome.

*

The lanista Lenticulus wasn't happy at first. The man who had hired him – Calidus, was it? – didn't want a big show. The amphitheatre was huge and bouts there would draw big crowds. They would expect blood. That was not what Calidus wanted because old Nerva hadn't wanted it. Was that reasonable, Lenticulus had asked him? When all Rome wanted bread and circuses? When old Nerva was known to be a traditionalist of the old school? The munera was inextricably linked with death. If you commemorate the passing of a great man, you must see that others pass too, swiftly and viciously by the sword or trident. And more, this was the Saturnalia – sacrifices to the god went with the territory.

But Calidus wouldn't be moved. He was following his master's wishes to the letter. Three friendly bouts, where skill, not brutality, was paramount. So, they wouldn't be staged in the amphitheatre but a temporary arena outside the Ostian Gate. There would be seating for a hundred, no more. The occasion would not be advertised and would be by invitation only. Lenticulus had cheered up when he realised the men he had trained up would live to fight another day – his mind whirling, he wondered how he could promote this kind of fighting to make it more widespread; to be a gladiator who died of old age could become the newest fashion.

Flavia had never really enjoyed gladiator shows, the barleymen grunting and sweating as the crowd roared. The smell, the blood, the nearness and swiftness of death, they all sickened her. Perhaps that was why, at the end, when it had come to writing his will, Gaius Lucius had specified no killing.

That was fine by the fighters, who could go through the motions while giving the crowd their money's worth. Everybody who had been invited knew the score. Betting was pointless. It was one thing to throw your money away if a glorious kill was in the wind. But this – this was practice, like schoolboys playing with wooden swords. It was only loyalty to the dead man that made them turn up at all. Marcus Maxentius didn't – he sent a slave to the Lady Flavia pleading a headache.

It was dusk as the first guests arrived, slaves carrying torches to light the way along the road from the Ostian Gate, pinpoints of light dancing past the crumbling tombs of other great Romans who had passed this way and would pass no more. Calidus' people saw them to their seats. Slaves placed cushions, and the bitching started – 'Jupiter Highest and Best; he's brought *her*!'; 'Nasty hairdo,'; 'Well, he'd come to the opening of a sewer,' – it was endless.

'I see your friend is here,' Paula said, as she caught sight of Julia Eusabia. The tribune's woman looked beautiful by torchlight – even Paula could see that. What worried her was that Calidus could see it too. Fabius Quintus wasn't wearing his simple pallium now but the parade armour of his rank in the Praetorian Guard. The scarlet cloak hung from his shoulders, glittering with medusa heads, and the white belt shone brightly against the bronze of the muscled cuirass. He unbuckled his plumed helmet as he reached his seat and helped Julia into her place beside him. His eyes scanned the crowd. Yes, they were all here, the crawlers, the hangers-on, all those boring old farts who haunted the Senate, smug in the superiority of their ancestry. If any of them was on fire, he wouldn't piss on them to put it out.

When all was ready, Calidus signalled to Lenticulus, and the lanista brought out his first pair.

'I give you the Thracian,' he announced to Flavia, sitting alone as a widow must, on a dais above the sand of the arena. 'Lanius', the man nicknamed 'The Butcher', was broad and swarthy, with a five-day beard and dark eyes. His oiled body, barley-fed for the five years he had survived in this job, shone in the dozens of torches that outlined the circle. His right arm was striped from shoulder to wrist with hinged iron plates, and a broad belt held his subligaculum tight around his bulging groin. There were nods of approval and murmurings among the ladies. Julia smiled and then sniggered with her friends, none of whom, Paula knew all too well, had any links to the dead man.

'And the secutor, Fulgur.' The gladiator called 'Lightning' stood alongside his opponent. Bronze greaves shone with their ornate carvings below his knees, and his shield was painted with the lightning bolts of Jupiter himself. He was heavier than Lanius, hairier and Greek-looking. The ladies were less impressed with him, if only because his face was encased in a bronze helmet, laced at the front with leather thongs. The hooded sights gave him the appearance of a rather malevolent owl.

Lenticulus turned to face the pair. 'Why have you come, at this hour and to this place?'

'We have come,' the gladiators chorused, 'to do honour to Gaius Lucius Nerva, the senator.'

Lenticulus spun on his heel and bowed to Flavia as the fighters saluted her with their swords. With a roar, the pair broke apart. The Thracian clapped his horse-hair plumed helmet on, and now he was as masked and anonymous as his opponent. They crossed blades briefly, the curved sica of the Thracian and the straight gladius of the secutor. Then they stepped back and faced each other in earnest.

'Twenty sesterces on the Thracian,' Fabius Quintus turned to his adjutant.

'Done.' Rufius shook his boss's hand, turning to smile at the girl at his side. 'Like taking honey from a baby. Trust me, I've seen the secutor before, in Capua. He's good.'

'I'll take your word for it,' she purred.

The gladiators circled each other, their bare feet sending up clouds of dust. Lenticulus had trained them well – lots of noise, vicious grunts and growls. 'You're animals,' he had roared at them in the gladiatorial school, 'and all these good people out there have come to see animals die. Don't you disappoint them, now. Snarl, you bastards. Tell them you're not going quietly.'

Lanius' blade banged the top of Fulgur's shield and scythed to catch his helmet. The secutor staggered, and Quintus slapped his thigh. Rufius' money was as good as his. Fulgur danced sideways, the clever footwork his stock in trade, and offered his shield again. Lanius hacked downwards, and the secutor dropped his shield to the ground, forcing the Thracian to drop with it. Then he slashed horizontally, hacking the plume off Lanius' helmet and sending him reeling into the torchbearers.

Rufius grinned, holding out his hand to Quintus.

'It isn't over,' the tribune shouted over the roar of the crowd, 'until it's over.'

Rufius threw back his head and laughed. With insight like that, it was no wonder that Fabius Quintus was one of the emperor's favourites. Shield clashed with shield, and the sword-hilts locked. Flavia looked around her. The normally sedate and dignified senators who had been her husband's colleagues were a rabble already. They knew there would be no deaths in the arena tonight but 'accidental' blood on the sand, that could hardly be avoided. Their wives and mistresses were shrieking too, roaring on whichever fighter was their particular favourite.

The sweating, grunting bodies swayed together, then broke apart in a flurry of clashes, swords clanging on armoured arms. The secutor was sneaky; there was no doubt of that. He feinted with his sword, then clobbered the Thracian with his shield. As Lanius reeled, Fulgur butted him in the chest, the bronze ridge of his helmet drawing blood for the first time that night. The crowd was on its collective feet, roaring and whistling. This was more like it.

Intense pain brought the Thracian back to the attack, and he strode forward, the curved blade licking under his opponent's arm and drawing a crimson line across his ribcage. Fulgur cursed under his breath and drew back. He parried furiously, but Lanius' blood was up now, and he wasn't taking any prisoners. He drove the heavier man back until the secutor was hemmed in by the torchbearing slaves and he lost his footing. Instinctively, the Thracian banged the sword out of his opponent's grasp, spun him round and straddled him, his sword-tip against the man's neck, under his helmet.

Lanius looked up to Flavia. All around him, the mob was roaring, *Kill! Kill!* – many of them drawing their thumbs across their throats to signify their wishes. But this was Flavia's call alone, and she knew her husband's wishes. For a moment, she hesitated. Then her hand came up and her thumb shot towards the sky. There was a groan of disappointment, and Lanius jerked back his blade, freeing the secutor, who struggled to his feet. There was blood on the sand from both men, but honour had been satisfied, and no one had died.

Fabius Quintus smiled, holding out his hand to Rufius without bothering to look at him. He was looking at Julia. 'Like taking honey from a baby,' he said. And the adjutant coughed up.

Lenticulus the lanista took centre stage again to announce the second bout. 'I give you,' he roared, drawing out each word to attract the attention of the crowd, 'the myrmillo, Veru!' The crowd was settling down again, laughing. The man was called 'The Skewer'. All well and good, but there wouldn't be much skewering tonight, not on current showing. The gladiator was already wearing his huge square-crested helmet with its fish-scale ridge and faceplate. His rectangular shield was scarlet, and a silver octopus writhed over the leather face. His right arm and legs were strapped with padding, and the gladius, long-bladed and heavy, was already in his hand.

'He's good,' Quintus murmured to Julia.

'Well hung, certainly,' she said, narrowing her eyes to admire the contours of the gladiator's body.

'Keep your mind on the job in hand,' the tribune chuckled. 'We're here to pay our respects to a great man, remember.'

She raised an eyebrow, yawning. 'How could I forget?' she asked him.

'And I give you ...' but Lenticulus never finished his next announcement. From the Gate of Life, a trident slung casually over his shoulder and trailing a gilded net in the arena's dust, a newcomer had batted aside the myrmillo's actual opponent and announced himself. '... the retiarius,' he called, in a melodic voice, 'Lucius Domitius Ahenobarbus.'

There was a gasp, then silence. The lanista, the nearest man to the net fighter, was the first to move. Then the myrmillo fell on one knee. Then the torchbearers, still carrying their flames aloft. Finally, the crowd. They were on their feet, bowing in ragged confusion, then slamming their fists to their chests and pointing their arms forward, rigid, like the slaves they all were.

'Jupiter Highest and Best,' Licinius Glabrio murmured to Publius Varro, standing beside him. 'It can't be, can it?'

It was. The Emperor Nero stood, smiling at them all, the arse-lickers, the cock-suckers. Three years ago, he had stood bareheaded before the Senate, pledging his willingness to work with them. 'I bring with me no feuds,' he had told them, 'no grievances, no desire for vengeance.' They were empty words – more, they were empty words written for the lad by Seneca, the philosopher who was his tutor. Had any senator dared remind him of these words and all that had happened since to undo those sentiments, he would have giggled, like the child he still was, 'I had my fingers crossed all the time, under my toga.' Tonight, the Emperor of Rome wore no toga. His legs were strapped with padding up to the knee, and his subigaculum was purple, fringed with gold. There was a dagger stuffed into his broad belt, and his left arm was armoured, a bronze plate on his shoulder to deflect any blows from the myrmillo. But it was the emperor's face that held the attention of all there. He wore a blond wig, the curls of which were held in place with the traditional striped headband, and his face was a chalky white, glycerine tears streaked from his red-rimmed eyes to his chin. He had come to mourn Gaius Lucius Nerva.

'I've seen him racing his chariot in the games,' Varro murmured, still holding the imperial salute, absent-mindedly, 'even the odd wrestling bout. But this is a first.'

'Mad as a snake,' Glabrio was shaking his head. His was the first hand to fall.

'I have come to honour my old friend,' Nero announced to them all, 'that great Roman, Gaius Lucius Nerva.' There was a break in his voice, impeccably timed.

The murmur of the crowd turned to polite applause. The applause became cheers and whistles, and Nero circled the sand, waving and acknowledging their obeisance. Then he held up his right hand, the trident pointing to the stars and shouted across the arena, 'Lay on, myrmillo. Give it your best shot.'

The merman bowed, and Lenticulus grabbed his arm and pulled him nearer. Out of the corner of his mouth, he said, 'He's the bloody emperor, for Jupiter's sake, go easy with him or we'll all be food for the fishes tonight.'

Veru nodded. His opponent may have blue blood in his veins and purple silk over his bollocks but he was, combat-wise, a spotty eighteen-year-old with flabby muscles and probably no co-ordination at all. For so many reasons, The Skewer couldn't skewer him, and it narked the veteran of sixteen fights that he would have to make himself look like a vegetable to be bested by Nero. There were two ways of looking at this, thought Veru, as he eased his neck muscles and stepped forward. In one, the emperor would be so pleased to win, he would let the merman live to fight another day, although mocked by all for his pathetic performance. In the other, he would kill him; and, the dead part aside, that was probably the better of the two evils. Never mind. 'I, who am about to die, salute you,' he muttered, to any god who might be listening and stepped forward to meet his fate.

Since the emperor had effectively announced the purpose of the bout already, Lenticulus raised his wooden sword in silence, and the gladiators faced each other. No money was changing hands on the terraces now. There was no sport in this. The only point of interest was to see whether the myrmillo would be bad enough to let the net-fighter shine.

Nero had not stooped to bare his feet in public, so he felt his sandals slip on the sand. The weights dangling from his net were solid gold, but they hurt like lead, and Veru was ready for them as they whirled over the emperor's head and lashed into his shoulders. He shrugged off the attack and moved in with his heavy shield, covering his body. Nero swung the net again, faster than anybody expected, especially Veru. He felt the shield being hauled from his grip and he was facing the trident with only his sword. Luckily for his reputation, the crowd assumed it was all stage-managed anyway, and they applauded politely.

Nero sneered at them, his white-painted face streaked with sweat now. Was that all they could manage? A half-hearted ripple. He'd give them something to cheer about. He didn't give Veru a chance to regain his shield but caught him round the ankles with the net, and The Skewer went down. Nero closed in and felt a numbing pain as the flat of the myrmillo's blade slapped against his shin. An inch or two higher and Veru could have shattered the emperor's kneecap and he knew it. Nero pulled back.

The myrmillo was on his feet again. He'd lost a shield before against a retiarius. It was nothing. And this lad wasn't really a net fighter; he'd just got lucky, that was all. He swung into the attack, almost lazily, hooking his straight blade against the forks of the trident and twisting it so that Nero was thrown off balance. Still, the crowd was impressed. Oh, they'd congratulate the living god later, of course, because they knew better than not to, but this was all just a play. They could see better at the theatre any night, with the Miles Gloriosus character beating up Senex, the old man. *And* it wouldn't have cost so much.

Nero steadied himself and thrust the trident. It bounced off the myrmillo's helmet, and the gladiator came back with a lightning series of blows that drove the emperor back. He was stumbling over his own net, always a problem for a beginner, and everyone wondered how he could come back from this. They expected the myrmillo to hesitate or miss wildly or stumble to let Nero gain his footing again, but that wasn't happening. Two slashes, three, delivered with speed and power, and the trident sailed through the air to land with a thud in the sand. Nero was down on one knee, and the contest was over.

Veru paused for breath, and as he did so, Nero lashed out with both feet and brought the man down. In an instant, the emperor's knife was glinting at the myrmillo's throat, his head wrenched back to bare his flesh to the blade. Now the crowd was on their feet. The polite applause had become an almost hysterical wave of shouting and cheering. If this was rehearsed and planned, it was bloody well done. The emperor looked up at Flavia, still sitting on her dais, still horrified by her surprise guest and not quite able to take it all in. She realised that all eyes, not just the emperor's, were on her, and she collected herself. It was too late for her to just close her own eyes and wish it all away. She must, at least, look normal, no matter how she felt. There were wolves in the night air on all sides, baying again for blood. She held her thumb horizontally, signifying mercy; signifying life.

Nero's face didn't change. In fact, he hardly moved, just slicing his blade slowly across the myrmillo's throat, so the blood spurted in a crimson arc, the arteries severed by the most powerful man in the world. The merman gurgled once and slumped forward. Flavia sat rooted to the spot, nearly as pale as the painted emperor, while all around her, senators and wives, courtiers and mistresses shrieked their delight. Blood at last. Blood after all. And who had provided it? Their own emperor, their darling little Nero.

He held up his hand until the cheering and the shouting had stopped. He stuffed the bloodied dagger into his waistband and crossed to retrieve the trident. 'Gate of Death, lanista,' he ordered, and Lenticulus' people, who hadn't expected this job tonight, began to haul the dead man onto their cart. Nero walked towards Flavia's dais. 'Madam,' he said. 'Tell me who has organised this munera? Who has honoured Gaius Lucius in this way?'

Flavia's eyes narrowed. She had never liked Lucius Domitius Ahenobarbus. Calling himself Nero and wearing the purple had changed nothing. He was still the half-mad, flaky misfit he'd always been. There were nasty rumours about Nero and his slaves; nastier ones about Nero and his mother. She didn't know why he was asking, but she wasn't taking any chances. She wasn't going to hand this lunatic Calidus' head on a plate. So she said nothing.

Nero fidgeted with the trident. He had just asked this wretched old crone a question. All he got was the treason of silence. And Calidus could not stay quiet in a moment like that.

He broke through the cordon of torchbearers and made for the emperor.

In an instant, a hedge of spears faced him. He had barely noticed them until now, what with the events of the last few minutes, but here they were. The emperor's German bodyguard, huge and bearded, had formed a solid phalanx around their master.

'No,' Calidus heard Nero say. 'Let him through.'

They parted, spears still at the ready, and Calidus fell to one knee in the sand, head bowed.

'Who is this?' he asked Flavia.

This time the woman did answer. 'This is Gaius Lucius Calidus,' she said. 'My late husband's freedman.'

'You organised this?' Nero looked down at him.

'I did, Sire,' Calidus said.

'And the hunt this morning?'

Calidus nodded.

'And the oration?'

He nodded again. Nero smiled. 'Yes,' he said, passing his trident to a German, 'I heard all about the oration. Very … moving. So moving,' he was untying his headband and shaking the wig under it, 'that I put some of it to music.'

'You know what I said, Sire?' Calidus asked.

'Speak when you're spoken to,' one of the guards snarled in guttural, bad Latin.

'No, no, Statius,' Nero scolded gently. 'No need for that.' Nero's eyes had wandered up above Calidus' head to the crowd from where he'd come. 'I wasn't there, of course.' He flicked an ingratiating smile at Flavia. 'Too busy, I'm afraid. In a busy life, the cares of state – you know, madam, how it is.'

Flavia knew all about the cares of state, but she doubted whether Nero actually cared at all, about anything except Lucius Domitus Ahenobarbus.

'I have my people,' Nero went on, by way of explanation to Calidus, 'my eyes and ears. Tell me, freedman, who is that girl you were with over there?'

'Er … my wife, Sire.' Calidus didn't much care for the question.

'Your wife?' Nero repeated. 'How insufferably sweet. Well, wait on me tomorrow at the palace. The third hour. You must listen to my song. Oh, and … er … bring your wife with you, there's a good freedman.'

IV

Sextus Afranius Burrus had only one good arm, but with it, he commanded the Praetorian Guard, and with that, he commanded the emperor. It was the month of January when Calidus went to see him, on his way to see Nero. The day was nine and three-quarter hours long, the sun in the sign of Capricorn the goat. In the fields around Rome, the stakes were sharpened, and along the Tiber, men bent their backs, cutting reeds and willow. As he followed Burrus through the emperor's atrium on the Palatine, Praetorians clicking heels as their commander strode past, there was a squawk of poultry and the fluttering of wings. Blood was spraying from a mangled chicken in the hands of the priests, spattering the statue of the household gods, who demanded sacrifices at this time of year, now that the Saturnalia was over.

'Whatever you find in here,' Burrus was leading Calidus and Paula up a broad flight of stone steps onto a balcony, 'just play along. Don't speak unless you're spoken to. And, whatever you do, don't mention his mother.'

It hadn't crossed Calidus' mind, but Burrus felt he had to explain. 'The Augusta is not exactly the flavour of the month at the moment. Other women are filling his mind, but that needn't concern you.' Burrus stopped abruptly and turned to Paula. 'It might concern you, though. You'd better stay here.'

'His Imperial Majesty specifically requested my wife,' Calidus felt he had to say.

'Yes, precisely. And when he does that, what are you going to say, uh? The most powerful man in the world lies beyond that door, boy. He's younger than you are and can afford to indulge his every whim. My job?' He rolled his eyes to the ceiling, sighing, 'My job is to stop him.' He rapped on the door with his staff of office, and a muffled voice said something that Calidus couldn't catch. Burrus swung the door open and thumped his chest, the soldier's salute to the emperor.

It was dark in Nero's bedroom, the winter sun peeping through a slit in the curtains and falling on a couple in bed.

'Calidus the freedman, Sire,' Burrus announced.

Nero popped his head out of the covers. 'Bugger off, Burrus. I'll call if I need you.'

'Sire,' the Praetorian nodded and gave Calidus an old-fashioned look.

Calidus saluted his emperor, who sat up in bed. He noticed the freedman looking at his companion. 'This is my husband, Doryphorus,' Nero laughed. 'What is it about you freedmen?' he asked. 'Either disgustingly punctual, like you, Calidus. Or bone idle, like this one.' He kicked the man, who squealed loudly and leapt out of bed, stark naked. 'Go and get me some wine, husband.'

'You have slaves for that.' Doryphorus stood there, smouldering with fury.

'Yes,' Nero yawned, leaning his head back against the wall. 'And you're one of them. Now, piss off.'

Doryphorus hesitated, scowling at Calidus, then grabbed a robe and swept out of the room.

Nero chuckled, shaking his head. 'He's impossible. Ideas, I fear, above his station. Er …?' He held the covers up and patted the mattress.

'Um … I'm happily married, Sire,' Calidus was quick to remind the most powerful man in the world.

'Yes,' Nero sighed. 'So am I. Did you know?' the emperor changed the subject entirely, as he caught sight of the rays of the sun on the pillow, 'that on the day I was born, I was enveloped in the sun's rays as I took my first breath? Odd, isn't it? It was the middle of the night at the time.' He looked his visitor up and down. 'Gaius Lucius Calidus,' he said, savouring each syllable of each name. 'That means smart-arse, doesn't it? Not altogether flattering. Why did you do it?'

'Do what, Sire?' Calidus was learning that to keep up with Nero it was better to untether the brain from sanity and try and run and dodge to and fro as he did. It was still hard to stay abreast, though.

'That nonsense of the hunt. I heard all about it.' Nero got out of bed, as naked as his freedman had been and crossed to a side table. There was a jug of wine here, even though he had just sent his husband in search of some and he poured a cup. There was none for Calidus. Without his retiarius outfit and his blond wig, the emperor was just a man. Not even that; he was still a boy. His body was smooth, with no hair, except on his head, and a rather feeble attempt at a beard that resolutely refused to grow on his chin. His skin was blotchy and rough, and Calidus could smell him from where he stood.

'On my accession,' Nero swilled the wine around his mouth and spat it out. 'Jupiter Highest and Best, that's gone!' He crossed to the window, hauling the curtains back and threw the wine, jug and all, out into the courtyard below. 'On my accession, we had a hunt. Four hundred bears, three hundred lions, all killed by my lads. That's what a hunt's supposed to be, Calidus, in the arena, not a handful of wolves along the Tiber. What were you thinking?'

'It was my late master's wish, Sire,' Calidus explained.

'Ah, yes, your late master.' Nero turned to face the freedman. 'I'll be frank with you, Calidus,' he said. 'Gaius Lucius Nerva was a pain in the arse. What's going to happen to his villa?'

'The one in Rome, Sire, or the one in Tibur?'

'Sod Tibur, man – the one in Rome, of course.'

'The lady Flavia still lives, Sire,' Calidus reminded him. 'It is her home.'

'Yes.' Nero fumbled for his robe. 'Sour old bitch, if memory serves.'

Calidus felt a nerve jumping in his jaw. Nothing would give him greater pleasure than to see the most powerful man in the world follow the wine jug out of the window.

'See if the thing's for sale,' Nero said. 'Ask her. I'll go to … oh … ten thousand sesterces.'

'It's worth ten times that, Sire.'

Nero crossed to him, his eyes flashing fire. 'Is it, freedman?' he hissed. 'Is it really?' Then he relented, forcing a smile. 'Well, then, ask the old girl, the Lady Flavia, to name her price. As my many friends will tell you, I'm a generous man. Oh, by the way, where's that rather luscious wife of yours?'

'Unwell, I'm afraid, Sire,' Calidus smiled. 'She sends her apologies.'

'Does she?' Nero looked disappointed. 'I hope those apologies were *abject*!'

'I apologise too, Sire. I should have said. *Abject* apologies.' Calidus could not believe that people grovelled at the feet of this man. And yet, here he was, doing it himself; it was probably something to do with a part of the brain, where self-preservation resided, taking over the body.

'Never mind,' the emperor said, flinging himself back onto the bed. 'There'll be another time. Don't forget now, whatever price the old girl has in mind, I'm good for it. Can you see yourself out?'

Calidus bowed and walked backward, head down, to the door.

'Oh,' the emperor stopped him.

'Sire?'

'If you see Doryphorus on your travels, send him in will you?' Nero gave an evil chuckle and checked beneath his robe. 'Yes, and tell him …' and he roared with laughter, 'tell him it will be more than worth his while.'

*

A chill wind blew over the olive groves of Tibur the next day. For two generations, rich Romans had made their homes here, where the waters of the Anio cascaded down from the Umbrian mountains, splashing over ancient rocks, hurled there before time began, by gods in a playful mood. Calidus had been born here in the reign of the Divine Tiberius, and he was never happier than when he rode the dripping rounds, supervising the clearing of the woods and chatting with the shepherds on their lonely hillsides. Whenever he was in Rome, with its noise and its bustle and its smells, his mind would wander here, trailing the river bank with Paula by his side and his little girl toddling ahead, falling over in the tall grass just for the fun of it, a daisy chain on her brow.

A steward of a great house had precious few moments like this, and Calidus took them as often as he could. Only now, now that the old man was dead, and he himself was free, did he have time to look to the future. But that would come later, as the future always did. This was the present, and as Calidus turned his horse into the weather and trotted back to the low, red-tiled villa, he couldn't shake his belief that Gaius Lucius Nerva had been murdered.

He didn't like what he was doing, as he settled himself down in the old man's tablinum, but it had to be done. On the table in front of him was the list of Nerva's staff, the slaves of the field and house. Calidus had known them all his life; could it be possible that one of them was a killer? He looked across to the shelf where he had hung his dog-tags, the symbol of the slave, with his name and Nerva's inscribed – the owner and the owned. He knew all about the wolf by the ears, that slaves outnumbered freed men in Rome by four to one. You heard such stories. Only last year, the prefect Lucius Pedarius Secundus had been hacked to death by a slave. The emperor had stood by the ancient law he scarcely understood and had all the man's slaves put to death. But Secundus was a professional bastard, flogging his people if they so much as looked at him funny. Gaius Lucius Nerva was the mildest of masters.

Even so, Calidus was his steward, the man who had run the domestic side of the man's life. The last kindness he could do for him was to find the one who had reduced him to ashes. Those ashes waited at the Esquiline villa now in a marble urn, against the day when the sculptors had finished the mausoleum for him to lie in; for *them* to lie in, for the gigantic marble edifice would be Flavia's resting place too. Calidus crossed out all the children of the estate with his stylus. They killed flies and stole birds' eggs, but that, for now, was the height of their criminality. No one ended up in the tullianum for that. No doubt, many of those incarcerated there would claim to be as innocent as a babe yet unborn, but Calidus was being practical, and the children were not suspects.

What about the women? Old Nerva had sat the boy down once and told him all about women. He loved his Flavia dearly, and of course, he had the usual smattering of mistresses as any self-respecting senator did, but essentially, women were evil incarnate. The Vestal maidens, of course, had been above reproach, but a *powerful* woman? That was the kiss of death. There were once wild women, the old man had told him, who worshipped drunken Bacchus and lived in the mountains, tearing beasts apart with their bare hands and whirling in a frenzy of the dance. Then there was Cleopatra.

She was a deadly monster who had made a woman of Marcus Antonius, made him hoist sail at Actium and embarrass a great nation. The Divine Augustus had not fallen for the bitch's charms, however, and in the end, she did what was fine, what was Roman, and had taken her own life. 'With a snake,' Calidus could hear the old man hiss, as if the viper itself had hold of his tongue. Calidus looked about him in the chill of the tablinum. Had he just spoken those words aloud? He shook himself. He remained faithful to old Nerva's viewpoint and did not cross out any of the women. When he came to Paula's name he threw the stylus down, disgusted with himself. Then he picked it up and crossed the name out. Had it come to this? Did the death of one old man lead to such doubts, such spiteful recriminations, without a word being spoken?

He looked down the list of men's names: Sarranto, Nerva's groom; Titus, the scribe; Victor, the cook. The cook? A man with access to the old man's food. The gods alone knew what arcane secrets lay in that man's kitchen, along with the herbs and the olives and the dangling hares and chickens. There again, Titus could have doctored a bottle of wine. Calidus slammed the stylus down again. This was ridiculous. He stood up and crossed to the window. Some lads were harnessing up the oxen to haul away a stand of newly felled cedars, their children running with them, teasing the yapping dogs. Calidus shook his head. He would find no answers here. His answers lay in Rome.

*

'We've had an invitation, Calidus.' Flavia was waving a scroll at him. 'From the palace.'

'We have?' Calidus didn't like the sound of this.

'All of us.' Flavia raised an eyebrow. 'Me, you, Paula. Would you like to tell me what's going on?'

Calidus looked at the woman he had always worshipped. She had been more than a mother to him almost since the day he was born, and there was nothing he wouldn't do to save her pain, to save her trouble, to keep her safe. Lately, that had meant keeping things from her, for her peace of mind, but the time for this cat to jump out of the bag was here. 'He wants this villa, Mater Flavia,' he said. 'The emperor said you could name your price.'

She nodded. 'Yes, the little pervert thinks everything has a price tag. Well, he's wrong. You go, Calidus. Dear Gaius never accepted an imperial invitation to dinner in his life. I'm not going to break faith with that. Tell the emperor, in simple words that he will understand, that the Villa Nerva is not for sale, to him, or anyone. That's my decision and it's final.'

Calidus smiled. *Powerful women*, he heard old Nerva say again, *they're the kiss of death.*

*

The emperor lounged on his couch later that day, absent-mindedly tracing his fingers over the lion's head carvings. The wine was good, the fire was spitting and crackling in the centre of the room and all was, nearly, right with the world. Or it would be, if only Burrus would shut up.

'I do worry about Corbulo,' the Praetorian prefect was saying. 'He's taking liberties.'

'What?' Nero hadn't really been listening.

'Gnaeus Domitius Corbulo.' Burrus was shaking a vellum report at him, dangling with army seals. 'He's advancing into Armorica.'

Nero looked blank.

'Armorica, Sire,' Burrus spoke slowly, as to a child. 'In the East. To the north of ...'

'Don't patronise me, Burrus, you old cripple!' Nero snapped, his voice squeaking as it always did when he was annoyed. 'I know *exactly* where Armorica is. And anyway, isn't Corbulo legate of Cappadocia and Galatia?'

'He is, Sire,' Burrus acknowledged. 'You, in your greatness, appointed him yourself.'

'Well, there you are then.' Nero held out his cup for a slave to refill. 'Man's just doing his job.'

'But there are ramifications, Sire ...' Burrus tried to explain. 'The Parthians ...'

'... are cowardly bastards who shoot arrows from under their horses' necks while running away. Yes, I know. Corbulo knows what he's doing. Now,' he took a hefty swig, 'about the dinner.'

'Sire?'

'The banquet. Next dies Martis. Have we heard from old Nerva's widow yet?'

'Not yet, Sire,' Burrus lied. One of her slaves had brought her refusal the day before, but Burrus needed time to pass the information on. Like everything else with Nero, the timing had to be right.

'Well, send somebody, man. Chivvy her along. You know, I have such plans ...' and he lay back, beaming at some inner joke, visions swirling in his head.

'I will, Sire,' Burrus said. He got up, bowed and gave the imperial salute before spinning on his heel and leaving the Presence. In the vast atrium where the olive trees reached up gnarled arms to catch what sun they could, he caught sight of his, for want of a better word, colleague, the emperor's adviser, Lucius Annaeus Seneca.

'Ave, Lucius,' Burrus nodded. He looked drawn and tired.

'Bad day, Sextus?' the older man raised an eyebrow.

'He's obsessing about Nerva's villa now. Determined to buy the place.'

'Ah, the Golden House.'

'Oh, yes,' the Praetorian commander usually busied himself with military matters and foreign affairs. Domesticity he left to Seneca, the tutor, the philosopher. 'He's been dreaming of that for months.'

'It'll never happen,' Seneca said. 'The imperial butterfly's too busy flitting from flower to flower. Who is it this week?'

'He's been on about some tart that he clapped eyes on briefly at Nerva's munera the other day; ex-slave, apparently. He's invited her – and her husband, of course – to the bash on dies Martis next.'

'He'll probably give us all a thrill by poking the girl over the sucking pig. The husband will put up with it. We'll all applaud the size of his dick and his incredible prowess in matters extramarital, and Octavia will sulk, again.' He shrugged. 'It isn't as if it will keep us off our food for long. A blink of an eye and it's all over bar the shouting. I hope she *is* a shouter – you know how he loves some ... is appreciation the word I seek? ... from his partners. Have I missed anything out?'

'Seneca, you old cynic,' Burrus scolded, laughing. 'I can see why men rate your philosophy so highly.'

'They do, they do.' Seneca clapped Burrus on the shoulder. 'That's because I never forget the three pees – patronise, patronise, patronise.' Even before he had reached the Presence, Burrus heard Seneca call out, 'I had not thought my day could be made brighter, but then I saw Your Majesty's noble countenance …'

Burrus chuckled. It was either that or vomit in the corner.

*

Cena with Nero was something that few men forgot. No woman did. With or without their husbands or fathers, they were all on display for the most powerful man in the world. And they were all there for his personal pleasure. He was not there, of course, when his guests arrived, and Calidus and Paula found themselves on couches alongside Publius Varro and Licinius Glabrio. The senators had carefully trained their fringes forward as best they could in the still-essential Caesarean way and had gritted their teeth while the slaves at the baths had ripped the hair from their chests and legs. Nothing so inelegant for their wives, whose coiffures had, nevertheless, taken hours to achieve. Paula felt underdressed, which quite possibly was what the emperor intended for later. Flavia had lent her her best stola, and she wore the gold dolphin earrings that Gaius Lucius Nerva had given her on her wedding day. She had not powdered her skin to make it pale, however, nor darkened her eyebrows. She would leave that to the older ladies of rank, who fussed and gossiped, at once astonished and annoyed to find the wife of a freedman among their number. It would have gone easier with her had she followed their lead and covered her flawless complexion with something to make it look false; as it was, natural peaches and cream would get her nowhere. She would have been wiser to thicken her hair by plaiting in straw or slaves' shorn tresses – her own glossy curls outshone most in the room, and it was clear, even to the old wife of Marcellus Paulinus, that they owed nothing to anything but nature itself.

Paula kept her eyes downcast, something which would have made Calidus laugh had he been near enough to see. Her life had changed when Gaius

Lucius Nerva took his last, shuddering breath, and she wasn't, as yet, certain whether it was for the better. True, she and Calidus were free, and Paulina would never know slavery, but it seemed to her that Calidus was being ordered from pillar to post just as before, but by much less kind a master – now, the entire populace of Rome seemed to be in that role, and she could tell he wasn't as happy. And Julia Eusabia … she risked a glance from under her lashes … not here yet, but she would be. She struck Paula as the kind of woman who would like to make an entrance. She stepped back, away from the staring women; she was sure she had felt at least one of them tug at her hair, surreptitiously checking whether it was real.

Calidus had been grabbed by Glabrio as soon as the man saw him come in. 'So, how did the emperor take your explanation of the hunt, Calidus?' he wanted to know.

'I believe he found it rather … stingy, sir.'

'Yes, well, when you own half the world, you do, don't you?' The senator was helping himself to food from a golden plate, held out to him by a beautiful youth with honey skin and tumbling curls the old women would have killed for. With his mouth full, he gestured towards the plate. 'Tuck in,' he muttered, through the food.

Calidus had tried octopus seethed in honey before, and he could take it or leave it alone. He shook his head.

'Don't let the emperor see you turn down his food,' Glabrio advised. 'Men have had their mouths sewn shut for less.'

'Sewn shut?' Calidus was horrified. 'That's barbaric.'

'Oh, you're too sensitive.' Glabrio grabbed a passing serving girl, though, as she was wearing nothing above the waist, it was hard to get a grip. 'Try one of these instead.'

Calidus looked doubtful.

'I know they don't look very attractive,' Glabrio said. 'Sea urchin. You just drink them from the shell. Like this.' And he tossed his head back, tipping the purple contents into his mouth. 'Delicious.'

Calidus couldn't get the idea of having his mouth sewn shut out of his head and took an urchin and swallowed it in one. He blinked. 'That's delicious,' he said, amazed.

'Well, yes,' Glabrio said, smiling. 'Of course. The emperor doesn't have any old rubbish on his table, you know. He has cooks from every corner of the empire to prepare even the simplest meal. And food tasters, of course; that's essential for a man in his position. That's why he is so suspicious of anyone not eating. Poor old Antoninus Vermillius had to leave Rome in the end; he would swell up and fight for breath every time he went near anything that had swum, and the emperor does love his seafood. It goes so well with the slaves, you see.' He glanced behind him to where lovely boys and girls were slipping like eels through the growing crowd. Calidus now noticed that they all wore very little clothing, and what was there was based upon shells and seaweed. 'It's his favourite costume.'

Calidus reached for another urchin. He would stick with these; it was certainly better than having stitches through his lips. 'Does the emperor *really* do that?'

Glabrio tore his eyes away from a girl who seemed to be dressed solely in three strategically placed oyster shells. 'Hmm?'

'Sew …'

'Oh, you don't need to worry about that,' the senator said, laughing. 'He doesn't do it all the time. In fact, as memory serves, it's weeks since he did it last. And it isn't *permanent*. Only until his guest has learned their lesson. A day or two. A week. Two at most.' He thought for a moment. 'Yes, I believe two weeks has been the most.' He grabbed another handful of octopi and examined them closely. 'Another thing to remember,' he said to Calidus, his hand halfway to his mouth. 'Check the octopus. The cook has instructions to put a live one on every other plate or so.'

Calidus cocked an eyebrow. 'And?'

'Deadly.' Publius Varro had come up on his other side. 'The suckers cling to your gullet. Dead in minutes. Not pretty. Glabrio,' he nodded to the senator.

'How are you, Varro?' Glabrio asked. 'Got over the wolf incident?'

Varro didn't know who to glower at first – the annoying bastard who always bested him in the Senate chamber or the little shit who'd saved his life. Glabrio didn't expect an answer; he was enjoying the joke too much.

Paula had made her way around the edge of the room and now stood at Calidus' elbow. Glabrio gave her his usual once-over, but there was no malice in it; he just liked to keep an eye on the ladies. Had one ever taken him up on his unspoken request, he would have run a mile; but very slowly, due to his age and general decrepitude.

She leaned in now, and Calidus smelt her perfume and felt the silk of Flavia's best stola brush his arm. 'Who's that?' she whispered. A statuesque woman swept into the room, surrounded by a gaggle of beauties, their skins radiant, as only the best snail cream could make it, their hair piled as high as it could go and still enable them to turn their heads.

'The Augusta,' Calidus told her. 'The emperor's mother.' He had seen her before, when her little boy had become emperor in the first place. She had taken Nero to the Campus Martius, the barracks of the Praetorians, and he had made a speech written by Seneca. The guard had cheered them both wildly, especially when the new Caesar had doubled the usual donatius. Amazing how loudly the rattle of coin sounds as it falls into greedy coffers.

'This should be fun.' Glabrio half rose and bowed as the Lady Agrippina caught his eye. 'Get up, Varro, you're looking at the mother of the most powerful man in the world.'

To Varro's amazement, the Augusta was making her way in their direction. Everyone was on their feet in an instant, before the women dropped to their knees. Agrippina held out a bony hand for Glabrio to kiss. Close up, the strain of being Nero's mother was beginning to tell. The make-up was heavy, and her cheeks under the chalk were hollow. The mouth was tight-set and a thousand beetles had died to give her lips their scarlet colour, which had already begun to leach cruelly into the million tiny lines that edged them.

'Glabrio, you old bastard. It's been too long.'

'It has, madam,' he said, stooping to kiss her ringed fingers. Any one of those gems could have bought Nerva's Tibur villa twice over. 'And the night of my loneliness is made radiant dawn by your presence.'

'Bollocks!' she chuckled. 'Why hasn't my son made you a proconsul or something?'

'I would count it an honour to hold His Majesty's horse, to crouch as he mounted.'

'Yes, yes, all right, Glabrio, don't overdo it. Who's this?'

'Publius Varro, madam,' the senator said, bowing low.

'Not you,' Agrippina said. 'You.' She was pointing at Calidus. 'A new face. I like a new face.'

'This is Gaius Lucius Calidus, madam,' Glabrio introduced him. 'The steward of the late Gaius Lucius Nerva.'

'Ah, yes.' The Augusta held out her hand to Calidus. 'The end of an era. You're very good-looking, young man.' And she smiled her crooked smile.

'Thank you, madam.' Calidus bowed and kissed her fingers. Her nails were beautifully manicured, unlike her son's.

'Is this the little woman?' the Augusta nodded to Paula, who was still kneeling.

'My wife, madam,' Calidus said. 'Paula.'

'Hmm.' There was no hand this time. New faces Calidus and Paula may have been, but a Roman matron of a certain age, and with a unique standing, had no intention of being upstaged by someone prettier and younger. 'Hmm. Charming.' And she swept away.

'Jupiter Highest and Best,' Varro hissed, once she and her entourage were out of earshot. 'I'll swing for that woman!'

Glabrio laughed. 'Don't take it personally, Varro. We're all of us expendable.' He looked at Calidus. 'Even you. After tonight, remember, you won't be a new face anymore.'

No sooner were the ladies settled on their couches than a tribune of the Praetorian Guard crossed to them. Fabius Quintus was duty officer tonight; he wore the parade armour of his rank, minus the plumed Attic helmet, which he had left with an attendant. Alone among the emperor's guests, he carried a sword at his hip. Assassination was a Roman way of life as much as it was a Roman way of death; you couldn't be too careful.

'Calidus.' Julia Eusabia shimmered on the tribune's arm. Her stola was a blinding white, gathered under her full breasts with a golden belt, set with emeralds, the gift of an admirer. There was a golden diadem in her dark hair, and her eyes flashed like fire. She held out her hand, and the steward kissed it. She glanced at the girl beside him. 'You must be Paula,' she said, with a smile so condescending it made the others wince. 'I've heard *so* much about you. Can I whisk your husband away? There are people he just *has* to meet.' And they were gone, Calidus shrugging his apologies, leaving Paula with an open mouth and an ugly flush rising up her neck until she could feel her cheeks as hot as Hades' flames.

'Come and sit by me, my dear,' Glabrio suggested, patting the couch he had subsided on. He caught sight of his frumpy wife looking less than enchanted at the idea, and he smiled across the table at her. 'She's about the same age as our Livia, isn't she, Ulpia, dearest?' he asked her. The woman was not fooled, but this was no place to cause a scene – she could keep this along with all the many other insults, real and imaginary, to throw at him later, when she got him home. Glabrio picked up a plate and offered it to Paula. 'Quail eggs in pine nut sauce,' he said, sniffing it as he passed it across. 'Delicious and not too filling. We still have the main course to come.'

Paula took one and popped it in her mouth. No doubt it was delicious, but to her, it tasted like a stone. She made small talk with the senators and their wives, wishing the ground of Nero's palace would open up and swallow her whole. The room was full of clash and carry, slaves passing with silver tureens, ewers and wine by the gallon. Gradually, the sweetmeats and tempting little morsels were replaced by large platters, holding baked fish, the centrepiece to each table being a young dolphin, holding the tail of a bass in its mouth. In its turn, the smaller fish had the tail of a smaller fry in its mouth until, at the end of the food chain, an anchovy held a single shrimp. Paula should have been enchanted, but she couldn't concentrate. The Falernian was the best that money could buy, from the vineyards to the south, and it had gone straight to her head. A single quail's egg does not line the stomach to any great extent, and she had been too busy getting ready to eat before she came out of the house. She looked through the crowds. She couldn't see him. Or her. That arrogant shit of a Praetorian was there, quaffing wine and telling tall stories to an admiring group of guffawing diners. But Julia had vanished. So had Calidus.

V

In the darkness of the anteroom, with the sound of partying coming through the walls, Julia reached up to kiss Calidus full on the lips. He held up his hand. 'What was that for?' he asked her.

'Old times' sake,' she said, softly. 'Or perhaps a "welcome back".'

'I'm married, Julia,' he pointed out. 'And you, you have …'

She brushed Fabius Quintus away as she would a mosquito. 'Cal,' she said, tapping him on the chest with a manicured finger, 'you were always so old-fashioned. I have no illusions – I'm the plaything of Fabius Quintus, I know that. He's rich, he's powerful, he's hung like a mule. And I shouldn't be at all surprised if Nero doesn't make him Prefect of the Praetorians one day. But you…' she leaned against him, 'you, Gaius Lucius Calidus, you, I love.'

She looked up at him, her eyes closed and lips parted. The perfume and the memories swept over him as he felt her hands fondling his chest, tucking her fingers inside the hem of his pallium and curling the hairs she found there. Her other hand was curled into the hair of his head, and she was pulling him to her.

'Paula,' he said, holding himself back. 'Julia … no …'

She shook her head. 'Paula was then,' she whispered. 'Paula was minutes ago. Your past … your past, slave, belongs to me. Remember Neapolis?'

He did. The girl in front of him now, barefoot then and a slave like him. He heard her laughter, her jokes, felt her love and the warmth of her. The wild gyrations as she had danced in front of him.

'And Terracia?'

He laughed in spite of himself. 'They nearly caught us then,' he remembered.

'You told old Nerva we were looking for truffles. And he said …'

'"You don't look for truffles lying on top of people, boy,"' Calidus dropped his voice, echoing the old man.

She laughed. 'No one could take off the master like you.'

'And no one could use a lash like him, either.' Calidus still felt the leather thongs with their ivory tips slicing through the flesh of his back. She was suddenly serious, reaching up to stroke his cheek. 'You took those strokes for me,' she said. 'He wanted to whip me too, but you said no. Did you love me, Gaius Lucius Calidus, once?'

He found himself nodding. This wasn't happening. 'Yes,' he said. 'Once.'

She pulled his face closer, and their lips met. 'And again?' she asked, after a moment.

'Julia …' he struggled to find the words. Paula flashed before his eyes, wide-eyed and laughing. Paulina sat on his lap, wriggling and writhing in an ecstasy of excitement as he tickled her.

'Paula belongs to your recent past,' Julia said. '*I* am your distant past. And,' she pulled him to her again, 'I am your future.' And they kissed again. He felt her hand sliding downward, below his belt, scratching lightly as she reached beneath the fabric, onto the skin. His throat was dry, and his head was reeling. He must say no, but somehow, the word wouldn't form properly on his tongue. *How was this happening?*

A fanfare shattered the moment and brought him to his senses. He held Julia's arms firmly in both hands. 'The emperor,' he said, as he spun on his heel and left.

'Shit!' she hissed and straightened up her hair and gown before sliding through the curtain into the world of light.

*

'Jupiter Highest and Best!' Licinius Glabrio couldn't believe it. Everyone was on their feet as the trumpeters stood aside, and Tiberius Claudius Drusus Germanicus Nero stood there, dressed to kill as Neptune, God of the Sea and All the Waters. His skin had a pale green sheen, and over his bare shoulders and chest, diamond dust had been sprinkled, in the shape of scales. He wore a false beard, snaking down almost to his waist, which along with the wig he wore, was twisted through and through with golden wires, to make them look as though they were caught in a current of an invisible ocean. He wore a loin cloth of silver tissue, twisted around his legs to look like a fish's tail, and in one hand he carried a trident, in the other, a whip.

'Forgive me if I'm wrong,' Varro muttered to Paula, 'but does Neptune usually carry a whip?'

She was staring, eyes wide, as the slaves who had been serving them the food gathered around their master and, bending at the waist, undulated up and down like the surface of the sea. Every now and then, one would stand up and make sinuous movements with their hands, then would disappear into the rolling deep. She shook her head at Varro. 'No,' she said, after too long a pause. 'No, I don't think he does.'

'Then I think we should watch out for it,' Varro said, quietly. 'He obviously has plans.'

As he spoke, the whip snaked out, like an angry hand smacking a cheek, touching now here, now there, and leaving whoever it touched bleeding and in pain.

'Sorry!' Nero beamed cheerily and threw the whip down. 'All fun, all fun.' He threw up his arms, and those nearest the trident flinched. 'People,' he said, 'and Mama!' he bowed to Agrippina. 'I have an announcement.' He waited for the hubbub of his arrival to settle. The courtiers knew this was an exact science. If they were too quiet, he could throw a tantrum because his costume had not sent them into paroxysms of delight. Too loud for too long and another tantrum would ensue, this time because they were not concentrating on their divine ruler. When silence was almost absolute – no one expected Septimus Numidius to stop talking, even for Nero – he sprang onto the nearest table and stood, arms folded and legs apart, as far as his tail would let him. 'Five years ago next Aprilis, I received my first shave. In honour of that, I intend to stage new games – the Games of Juvenal!'

There was a muted roar of approval. Games cost money. Money that the senators in the room would have to find from somewhere. The plebs, of course, would love it. It was all they lived for, bread and circuses. But at their, more sophisticated, end of the political spectrum, they all knew that Nero was buying his way to a glorious afterlife, probably at their expense.

'I myself am to play some small part in the proceedings.'

The applause was more rapturous now, perhaps because a handful of the Emperor's German Praetorians had wandered into the room, adding appreciably to the number of weapons present.

'Now,' Nero took up somebody else's wine cup and drank deeply, letting the ruby contents mingle with his flowing beard. 'Eat, drink and be merry. For tomorrow … we dine!' And he burst out laughing, thumping an aged senator on the back so hard that the poor man had a coughing fit. As the emperor began his slow royal progress around the room, everybody resumed their places.

'Where have *you* been?' Paula hissed under her breath to Calidus.

'Reliving old times,' he told her, noting all too keenly the look on her face. Out here, in the light of the palace triclinium, the spell of Julia was broken. He couldn't even see her among the handsome men and the beautiful women, the knots of them thickest wherever the emperor was circulating.

'Give us a moment,' Nero said to his adoring courtiers as he reached his mother's couch. And they retreated to a respectful distance.

'Still the good entrance, eh, Nero?' she murmured through the thin lips. She reached up and twirled a tendril of the green beard around a finger. 'You have almost outdone yourself.'

'*You* taught me, Mama.' He sat next to her, kissing her hand as though she had the plague.

'Yes, I did, didn't I?' she arched her neck. She was the sister of Caligula, for the gods' sake, the widow of the deified Claudius, the mother of the monstrosity now on Rome's throne. Could there be a finer pedigree? 'Where's Octavia?' She looked around for her daughter-in-law.

'Who cares?' Nero had grabbed someone else's wine again and was slurping cheerfully. 'She doesn't share my bed. Why should she share anything else?'

'I see,' Agrippina nodded, smiling like a basilisk at various guests. 'And who is the current apple of the emperor's eye?'

Nero grinned. He leaned in closer to his mother. 'See that girl over there at Glabrio's table? The blonde with the blue stola?'

'The freedman's wife,' the Augusta nodded.

Nero sat upright. 'It still amazes me, Mama,' he said, 'how you know *everybody*.'

'No,' she said. 'I'm just nosey, that's all. What's in it for you?'

'Are you serious?' Nero blinked. 'Have you seen her face? Her body? I shall have to pin her down over a table tonight, or I shan't feel satisfied.'

'You're disgusting!' she shook her head. She knew that her son could have any woman he wanted to, in that room or any room. Come to think of it, he could have any man too, and often did. And such dreadful acne. 'Let her go.'

'Why?' Nero frowned. He had never liked having his toys taken away from him.

'Because I say so.' She looked at him with a level gaze. Nero looked back. There had been a time when he would have walked through fire for this woman. She had given him life, of course, but that was a trivia. It wasn't about biology. It was about a common bond. A bond that was based on power. And mushrooms. Never forget the mushrooms. The first coins struck had shown them both, the emperor and his mama, smiling at each other. More recent ones still showed that, but his head was above hers. And, unbeknown to Agrippina, the new design that Nero had just sanctioned, didn't show her at all. He was a man now, with advisers of his own. With Burrus and Seneca, the apron strings had been well and truly severed.

'Not enough, Mama,' he shook his head. 'Not anymore.'

'She's an ingenue, Nero.' She tried gentler logic. 'A chit of a farm girl. What about her, over there … what's her name?' She nodded to an elegant woman whose breasts were almost visible beneath her diaphanous stola.

'That's precisely the point,' he said, swigging again. 'I feel I need a bit of rough. Somebody who smells of pigs and hayricks. Anyway, that's Herminia Scaevola – I've had her already. Enjoy your meal, Mama.'

And he was gone.

It took Nero nearly half an hour to complete the circle of the room, pinching backsides, stroking breasts, cracking lewd jokes at the expense of his guests. During that time, Calidus and Paula hadn't exchanged two words. Nothing had happened in that darkened anteroom. Yet something had. An old flame had sparked to life again, like the Vestal fire in the Forum. It had not crackled and roared to a conflagration, but it was there, and it would be a while before Calidus could summon the will to extinguish it.

'Sire!' Licinius Glabrio was on his feet, only seconds behind Publius Varro. Everyone at the table rose and bowed; the women were on their knees.

'That's an interesting position,' the emperor smiled down at Paula, 'but I was hoping for something more face to face.' He teased the golden curls on the girl's head and pulled her up.

'Take your hands off her.'

People around the table were not sure they had heard right. And if they had, they didn't believe it. They all looked at Calidus. Old Nerva's freedman stood like an ox in the furrow, his eyes fixed on the spotty, strutting oaf who expected to have his wife. Paula was on her feet now, her eyes wide with panic, heart thumping. The great honour of a dinner with the emperor had suddenly turned into a death sentence for them both.

No one moved. No one blinked. Half of the emperor's guests didn't even breathe. Then there was the rush of iron as Fabius Quintus crossed the room in three strides and held his sword point at Calidus' throat. His Germans drew iron too, and the emperor was surrounded by his guards.

'No,' Nero held up his hand, a rictus grin on his face. No one, *ever*, had spoken to him like that; still less a jumped up little freedman. But tonight, the most powerful man in the world was in a playful, forgiving mood. 'No, it's all right,' he said, still looking at Calidus. 'A pity your former mistress was indisposed and couldn't come tonight. But that's the way with mistresses, isn't it? They can't always come.' He leered at Paula, whose throat had all but closed in fear.

Calidus moved forward, despite the swords at his chest, but Glabrio intervened, diffusing the moment. 'Great Nero,' he called to the slowly retreating emperor, 'An ode. Some lyre playing. We've all come to hear you play.'

Publius Varro joined him in the demand, and soon the whole room was shouting, cheering, urging the greatest lyre player in the world to hold forth. He raised his hand, beaming like a cat that had got the cream. From nowhere, a slave had brought an instrument, and Nero sat cross-legged on a table, striking a noble pose and a chord at the same time. The diners settled down for an excruciating hour or so.

'This'll take a while,' Glabrio murmured to Calidus. 'Sit tight until he's finished.'

'*Nobody* leaves when the emperor plays,' Varro said. 'Virilis Casca's wife gave birth to twins during a Nero recital this time last year. The emperor took her screams to be hysteria over the brilliance of his playing. When he heard about it, he took the credit for it being twins – divine intervention, I suppose it was deemed.' Paula's eyes were wide – it took people time to get used to Varro's sense of humour, if that indeed was what it was.

'But as soon as he's finished,' Glabrio hissed, 'you and Paula get the hell out. And don't go to the town house. Get to Tibur, and keep your heads down. Let's hope he's got a short memory.'

Calidus nodded, tight-lipped. He held Paula's hand and saw her lip tremble. She wasn't looking at him. She couldn't.

'Short memory?' Varro muttered to Glabrio. 'Nero?'

The older senator shook his head and reached for his wine. 'Got to give a drowning man some hope, Varro,' he said. 'Oh, look, the Augusta's waving at us.' And he waved back.

*

Gaius Lucius Calidus loved the Tibur, but he couldn't follow Glabrio's advice and stay there. He had a murderer to catch and he knew he would not find him in the country. Old Nerva had accepted an invitation to cena at the house of Egnatius Gellius on the Aventine three days before he died. It would have been nothing like the opulent vulgarity of the Imperial Palace. Peacock rissoles would have been as far as the cook would have pushed his culinary luck, not because Gellius was a mean host but because he was not Nero.

'I'll be frank with you, Calidus,' the senator told him as they lounged together in the echoing warmth of Agrippa's thermae, 'I'm not altogether happy about this.'

Agrippa's baths were the second oldest in Rome, and anybody who was anybody could be found there, especially after a hard day's debate at the Senate House. The steam swirled in the sudatorium, conjuring fanciful shapes that the augurs and other hysterics might well interpret as an omen.

'I mean no disrespect, sir,' Calidus assured him. He was sitting on a bench drinking the senator's wine, the sweat trickling in rivulets from his forehead and beading his hair. Egnatius Gellius had no hair, so he didn't have that problem, but his head was slick, and his upper lip shone. The folds of his fat flowed over where his waist had once been and he was puffing visibly. Younger, fitter men than Egnatius Gellius had keeled over in the heat before now, but he wasn't going to be beaten; only weaklings couldn't survive Agrippa's sudatorium. The senator wiped his face with a towel and frowned at Nerva's steward.

'You accuse me of poisoning an old friend, and I'm not supposed to take umbrage?' he bellowed.

One or two of the other bathers looked at him, but he ignored them.

'You misunderstand me, sir,' Calidus said. 'I merely wanted a guest list for the meal in question.'

'Classified,' Gellius snorted. 'I'm a senator, for Jupiter's sake; I can't go around giving out that sort of information.'

Calidus closed to the man, trying to ignore the heat that came off him. Should his cheeks be that shade of purple? 'Nerva, you said, was an old friend.'

'So he was. I ...' Gellius hauled himself upright, beckoning. 'Come into the massage room. Got to get rid of the smell of Rome.'

The pair strode through the steam, away from the bubbling water. The coolness of the massage room hit them both like a wall, and they lay down on the wooden benches, side by side. Attendants came to them, slid the curved strigils over their glistening skin, towelled them dry and then smeared the scented oil into their muscles, or, in Gellius' case, their fat.

'Gently, Severian,' Gellius scolded. 'Old war wound there. Have a care.'

Both Calidus and Severian knew perfectly well that Egnatius Gellius had never fought a war in his life. His mother, it was widely rumoured, had once entertained several contubernia of the Valeria Victrix, all together in a single session, but men like Gellius made enemies and it was probably untrue.

'I don't know which is worse,' the senator went on, as Severian rolled him over and started work on his chest, 'accusing me or accusing my friends.'

'No one is being accused, sir,' Calidus insisted. 'I just need to understand what happened.'

Gellius propped himself up on one arm while Severian scraped and oiled his flanks. 'What happened, steward, is that your master died. He was older than Jupiter, and it was his time. Why can't you accept that?'

Calidus shrugged, sitting up by now as he was. 'Just stubborn, I suppose,' he said.

The senator rolled onto his feet again, waving Calidus away. The conversation was at an end. Calidus didn't waste time cooling off in the tepidarium. Instead, he made for the changing rooms and got dressed. Most of his fellow bathers were unimpressed; the man was dressing himself. Had he no slave? What *was* the world coming to? Those who had old wives shook their heads; the tale was that a man courted ague or at the very least a nasty attack of the rheum by not cooling off before going outside.

It was on his way out that Calidus saw a face he knew. Sitting on the communal toilets beyond the archway, Piso the purse-lifter was leaning back against the wall, his eyes closed, dreaming of who knew what? As Calidus sat down next to him, Piso opened one eye. He started to get up, but Calidus held his sleeve.

'If it weren't obvious,' he said, 'I'd ask you what you are doing here.'

Piso looked quickly from left to right and back again, just for luck. 'The apodyterium,' he murmured.

'The changing rooms?' Calidus frowned. 'Ah, silly me.' Instinctively, he checked the purse at his belt. All was well. 'Rich pickings, eh?'

'Well, we're neither of us here for a shit, are we? I mean, I wouldn't even have a piss with some of the people in here.' He looked around him. 'In fact, I wouldn't piss on them if they were on fire.'

'I'm with you there,' Calidus nodded. 'Piso,' he leaned towards the man, 'remember when we first met?'

'Vividly,' Piso grunted. 'You were all for cutting my hand off.'

'I still am,' Calidus smiled, 'and I'm calling in the favour.'

'Ah.'

'You know people – litter bearers and so on.'

'Well, I wouldn't normally soil my hands with people like that, of course; but yes, I know a few.'

'Find a few who took people to a dinner party at the villa of Egnatius Gellius on the Esquiline, last December, the Ides. Who knows, there could even be a drink in it for you.'

'Joy,' moaned the purse-lifter. 'Oops, gotta go.' And before Calidus knew what was happening, Piso had gone, not making for the changing rooms but the way out. There was a commotion in the great hall, raised voices and cries of outrage. Armed men of the Emperor's German Guard were marching into the toilets, spears upright, shields locked against their bodies.

'What's going on?' somebody bellowed.

'This is outrageous. The emperor shall hear of … oh …'

The last complainant had been stopped in his tracks by the appearance of Fabius Quintus, the tribune, at the head of the men. He ignored the mumblings and made straight for Calidus.

'Gaius Lucius Calidus,' he said, in a voice that carried through all of Agrippa's baths. 'You will come with me. You are under arrest.'

Calidus looked at the grim faces under the helmet rims. Men with no sense of humour. Men without qualm or scruple. He didn't intend to die today. And certainly not on the toilet. He stood up and the guard escorted him from the building.

'Who was that?' somebody asked.

'Never seen him before,' somebody else said.

'His name's Calidus.' Gellius had waddled through, still stark naked, making for the tepidarium. 'Gaius Nerva's steward.'

'Not him,' the man said. 'The arresting officer.'

Gellius blinked. Who didn't know Fabius Quintus? 'Fabius Quintus, wasn't it? Praetorian tribune?'

The man spat. 'Tribune, my arse! How did he get that little number, eh? Can't even make a proclamation right. *He* didn't rise through the ranks, I can tell you that for nothing.'

'What do you mean?' Gellius asked.

'Well, I've seen this sort of thing before – we all have. My little lads playing soldiers can get it right. The tribune *should* have rounded it off with "in the name of the emperor" but he didn't. I'm not even sure it's legal without it. Another arse-licker, I suppose; somebody's little boy, favours asked, favours given.' The man tossed his head and clicked his tongue. 'I don't know what this country's coming to,' and stormed out in high dudgeon, something very hard to do when wearing not a stitch of clothing and carrying enough spare flesh to make an elephant proud.

*

'Somebody's little boy' said nothing to Calidus as the knot of guardsmen and their prisoner swept through the city. The sun was setting by the time they reached an opulent villa on the Palatine. Calidus was dumped roughly in an atrium, and one of the Germans, in appalling Latin, told him to wait.

The steward had been expecting this. He hadn't taken Glabrio's kindly advice and skulked in the Tibur. Instead, he'd stayed in Rome, risking a clash with Nero at any time of the day or night. Worse, he'd been asking questions, pestering senators, magistrates, slaves and acquaintances – *anybody* who had known Gaius Lucius Nerva in his last days. And here he was, under what appeared to be house arrest. The question was – whose house was this?

Even as the question popped into his head, he was answered. A tall, elegant woman walked into the room. There were no attendants. Not even any jewellery or make-up. Even so, Calidus knew immediately who she was, and he bowed.

'Madam,' he said. 'What an honour …'

'Spare me the gushing, steward. I am the Augusta, mother of the emperor, and you are something on my sandal. That's how it is and how it always will be. Are we clear about that?'

'Of course, madam.' He bowed again.

She looked at him, eyes narrowed, mouth set firm. 'How old are you?' she asked.

'Twenty-one summers, madam,' he told her.

'Twenty-one.' The hard face softened. 'When I was your age, I had vine leaves in my hair and a stola of finest fox skin. I was the wife of Gnaeus Domitius Ahenobarbus. He was an utter shit, vicious and sadistic. But he gave me one unique gift – my son, Nero. When I was your age, the little darling was still bouncing on my lap.' She smiled. 'Where did the years go?'

Calidus looked at the woman. He had heard the rumours, that she shared Nero's bed, that she had had her second husband, mad old Claudius, who was only mad north by north-west, murdered. And then there was Britannicus, Claudius' son. He had the falling sickness, men said. But he was a rival to Nero, and when he *did* fall, it had to be admitted, at a very convenient time, over dinner two years ago, there was no one who stood between Nero and the purple.

Agrippina waved Calidus to a seat, and she sat beside him. She clapped her hands, and a maidservant appeared with wine and two goblets. She poured for them both.

'Shall I drink from both cups?' the Augusta asked Calidus. 'I assure you, you are safe in this house.'

He held up his goblet and drank. Agrippa's Falernian was every bit as vintage as her son's. The fire was crackling in the grate, the logs spitting in their fury at being consigned to the flames. A wolfhound was curled up in front of it, unaware of the danger of the fire, unaware of whose house he lay in. The Augusta fed and petted him. Could he, could any Roman, come to that, ask for more?

'Why am I here, madam?' Calidus asked.

She savoured the wine for a moment before she spoke. 'Because I was impressed,' she said. 'Your little performance at the palace the other night.'

'I'm sorry if I embarrassed anyone,' he said to the woman whose son had turned embarrassment into a fine, not to say lethal, art.

She laughed. 'I have never seen my boy so nonplussed,' she said. 'He really didn't know where to put himself. The irony is, your little wifey isn't his type at all. He likes them ... bigger. All right, Octavia's virtually a dwarf, but Octavia is politics.'

Calidus was surprised. He was a *little* taken aback to hear the emperor's wife dismissed in such terms.

'Acte, now,' Agrippina went on, 'my "daughter-in-law, the maid" as I used to call her. She was more his cup of wine, but she was Seneca's favourite, and I couldn't have that. For a few days, it was your wife. Tomorrow? Who knows?' She drank deeply. 'I find it difficult to keep up.' Her acid smile had vanished. 'You've met Burrus?' she asked.

'I have,' Calidus acknowledged. It was important not to say too much around this woman. Bare facts, that was the only way to stay safe, or as safe as was possible.

'What did you think of him?'

'Good soldier,' Calidus said, carefully. 'Wise counsellor, I should think.'

Agrippina nodded. 'You've not only got guts, Gaius Calidus,' she said, 'you've a shrewd head on your shoulders. Hard to believe you're only three years older than my boy. What about Seneca?'

'I haven't had the pleasure,' Calidus said.

'Count yourself lucky. The man's a teacher, for Minerva's sake; you know the sort – believes his own rhetoric. Smug hypocrite. You wouldn't think he's been exiled by not one but two emperors, would you?'

'Madam,' Calidus said, 'it's not my place to …' Negotiating this swamp was tricky; step on the wrong tussock and it could turn out to be a crocodile.

'Exactly!' she cut in. 'It's not your place I'm after Calidus, it's your quick wits and, I suspect, a dagger just as quick.'

'I don't understand,' he said.

Agrippina got up and crossed to the window, watching the pale sun setting on the columns of the Basilica Julia and the streets growing dark and dangerous. 'I won't deny,' she too was choosing her words carefully, 'that I worked hard to get my boy where he is today. What mother wouldn't? I've done things I'm not very proud of, Calidus.' She laughed brittley, bitterly. 'That's Rome for you, I suppose you might say. But it's all turning to ashes in my mouth.' She looked down at the darkness of her wine and her pale reflection in it and put down the goblet with deliberation. Then she looked up at the man who was so different from all the others she had ever met. 'To put it succinctly,' she said, 'Burrus and Seneca between them have corrupted my little boy, filled his, admittedly, empty head with rubbish, turned him against me. *Me*! I *made* him. Without me, the most powerful man in the world would be a snivelling wimp who writes bad poetry and can't carry a tune in a bucket.'

She crossed to Calidus, who jumped to his feet, ready for anything. The Augusta had a reputation which he didn't know for sure was deserved, or was the product of gossips' wild imaginations, but he reacted automatically. She reached up and he flinched back, but she caught his cheeks gently between her palms and looked deep into his eyes. 'They're trying to kill me, Calidus,' she said. 'I know it. I'm asking you to keep me alive.'

For a moment, Calidus was lost for words. 'Madam,' he said. 'I am a steward of an estate. Until recently, I was a slave. I know nothing … What about Fabius Quintus? He's a soldier. He can handle himself. People will talk to him when he …' the right phrase was essential, '… asks them things.'

'Yes,' she half-smiled and let go of his face with a gentle pat. 'Fabius is a sweet boy, but he works for *my* sweet boy, and my sweet boy has had his head turned by self-serving bastards. The only reason Fabius brought you to me tonight is that he seems genuinely fond of me. I remind him, apparently, of his mother. As if we haven't mothers enough! Where's yours, Calidus?'

'With her ancestors, madam,' he told her. 'She died when I was young. I have no memories of her, just a carving on the stone.'

Agrippina nodded. 'There's no one here I can trust,' she whispered. 'No one at all.' She stood back and looked at him. 'Now, your price,' she said.

What was it about this family, Calidus wondered. This was the second time he had been asked that by a Claudio-Julian.

'I have a post,' he said. 'A family.'

'Your post can be filled by somebody else,' she told him. 'As for your family, bring them with you.'

'Where?' he asked.

Agrippina held out her arm. 'You see this?' she pointed to a gold bracelet dangling from her wrist. 'Nero has one too. It's made of snakeskin. You'll have heard the rumour. When that promiscuous bitch Messalina, my Claudius' third wife – hah; he really got through us, didn't he? – when she tried to have little Nero killed, a snake saved him. The assassin was poised to strike, dagger in hand, and a snake came out of the bed covers. Juno alone knows how it had got there, but it saved his life. The assassin, it transpired, had a thing about snakes and couldn't get out of there fast enough. As long as I'm wearing this, I'm safe. It never leaves my wrist. It – and I – will stay here. Not even Burrus and Seneca will dare harm me here – I am too loved by the people. And I want you here, Calidus, with me.'

Calidus looked into the dark eyes of the Augusta. 'I have my own destiny, madam,' he said. 'I am looking for a killer.'

'A killer? Who?' She looked at him keenly – was he who she had thought, or was he already in the pay of someone else?

'I don't know,' he told her. 'That's just the point. He poisoned my master, I'm sure of it. One moment I think I'm getting somewhere. Then the next …' he spread his arms wide.

'Will you at least think about it, Gaius Lucius Calidus?' she asked. 'Consider my offer. I will keep your family safe if you keep me alive. Will you consider that?'

Calidus put down his wine. 'Yes, madam,' he said. 'I will.'

VI

Poppaea Sabina let her slaves take the robe from her, and she lowered herself into the bath of asses' milk. It was just the right temperature, and she closed her eyes. The candles flickered in the soft breezes from the window, and she was soon dozing, watched over by her attendants, pampered and content.

Beyond the curtain, out of her earshot, the Emperor Nero was smiling. More than that, he was virtually licking his lips and didn't bother to hide his erection from Burrus, standing embarrassed by his elbow.

'So *that's* why old Otho's so infatuated with her. Gorgeous.'

'She *is* his wife, Sire.' Burrus thought it was wise to point it out.

'Oh, yes, I know, but, Jupiter Highest and Best, I could shaft that. She's wasted on that bandy, splay-footed arsehole. I want him out of the way, Burrus. Can't we find him a post somewhere? Anywhere, as long as it's well away from Rome.'

'Well, we need somebody in Lusitania. There's a vacancy …'

'Excellent.' Nero clapped, then remembered where he was and ducked back as Poppaea looked up at the sudden noise. 'Get him out there. He'd like that, a governorship. Simple soul, is Otho. Meanwhile …' he straightened his pallium, tucking his erection out of sight. 'How do I look?'

'Divine, Majesty,' Burrus sighed and slid away as Nero burst in on the bathing wife of his old drinking partner. He had paperwork to do.

*

'This is nice!' Piso the purse-lifter was admiring the frescoes in the Villa

Nerva's atrium. 'I could get used to this. Oh, that's Horatius, isn't it?' He pointed to a huge warrior in terracotta on the wall. 'Defending the bridge in the brave days of old? Nice. Very nice.'

Calidus looked at the man, as out of place as it was possible for a person to be, and yet, strangely, he looked completely at home as he wandered around, appraising Flavia's belongings. 'No, you can't sneak the wall under your cloak, Piso,' he sighed. 'What have you got for me?'

'Well.' The cutpurse made himself comfortable on Flavia's favourite couch and absent-mindedly fondled the carvings on the arm. 'I want you to know,' he said, 'that this information doesn't come cheap.'

'Piso,' Calidus growled. 'Remember the hand …' and he waved his own, just to show Piso that he still could.

'Yes, all right.' He cleared his throat. 'Guests at the Villa Gellius on the night of the Ides of December last. First to arrive … er … Septimus Numidius.'

'The senator,' Calidus nodded, picturing the man.

'*Ex*-senator,' Piso corrected him. 'Mad as a tree, they say. Older than Jupiter. Unsurprisingly, he came alone.'

'Who else?'

'Licinius Glabrio,' Piso said. 'A current senator.'

Calidus nodded. 'Was he alone?'

'No. He had his missus with him. Funny old girl. Rude to the litter bearers.'

'Dreadful,' Calidus muttered. 'Next.'

'Um … the tribune, Fabius Quintus. Arrogant shit, he is. Ah, but I don't have to tell *you* that. What happened there, by the way? The arrest at the baths, I mean.'

'Mistaken identity,' Calidus lied.

'He had his piece with him; Julia somebodyorother. Quite a cracker, according to the litter bearers.'

Quite a cracker indeed. What with Mater Flavia, Paula, Julia and the Augusta, there were just too many women in Calidus' life at the moment.

'That pain in the arse Publius Varro was there. With *his* missus, before you ask. The litter bearers thought she was very nice.'

'Lovely,' Calidus murmured.

'Marcus Maxentius,' Piso went on. 'It must have been like an extra-curricular meeting of the Senate. He had some tart with him, but the litter bearers didn't catch her name. Now then,' he leaned back so far, he almost fell off the couch, 'I've saved the best 'til last. One Marcus Salvius Otho, couple of years older than you.'

'I've heard that name.'

'You should have. He's an old mate of Nero himself. He had a cracker with him too. Said she was his missus, but nobody believed him. Poppea Sabina; they say she goes like a weasel and looks it, too.' Piso went off into a reverie, and Calidus left him to it.

'Make sure that that man leaves empty-handed,' he said to the slave on the gate. 'Search him if necessary – but don't disturb him now. He's having a daydream, and he's welcome to one of those, at least.'

*

The most powerful man in the world rolled off the woman and lay flat on the vast bed. The snake bracelet glittered in the candlelight as he reached across her for more wine. He was out of condition; time to get back to the chariots.

'Tell me,' she propped herself up on one elbow, facing him and tracing a lazy index finger around his nipple. 'How many women are there in your life?'

He paused with the goblet nearly at his lips. 'Only one, my darling,' he murmured. 'You.'

'Sweet,' she murmured back, blowing him a kiss. 'But that's not quite true, is it?'

Nero frowned. 'What do you mean?'

'Know what my favourite month is, Cuddles?'

'No.'

'October,' she said, rolling over to lie on her stomach. 'Sacrifices to Bacchus.' She tapped his cup and raised an eyebrow. 'Mars Ultor in the ascendancy. And the sun in the sign of Libra, the scales.'

'I don't follow.' Nobody said that the most powerful man in the world had much of a brain, least of all Seneca, who had spent years trying to find it with scant success.

'The scales,' she smiled, holding up one hand. 'Here is Poppaea Sabina, little me.'

'Gorgeous,' he leaned over and kissed her bare shoulder, breathing in her heady perfume.

'Bless you,' she chuckled. 'But here,' she held up her other hand, 'Octavia and Agrippina.' She let one hand fall while keeping the other high. 'No contest, is it?' she asked him. 'I am outweighed. They're too heavy, Cuddles. I can't compete.'

Nero put his cup down and rolled the woman over. 'You compete very well,' he said, running his hands over her breasts. He winced as he felt her fingers grab his balls and start to slowly squeeze, reserving application of the fingernails for later.

'But you control the balances, heart,' she said, raising an eyebrow. 'Only you can tilt the scales.'

'Really?' Nero enjoyed a *bit* of pain, but this was becoming too much. He tried to keep his voice low and level. 'How do you propose I do that?'

'Octavia is easy,' Poppaea relaxed her grip just a little. 'Divorce her.'

'Hmm,' Nero hedged. 'I won't pretend I haven't considered it.'

She released her grip and turned on her front again, nuzzling what passed for a beard on his chin. He edged his hips away from her just a little, enough to give him some room to avoid her fingers if she tried that one again. 'It's easy for you men,' she said, as though she was planning a new fresco for the atrium. 'All you have to do is turn round three times and say, "I divorce you." Say after me, "Nuntium mitteo." Go on,' she poked him sharply in the ribs.

'Nuntium mitteo,' he laughed.

'Twice more,' she said. 'Go on.'

'This is ridiculous.' But he was still laughing.

'Say it!' she hissed. This time, her poke in the ribs was delivered with her nails, and she drew blood.

'Ow.' He was still aching from the pressure on his balls, and he did as he was told.

'Good,' she said, flopping onto her face, her arms out to her sides.

He tried to roll her over again.

'We haven't talked about Agrippina yet,' she reminded him, her loose limbs resisting his attempt.

'A man can't divorce his mother, Poppaea,' he smiled. 'Can he?'

'No,' she said, running a lazy forefinger along his thigh and making him flinch. 'I had something more permanent in mind.'

'Permanent?'

'They named a town after her,' she said, rolling over suddenly and almost kicking him off the bed. She looked up at the huge phallus of Jupiter that rose in the fresco over the bed. It looked a lot like a criticism to Nero, who, dim as he was, knew he was losing control of this conversation.

'Is that so awful?' he asked.

'What was wrong with Ubiorum?' the woman wanted to know. 'Colonia Agrippinensis – ugh! So plebeian.'

'I'll name a town after you if you like,' he offered.

But a list was running through Poppaea's head, and she wasn't being diverted now. 'She backed Gaetulicus in his rebellion against her own brother,' she said. 'What kind of sister does that?'

'True, but her brother *was* barking, dearest.' Thanks to Seneca and much repetition, Nero had a *reasonable* grasp of recent politics.

'And what about Claudius?' She looked the emperor full in the face.

'What about him?' Playing the innocent didn't come easily to Nero. Claudius had been his stepfather, a stammering, snowy-haired freak with a gammy leg. The praetorians had elected him Caesar, and he had been in their purses ever since. Until that fateful day that the old man had swallowed mushrooms in a toxic marinade. He had become history, and little Nero wore the purple. 'I had him declared a god,' he whined.

'Sweet of you,' Poppaea nodded, smiling, 'but your mother killed him.'

'Now, there's no proof of that ...' the emperor began.

'Now, Nero,' she placed a finger on his lips. 'We are not talking about proof. Or justice. Or any of those things that we Romans are supposed to be so proud of.' She sighed and sat up. 'Well, it's late. And I have miles to go before I sleep.'

Nero sat up too. 'Where are you going?'

'Lusitania,' she said, getting off the bed, 'to find my Otho.'

'He's history,' Nero snapped.

'No, he's not,' she told him. 'He's governor of a province; not the same thing at all.' She reached across and patted his cheek. 'It's been … wonderful, Cuddles,' she said and smiled at him. The sight of Poppaea's voluptuous body disappearing into her robes was suddenly too much for the most powerful man in the world.

'All right,' he shouted. 'What do you want?'

'I've told you,' she said, freeing the ringlets of her hair from the stola. 'Octavia. The divorce.'

'That's a done deal,' Nero said. 'She's gone. I'll get my people on it.'

She stopped dressing and looked into his eyes. 'And Agrippina?'

Nero blinked and licked his lips. The woman had once been everything to him, had given him life and brought death to others, he knew, to prolong that life. But now … now he was a man, and a man who owned half the known world. Time to move on. 'All right,' he said softly, and the words fell like hammer blows in his head. 'I'll send for Locusta. Get the fox skin on it.'

There was a silence between them.

'Now,' he said, taking the stola and pulling it off over her head, 'let's get back to bed.'

She threw him backward onto the mattress and stripped herself in one fluid movement. It was the work of moments before he was ready again, and she straddled him, riding the most powerful man in the world for all she was worth.

*

'I'm not coming, Cal,' Paula was looking out of the window into the garden. 'It wouldn't be right.'

They had talked away much of the night until there was nothing left to say. She turned to him. 'You have to decide. This,' she waved her arm around the room, 'Paulina and me. Or the woman who kills emperors.'

'There's no proof of that,' Calidus reminded her.

Paula crossed the room to him. 'I grew up on this estate,' she shouted at him, 'as did you. The master taught us both a lot. And the most important thing he taught us was that emperors – and their families – were not to be trusted.'

'He was an old man,' Calidus said. 'We can't live forever in his shadow.'

'Can't we?' she said. 'Why not? Mater Flavia is still here. I'm still here. Nero hasn't bought this place yet, and he probably never will. Nothing has changed.' Her face darkened. 'Except you, Calidus. You've changed.'

'I have?'

She nodded. 'You're obsessed with the master's death.'

'Murder,' Calidus corrected her.

'If you say so,' Paula sighed. She held his arm. 'You know Paulina wrote her name yesterday.'

'She did? That's marvellous. Can I see it? Did you keep the tablet?'

'Of course I did,' she said. 'She wanted to show you at once, but you weren't here, were you? You're never here. And if you go to work for Agrippina, you never will be.'

'But *you'll* be with *me*,' he said, exasperated.

'No,' Paula said coldly, shaking her head. 'No, we won't.' She crossed to the window again, not turning to face him. 'Come and see us sometimes,' she said, 'when you're passing the Esquiline. I'll make sure Paulina remembers who you are.'

*

The rat sniffed the air, ears erect, nose twitching. Its yellow teeth, sharp as needles, shone in the candlelight. It pattered forward, slowly at first. Then scuttling. Food? Definitely. Cheese? Almost certainly; and yet …

The woman watched him, the grey-brown survivor of Rome's sewers, the shit-carrier of the Tiber, the amber of her gown glowing in the candlelight that made jewels of the rat's eyes. His fur was matted with everything that floated in the filthy waters he lived beside. The rat had reached the cheese, sniffing and prodding it with his nose. The yellow teeth bit into the mellow softness. Many a rich Roman's table would have been graced with cheese like this. It had come all the way from Sicilia in the far south and was worth a senator's ransom. Especially as there were quite a few senators who would gladly pay any price for cheese exactly like this.

The rat squeaked and drew back. Its eyes narrowed, and its front paws dabbed its whiskers, trying to stop the agonising burning in its mouth and throat. The fire spread to its stomach and it doubled up in pain, its tail lashing and its eyes closing. The woman watched, her eyes as bright as the rat's had been before death misted them over, her teeth, whiter and less sharp, gleaming in her broad smile.

There was a polite cough behind her, and a messenger of the Praetorian Guard stood there, his cloak heavy with the day's rain.

'From his Imperial Majesty, lady.' He held out a scroll.

'From Nero?' she trilled. 'How delightful.'

He nodded.

She tore open the seal of the she-wolf and read the contents. It was in Nero's own hand, semi-literate and very much to the point. 'I have need of your services, Locusta. Usual rates. Nero.'

She smiled, glancing down at the rat that squeaked no more. The Tiber's shit-carrier lay with its feet drawn up against its body in a paroxysm of agony. It would never see the river – or anything else – again. 'Tell the emperor I shall be delighted. Tomorrow at the palace.' She reached down carefully, lifting the half-nibbled cheese with a pair of tongs. She sniffed it and pulled a face. 'Just as soon as I have solved this little problem.'

*

The villa of the Augusta was very much like that of old Nerva. Except that it was larger and more opulent; and, or so it seemed to Calidus, it had more dark corners where an assassin could lurk. He was less than happy. Try though he might, he couldn't persuade Paula to cross the city with him, and he couldn't think of taking the little one away from her. Mater Flavia could cope; there were other staff who could do the work of steward, and although she had not really approved, she hadn't stood in Calidus' way.

Few people came to visit Agrippina, and those who did were vetted carefully by Calidus. They were mostly old friends or hangers-on who had somehow upset the emperor and longed to find favour with his mother. It was all rather desperate and not a little sad; but this was Rome, and a man had to climb the rickety ladder any way he could.

As the weeks passed and the visits fell away, Calidus risked leaving Agrippina alone. She had her personal bodyguard, reduced to a handful by order of the emperor, who claimed, while dining off gold plates, that the Treasury could not run to such expense. But those who remained were loyal to her, and they could handle themselves. It would take at least a cohort to get to the Augusta through them.

The murder of old Nerva still gripped Calidus like a vice. His dreams turned to nightmares, with the old man rising from the grave and pointing at him, the sightless eyes rolling in his head. 'Vengeance, vengeance,' the master moaned, every bit as dramatically as anything that Calidus had seen on the stage. In the light of the morning, he shrugged them off, but in the darkness they came again, ice and fire at the same time, filling his brain and, at moments he was sure, stopping his heart and the very breath in his body.

It all came down to that last dinner, at the villa of Egnatius Gellius, he of the tight lips and Roman circumspection; the man who was giving nothing away. In the harsh light of the morning, Calidus had already written him off. Who shits, the old adage went, on his own doorstep? No, if guilt attached to anyone that night, it must be smeared over one of the guests. Perhaps, even …

'Ha ha, yes, they do tickle, don't they?' Septimus Numidius was sitting in his atrium that morning, his ancient feet in a pool of water while little fishes nibbled at his toes. 'Put a few more in, Hortensius; I can take it.'

Hortensius obliged, upending a bucket of the speckled creatures into the pool. The old man shrieked hysterically, a child again in a world of men.

'Er … about the dinner, sir?' Calidus had almost given up on this one.

'What dinner?' The old man looked about him, confused. 'Is it dinner already?' He wrinkled his brow. 'I'm not really very hungry yet. Am I, Hortensius?'

'I doubt it, master,' the slave replied patiently.

'The dinner at the Villa Gellius.'

'Jupiter, that was months ago,' the old man said, touching the world for a split second. 'Wasn't it, Hortensius?'

'Yes, master,' the slave said. 'The Ides, last December.'

'There you are,' Numidius said, still giggling about the fish as they swarmed around his gnarled old feet. 'He's a mine of information, this one. Clever slaves – what would we do without them? I'd be lost without mine.'

'Do you remember, sir,' Calidus persisted, 'about Gaius Lucius Nerva at the dinner? Was he well? Was he taken ill?'

'Squid,' Numidius crowed, as though he had discovered the secret of the universe. 'That'll have been it. Dodgy stuff, squid. It's all those testicles, you see.' He paused. Was that the right word? Probably, and if not, it would do. Septimus Numidius had noticed of recent years that people didn't correct him as much as they used to. 'Can't be good for a man, not in the long run.'

'Did you see him actually *eat* the squid, sir? And did he become unwell immediately afterwards?'

'Who?'

'Gaius Lucius Nerva.' This was turning into a long day by anybody's standards.

'Oh, he's dead, you know. A while back. When was it, Hortensius?'

'Shortly after the Ides of December last, master.' The slave was indeed one in a million.

'Yes. Shame,' Numidius sighed. 'One of my oldest friends, old … er … I went to his funeral, you know. Peculiar hunt. I didn't exactly get there, but they told me all about it. Nice speeches, though. Somebody gave a particularly good oration. Was that me? It might have been me.'

'Well, thank you, sir.' Calidus recognised defeat when it bit him, and he stood up to go.

'Not at all, my boy, not at all.' The old man shook the outstretched hand, 'And many thanks for all the fish. They're really doing the business.'

'I'll see you out, sir.' Hortensius led the way. At the villa's gate, he paused. 'I'm very sorry about that, sir,' he said. 'He's a dear old man, but I fear his pigeons have flown the coop.'

'Indeed,' Calidus nodded. 'Well, thank you, Hortensius.'

'Er … I was there, of course.'

'Of course.' Calidus turned back to him. Why hadn't he thought of that before? 'Do you remember anything odd?'

'I remember the late Gaius Nerva didn't touch the squid. He had rather a lot of wine, though.'

'Too much, you think?'

'Oh, he was stone cold sober when he left, but he complained of stomach cramps.'

Quinius had told Calidus that at the time. 'I know,' he said.

'The ladies made a fuss of him,' Hortensius remembered. 'The lady of the house in particular. And Poppaea Sabina; she was very solicitous.'

*

'I've just heard, Calidus. He wants to marry that slut.'

'Madam?' Calidus liked to cross his tees and dot his ies in conversation with Agrippina; the woman's mind was a snake pit, and there were, after all, many sluts in the world.

'Nero, our darling boy. He wants to marry Poppaea.'

Calidus was looking at her. That name was cropping up increasingly in conversation, and so far, it had related to Gaius Lucius Nerva.

'Poppaea Sabina,' the Augusta held out her cup for a slave to top up her wine, 'his latest squeeze. Only this time,' she held up a scroll, 'his letter tells me, it's the real thing. I'll have to go to him, get him to see reason. He'll listen to me; I'm his mother.'

'What do you know about this Poppaea Sabina, madam?' he asked her.

Agrippina knew everybody. That was how she had stayed alive for so long. She tasted her wine. 'She's Titus Ollinius' daughter. They named her after Sabinius, who was consul back in the mists of time. Her first husband was Rufrius Crispinius, if memory serves. He was a guard commander, but a bad influence; I had to get rid of him. Before I did, however, she was bouncing around on mattresses various under Marcus Otho, a particularly reptilian individual who used to like a drink with my Nero.'

'Used to?' Calidus had heard the rumours, but in front of him was the oracle herself.

'That bastard Burrus packed him off to the provinces. Although now, with this latest tart, I'm beginning to wonder if Nero didn't have a hand in it. And poor Octavia. Barren as a dead fig tree *and* a philandering husband. It's her I feel sorry for.'

Calidus had come to doubt that Agrippina had ever felt sorry for anyone. He longed for his Paula, and missed the babblings of little Paulina, dancing unsteadily under his feet. He longed for the Tibur, with its orchards and its waterfalls. But he had made a promise to this woman, and he knew he must keep it. 'It wouldn't be wise, madam,' he advised, 'to go to the palace.'

'Burrus and Seneca wouldn't dare ...'

'Let me take your letter to your son, explain your feelings. Then, he can come here.'

'Here?' she laughed. 'Do you know, Calidus, that Nero has never spent a night under my roof? No, he wouldn't come here. Besides, you don't imagine he's forgotten or forgiven your stand over your little wifey that time, do you? Oh, yes, he's moved on to Poppaea without ever enjoying Paula, but we can't believe it's permanent; monogamy was never my son's strong suit.' She looked him up and down. 'He probably has the odd design on you, too, so I wouldn't put temptation in his way. But a letter intrigues me; not to Nero but to Otho. He probably knows what's going on all too well, but I'll paint him a clearer picture than his imagination could provide. What do you think? Threesomes with slaves? Something with a dog? Or is that going too far?'

'What do you hope to achieve by that, madam?' Calidus hated the fact that he was enmeshed in the antics of this mad family when his own might as well have been in Lusitania.

'Perhaps nothing,' Agrippina said. 'Perhaps Otho will come and collect his wife, Nero will reconcile with Octavia, and we'll all live happily ever after. What do you think? Should I consult an augur?'

'That's one way,' Calidus said.

*

The lady Locusta didn't like the lady Poppaea. In fact, it was hatred at first sight. Poppaea was younger, more beautiful, sang and danced well. Locusta poisoned people.

It was difficult to tell Locusta's age. Vine leaves tangled her hair on nights when the moon was full, and animal pelts graced her shoulders. When she moved, it was to a hypnotic rhythm only she could hear. She had had a hard life, certainly, in the slums of Rome, but she had gone to bed, aged twelve, with an apothecary, and he had taught her all he knew, between the sheets and out of them. Her skills were considerable, but these days, she served only one master. The apothecary was dead, surprisingly, of natural causes, and she had moved his bottles, his phials and his elixirs to the hidden room in the rather fine villa that Nero had put her in, north of the Salerian Gate.

'I was rather under the impression that the emperor had sent for me,' she told Poppaea as they sat in Nero's vast tablinium with its wall-to-wall books, all unread.

'He's busy,' Poppaea said sharply, then, softer, smiling, 'the affairs of state, you understand.'

'Yes,' Locusta said, 'I understand the affairs of state. I assume I am here to help them along.'

'Tell me,' Poppaea sat down beside the woman and patted her hand in a sisterly way. 'If I wanted someone dead, how would you do it?'

Locusta blinked in surprise. 'That would depend,' she said.

'On what?'

'Who the target was.'

'Is that all?'

'That's everything,' Locusta told her. 'Everything else follows on from that.'

'Someone close to the emperor,' Poppaea said.

'How close?' Locusta could cut to the crux of the matter with the best of them.

'Closer than Claudius.'

Locusta smiled. 'What do you know about that?' she asked.

'Only what Nero has told me.' Poppaea smiled back, blandly. 'Mushrooms, wasn't it?'

'Unfortunately,' Locusta said, 'they just gave the old man the shits. He got rid of most of my potion in the latrine. Xenophon killed him.'

'Xenophon?'

'His doctor. You see, when it comes to an important target, an obliging doctor is essential. So is an absent food taster. Halotus the eunuch cost quite a lot to look the other way.'

'So it wasn't you, as such.'

'It was my mixture – and the ingredients, I'm afraid, are my secret; mine and Bacchus' – but it was Xenophon who actually administered it. Oh, I know the rumours – poison on the tip of a feather inserted into Claudius' throat as he slept. Please! It was just a bowl of old-fashioned chicken soup.' She sighed happily, in memory of a job well done. 'The old ways are best.'

'What about Britannicus?'

'What about him?'

'Well, you helped kill the old man. What about his son?'

'It wasn't my idea,' Locusta said, suddenly doubting, a little late perhaps, whether she could trust this woman who was talking so openly about murder with her.

'I didn't say it was,' Poppaea smiled. 'I'm interested in the *mechanics* of it all.' She sighed. 'I fear I missed my vocation.'

'It's not a vocation,' Locusta said, 'not in the way that you mean it. It's …' she paused, suddenly unwilling to give too much away. 'Britannicus died of the falling sickness.'

'Yes, and I'm a German Praetorian guard,' Poppaea laughed. 'I was there, Locusta, at the funeral in the rain. I saw Britannicus' body on the bier. It was covered in gypsum, wasn't it? Not your idea, I hope? The rain washed it off as the great and the good of Rome looked on. His corpse was bright red, like a lobster. I asked Nero what happened. He said the boy dropped dead at the dinner table. His eyes were glazed and fixed, his jaws rigid. He pissed himself in spectacular fashion, and everybody smelt bitter almonds. Yes, that's the falling sickness, all right.'

'What's the point of all this?' Locusta asked.

'The point, serpent-tongue, is that you have something I want – something the emperor wants.'

'My skill.' Locusta understood.

'That,' Poppaea said, standing up, 'and to bring about the death of Agrippina.'

Locusta stood up with her. 'No,' she said. 'That I cannot do.'

'Why not?' Poppaea frowned.

'I have my reasons.'

'Which are?'

'Mine,' Locusta told her. 'Mine alone and Bacchus'.' She moved towards the door. 'I cannot help you, Poppaea,' she said, 'but I know someone who can.'

VII

The *Galatea* rode at anchor in Augustus' harbour at Baiae, the prow, a dolphin, glittering in the sun. It was high summer now, the day with its fourteen and a half hours, the sun in the sign of Cancer, the crab. It was the month of the Neptunalia, and the fleet squadron from Misenium was celebrating. Every ship was garlanded with flowers, and sailors danced and sang on the decks, hot and dry under the baking sun.

Under the awning of the *Galatea*, the prefect Anicetus was sitting with his adjutant, sampling the finest wine that Neptune could buy. The image of the great sea god rose above the deck in marble, his beard matted with seaweed, his hair sprinkled with shells. The weight of the god was taking its toll as the *Galatea* lay low in the water, her ropes creaking against the tide.

'Funny how the boy still needs me.' Anicetus was talking to his second-in-command, Lepidus. He was holding a scroll in the hand that wasn't holding the wine.

'The boy?' Lepidus wasn't always sure what his boss was talking about.

'Nero, Lepidus,' the prefect said, 'the emperor. He needs my help.'

'That's nice.' Lepidus reached across for more lobster.

'Well, it would be, if only ... how many liburnians do we have?'

'Thirteen at the last count, at Misenium.' He pointed across the blue of the bay to where the ships of the greatest empire in the world rode at anchor.

'Seaworthy?'

'Eleven, give or take. Don't tell me the emperor's going to mount a campaign!' Lepidus laughed. War and Nero didn't exactly go hand in hand.

'What about Ravenna?'

'Two, I believe.'

'How long would it take to get one here?'

Lepidus looked at him. Tutor to Nero he may once have been. Prefect of Misenium he undoubtedly was. But one thing was certain; Anicetus knew bugger all about ships. The liburnians were the fastest ships in the Roman navy; with two decks of oars, built for speed. And there were thirteen of them in plain sight. 'With a good wind,' he said, 'three days, even allowing for that tricky bit around Sicilia.'

'Good. Where's the *Imperator* at the moment?'

Lepidus didn't have to go below to check his charts. The emperor's flagship was at Ostia. 'Undergoing a refit,' he said.

'Excellent!' Anicetus was dipping Nero's letter into a flame that burned to Neptune on the table. The flame burnt briefly, lighting his face. 'Send to Ravenna, then. I want a liburnian, stripped of everything military. Get the ballistae off the decks and sling the grappling hooks. As of today, that ship is under civilian commission.'

'For the emperor?'

'The emperor be buggered,' Anicetus chuckled, knowing that was highly likely. 'The liburnian is reserved for the Augusta. Oh – and, Lepidus …'

'Sir?'

'Don't pour yourself another one. You're off to Rome. A message for Nero.'

*

Rome was hotter than hell in August. Anybody who could afford to – and many who couldn't – found what shelter they could against the demon that was the midday sun. Even the dogs that scavenged the Via Sacra lay dumb in the shadows.

One of those still on the move was Calidus. His hair was plastered to his head, and his pallium was dark with sweat. There was nothing he would like better than to lie in the frigidarium of the baths somewhere, although he knew they would all be packed by now. And besides, he had more pressing matters. Unable to penetrate the ring of iron around the Augusta, all Piso the purse-lifter could do was leave a message at the gate.

The man who helped himself to other people's valuables had important information relating to a certain matter, if Calidus read Piso's wink in the direction of the nearest blind horse correctly.

He knew he was in the right part of the city. By the time he had passed the Forum Boarium, he had been propositioned five times, four of them by women. He was also aware that he was being followed and kept his hand on his purse and his dagger hilt. Technically, he was breaking the old law of Augustus by carrying such a weapon, but Augustus was dead, and these were dangerous times and even more dangerous streets.

The graffiti told its own story. *Ammianus fucks Virginia*, the walls said. And what Phaedrus gets up to with his pet donkey would bring tears to the eyes.

'That's not true, you know.' Calidus recognised the voice even before he had turned around.

'Piso,' the steward nodded. 'What isn't?'

'That line about Ammianus. I know Virginia, she's a six-ass girl. Ammianus couldn't afford her.'

'And Phaedrus?' Calidus' interest was purely intellectual.

'Oh, that's true. Thanks for coming, Cal … er … I can call you Cal, can I?'

'No,' Calidus said.

'Right-ho,' Piso smiled. 'Cheerful' could have been his middle name. 'This way, sir.'

Calidus followed the man through the twisting dark lanes of the lower city. The smell of the Tiber was appalling here, its sluggish flow reduced to a trickle over the hot stones of the summer. Somewhere, somebody was tapping a chisel against a wall, but the pace was slow and the noise erratic. Out of the shadows, a slim girl snaked herself in front of Calidus. She may have been fifteen.

'Not now, Celestina,' Piso said, pulling Calidus away. 'Er … unless the master …?'

Calidus shook his head.

'Good call there, sir,' Piso murmured. 'More lice than you've hairs on your head. Ah, here we are.'

He ducked under a low arch that separated one insula from another. At least it was cool here. In fact, it looked to Calidus as if the sun never shone on this part of the city at all. He found himself in an apothecary's shop, but one that looked as if an earthquake had wrecked it. There were broken pots and shards of glass everywhere. A middle-aged man sat trembling on a stool. A woman was busy patching his cuts and bruises, and it looked to Calidus as if his wrist was broken. The arm was purple to the elbow, and the hand hung limp and useless.

'This is Graditanus,' Piso said. 'The apothecary. He's an old mate of mine. Graditanus, this is another mate … er … acquaintance, Gaius Lucius Calidus.'

The apothecary tried to grin, but it came out as a sneer, what with the swollen lip and puffy eyes. Getting up was out of the question.

'Tell him what happened,' Piso said, trying to find somewhere for Calidus to sit.

'It was last night,' the apothecary got the words out as best he could. 'Don't ask me what time it was. There were at least twenty of them …'

The woman who was tending Graditanus stopped her ministrations and looked at him.

'All right,' he caught the glance, 'eight. There must have been eight of them.'

'And?' Calidus didn't really know why he was here.

'They were pissed, all of 'em. Little Alessandro tried to keep them out.'

'Alessandro?' Calidus stopped him. This was getting complicated.

'Graditanus' slave,' Piso stepped in. 'An orphan. Lives in the old shelter by Insula Eight. Is he all right, Grad?'

'I sent him home,' the apothecary said. 'Poor little bleeder's black and blue.'

'Poor little bleeder,' the woman agreed.

'They'd have had a go at Acrimonia here, too, if he hadn't stepped in.'

Calidus took a closer look at Acrimonia, her solid arms, her ample hips. It would have taken all eight of them, he thought, but it wasn't his place to say so. 'Who?' he asked. 'Who hadn't stepped in?'

'Him.' Graditanus was fuming all over again. 'His High and Mightiness.' His eyes were wild, and he was staring around the room at the desolation.

'Nero,' Piso whispered in Calidus' ear.

'The emperor?' the steward frowned. He'd heard the rumours, of course, but here, for the first time, was living proof.

'He's always at it,' Piso shrugged. 'In disguise, usually, throwing his weight around with his heavies. Courtiers, arse-lickers, some of those great hairy Germans from his Praetorian Guard. If he's not stoating somebody up a back alley somewhere, he's smashing the place to bits. There ought to be a law.'

'There is,' Calidus said. 'Unfortunately, he makes it. Graditanus, you said the emperor stopped the others.'

'Yes and no,' the apothecary said. 'When they knocked Alessandro about and started on us, Nero said, "That's not why we're here."'

'What then?'

'He stood where you're sitting now,' Graditanus said, 'and he said to me – I'll never forget it – he said, "Where do you keep the Wolfsbane?"'

'Wolfsbane?'

'Aconitum Napellus, we apothecaries call it. It's a poison.'

'Yes,' Calidus nodded. 'I know. What would the Emperor of Rome want with that? And why didn't he buy it like anyone else?'

''Cos he's not like anyone else, is he?' Piso reasoned. 'He's a bloody madman, that's what he is.'

'He said he'd run out,' Graditanus told them. 'Said he'd used up the last lot – at which his mates all fell about laughing – and he needed a top-up.'

'What did you do?'

'I gave it to him. Too many people who cross that arsehole end up chatting to Charon; I'm not going to be one of them.'

'Then?'

'Then, the bastard turned to his mates and said, "Carry on, then, lads. Last one back at the palace is a eunuch's dildo." They wrecked the place.'

'Here.' Calidus dug into his purse, careful to turn his back to Piso. 'For your trouble.'

Graditanus' eyes widened. So did Acrimonia's. 'Jupiter love you, master,' the apothecary said. He looked at Piso. 'Is this from him?' he asked. 'From Nero?'

'No,' Calidus told him. 'It's from his mother. She's going to spank her little boy.'

The apothecary snorted. 'From what I hear, he'd probably enjoy that.'

Outside, in the quiet of the noonday heat, Piso held Calidus' sleeve. 'Poison, eh? I thought you'd be interested.'

'What made you think that?' the steward asked. The events of the past weeks had taught him to trust no one, least of all a man who put his hand regularly into other people's purses.

Piso folded his arms and looked at him. 'You work – or is it worked – for the Villa Nerva, the paterfamilias of which dies in what some would consider suspicious circumstances. Said circumstances involving a slap-up dinner at the Villa Gellius. You asked me to find out who attended that dinner. Now, I didn't exactly shine at school – to the extent that I never went to one – but I know a man who's investigating a murder when I see one. And you think Nero did it.'

Calidus laughed, but there was no mirth in it. 'Do I?' he said. 'If only it were that simple.'

*

The litter bearers helped her across the courtyard into the atrium where the Augusta was waiting.

'Julia, my child.' Nero's mother waved aside protocol and lifted the girl up from her knees. 'This is a surprise.' She hugged her, and they swayed together for a moment, murmuring in each other's ears a tune only they knew, from before the dawn of time.

'How are you, Agrippina?' Julia asked.

'Still here,' the Augusta said, 'thanks to Calidus and my guards.'

'Calidus?' Julia paused on the way through to the private apartments. 'How is he?'

'You know him?' Agrippina asked, surprised.

'I used to,' she said. 'A long time ago.'

The Augusta looked at her fondly. 'You can't have a long time ago,' she said. 'You're still a baby! But … however long ago it was, does Fabius know about this?'

Julia tapped the woman's arm with the edge of her stola. 'You're a terrible intriguer, Agrippina,' she laughed.

'I know,' the Augusta smiled. 'It keeps me young. Wine?'

'Thank you.'

'How is Fabius?'

'Well,' Julia waited until the slave had poured the Falernian. 'He's why I'm here, actually. He couldn't make it himself, so he sent me.'

'Got you working already, eh?' Agrippina laughed. 'And no yellow shoes and red veil yet.'

Julia pulled a face. 'I'm not sure I really want either,' she said.

'It's a man's world, darling,' Agrippina said, 'whether we like it or not. What did Fabius want?'

'To see you. To make sure you're all right.'

Agrippina nodded, looking into her wine cup. 'Burrus and Seneca,' she said. 'You're at court. What are they up to?'

Julia laughed. 'As you say, Agrippina,' she said. 'It's a man's world. I don't understand politics. Burrus is usually at the Campus Martius, drilling his soldiers. Seneca … well, frankly, Agrippina, he gives me the creeps.'

'Seneca does? Really? Why?'

'Looks me up and down and talks Greek. I'm sure most of it's filthy.'

Agrippina smiled at the girl and patted her knee. 'I'm sure it is,' she said. She paused and looked at her. 'And what,' she asked, 'of Poppaea Sabina?'

'Ah,' Julia put her goblet down. 'You've heard, then.'

Agrippina nodded. 'Is it true?'

'That Nero's taken her to his bed, yes.'

'They say she bathes in asses' milk.'

'Yes, she does,' Julia nodded. She read the worry on the older woman's face. 'It's just a passing fancy, Agrippina,' she said. 'You know your son.'

'Yes,' Agrippina sighed. 'Sadly, I do. If he has to bed every courtier he passes in a passageway, why hasn't he chosen you? You're beautiful, you're clever …'

'Me?' Julia shrieked with laughter. 'Agrippina, the emperor wouldn't look twice at me. By the way – and Fabius told me I'm not supposed to tell you this, but I'm going to anyway – there's a picnic planned.'

'A picnic?'

'At Baiae. The emperor's going to invite you to celebrate the Festival of Minerva there.'

'He is?' Agrippina's eyes brightened. Could it be true? She had been disappointed by Nero so often. And yet … she still remembered the old days with the little soft pudgy hands in hers and the smell of his little neck under the soft blond curls of his hair. It could never be like that again, and yet …

'You didn't hear it from me,' Julia said solemnly. 'The invitation will be with you in a few days. Um … Calidus …?'

The Augusta smiled knowingly and topped up their wine. 'Where did you know him from?' she asked.

'Oh, here and there,' Julia hedged. 'I think I met him first at the Lupercalia at Terracia, ooh, it must have been four years ago.'

'You were lovers?'

Julia was a sophisticated lady of Nero's court now. But it had not always been that way. There had been nights under the full moon, swaying tresses and dancing feet. If Agrippina didn't know better, she would have sworn that the girl was blushing. 'Yes,' she said. 'We were.'

There was a silence. 'And would be again?' the Augusta asked.

'He's married, Agrippina,' she said.

The mother of the most powerful man in the world roared with laughter. 'So was Claudius when I netted him,' she said. '*And* I might remind you that Poppaea Sabina is married to Marcus Otho. The day we women bother about such niceties, we can all throw ourselves into the Tiber. It might be a man's world, Julia, but as long as we have our charms between our legs, we will *always* wear the pallium. Or even,' she reached out and patted the girl's hand, 'why not the purple, one day?'

Julia smiled. Not for the world would she offend the woman by admitting that her son made Julia feel physically sick. Even old Seneca was preferable.

'Calidus isn't here at the moment,' Agrippina changed the subject slightly. 'He's an excellent protector. You know how indispensable some of these freedmen are.'

Julia did.

'I think he's left his little wifey, by the way.'

'He has?' This was news to Julia.

'I invited her here, to join Calidus, but she refused. Stubborn *and* stupid – it's a common combination, I fear. So, you see, he *may* be available, should you be interested. When he's got over this nonsense about old Gaius Nerva, of course.'

'Gaius Nerva?' Julia asked.

'Thinks he was murdered. I ask you! I mean, who'd bother? He was older than the seven hills and about as important in Roman politics these days as Romulus and Remus. He and his wife, don't laugh, appeared to be devoted to one another; if he had mistresses, it was only for the look of the thing, she was the love of his life and he hers. So, it wasn't domestic.' She shrugged and forgot all about the little tragedy played out on the Esquiline. 'Now,' she took both Julia's hands in hers, 'what's all this I hear about this fellow … what's his name? Pliny? Something about stopping babies by using the worms from a spider's head wrapped in deerskin. How does *that* work?'

*

Rome was abuzz with rumours the next morning; so what was new? From the meat slabs of the Forum Boarium to the Porta Salaria, there was talk of little else: the great general Gnaeus Domitius Corbulo had taken two cities from the Parthians, and all Armenia was Roman. In the Curia Julia, the Senate had been debating it all morning.

'He's bound to want a triumph,' Marcus Maxentius muttered as he made for his litter.

'Who?' Septimus Numidius was trying to remember where he'd left his.

'An ovation,' Publius Varro was talking to Maxentius. 'That's enough, surely, for two cities?'

'You're such a cheapskate, Varro,' Licinius Glabrio chuckled, shaking his head. 'Nero's not going to let this one go. It's an opportunity to bask in some reflected glory. He'll be up there, at Corbulo's elbow, waving to the crowd. Half of them will believe he was actually there, kicking Parthian arse.'

'Cataphracts.' Numidius was trying to recognise his own slaves. Where was what's-his-name? Hortensius? There were senators everywhere, miles of toga cloth swirling and tangling in the midday sun.

'What?' Maxentius frowned. All morning the senile old bugger had been muttering in his ear as the Senate argued. He had reached the end of his tether.

'The Parthian cavalry,' Numidius enlightened him, 'armoured horse and man. Bloody difficult to hit. Except their thighs, of course. Your Parthian doesn't protect his thighs. Cha! Foreigners, eh?'

The others swept on. 'Anyway …'

Varro had found his litter bearers and a face he had come to dread. 'Jupiter Highest and Best,' he muttered. 'What does he want now?'

Gaius Calidus saluted him and took him aside. 'A word, sir,' he said.

Varro watched the others clambering into their litters and making for the baths. 'Can't this wait, Calidus?' he asked. 'I'm a very busy man.'

'The dinner at the Villa Gellius,' the steward said, looking the man in the face.

'Which one? I mean, Egnatius Gellius is a genial host. I've been there half a dozen times in recent months.'

'The Ides of December,' Calidus reminded him. 'Gaius Nerva's last.'

'Oh, yes, of course,' Varro scowled. 'Still on about that, are you?'

'Aren't you?' Calidus asked him.

'What? No, of course not. Look, I know the old man meant a lot to you, Calidus, but really …'

'Remember the wolf, Varro,' Calidus said. The 'sir' had gone, and the freedman stood head to toe with the senator. Varro gnawed his lip. This upstart was getting above himself. Even so, he *did* owe him his life, so for now …

'I don't know what I can tell you. I didn't know old Nerva all that well.'

'You saw him in the Curia,' Calidus said. 'Knew his friends, his enemies.'

'Well, yes, but … look,' the senator angled himself so that his back was turned to the bustle behind him, as the great and the good of Rome's politicians were still coming out of the Senate House. 'Things are a little fraught at the moment. The emperor, you know …'

Calidus knew the emperor, but that had not answered his question.

'To be honest,' Varro said, as though the notion came as a surprise to him, 'Gaius Nerva was a bit of an anachronism. Oh, I don't mean he was gaga like Numidius, but he was stuck in some sort of Republican netherworld. When he was your age, of course, Augustus was the emperor. Things were different.'

Calidus knew that. He also knew that the master had always referred to Rome's first emperor as Octavian, calling a spade a spade. He had no truck with emperors and opposed them whenever he thought it right.

'Always a bit of a rebel was old Nerva.' A smile, perhaps of fondness, played around Varro's lips. Then he scowled at Calidus. 'You don't *really* believe he was murdered, do you? I mean, what would be the point? I'm sure he got up the noses of any number of the gentlemen in the Curia, but not to the extent they'd actually engineer his death. Getting rid of old men one by one is a long road to travel – there are too many of us. And more men grow old every day, Dis Pater willing, I should say.'

'Somebody did *actually* engineer his death,' Calidus said and stared the senator down.

Varro turned to go, but the steward stopped him. 'Would your wife have any memories of the dinner at the Villa Gellius?'

'Now, look, Calidus,' Varro rounded on him. 'I've been patient. I've tried to answer your questions. And, yes, I *do* owe you. But you're to leave my wife out of it. Understand?'

*

The woman who was kind to litter bearers had married Publius Varro years ago when Gaius Caligula was a nasty stain on the purple and nobody's virtue was over-nice. Virinia Metella was far too good for her husband; everybody said so. She sat with Calidus in her atrium, spinning wool as they talked. A moment spent without spinning, weaving, knitting or some other task was a moment wasted to the mistress of the Villa Varro, and talking to this nice boy who had come to see her didn't warrant putting down her spindle.

'I really don't know what the weather's like in Armenia,' she explained, 'but I *do* know our brave boys out there aren't being looked after properly. If *my* boy was with the XII Fulminata, I'd want him to have wool next to his skin for the long nights.'

'Where *is* your boy?' Calidus was making polite conversation before getting to the point of his visit.

'With the Valeria Victrix in Britannia, I'm pleased to say.' Her spindle flew past Calidus' nose, and he edged a little further along the seat, out of harm's way. 'He says the weather is dreadful, but at least it's peaceful there. The Britons understand civilization when they see it, and they're *so* appreciative. Do you have sons, Gaius Calidus?'

'No, madam,' the steward told her. 'A daughter.' It had been months since he had seen the little girl, and her face was already becoming a memory. Had her hair grown long enough for a braid yet? Did she still have the little chubby creases at the wrist?

'See to it that she doesn't marry a soldier,' Virinia said. 'Too many worries.' She shook her head, winding the wool with renewed vigour. 'Now, how can I help you?'

'Gaius Lucius Nerva,' he said.

'Oh, yes,' she said, lowering her arm and reaching into the bag at her side for more carded wool. But instead of carrying on spinning, she flattened it out on her lap, stroking it over and over as if it were a pet animal. 'That poor, poor man. I was talking to him that night, and he suddenly stiffened. He went grey, young man, quite, quite grey with pain. He'd been fine before that, chatting with Publius about this and that. Publius never tells me anything, and, to be honest, I don't get out much. So I was really enjoying myself until that moment. Gaius Nerva complained that he had stomach pains. Quite doubled up, he was. I was sorry I couldn't get to the funeral.' She looked down at the wool on her lap as if suddenly remembering what she was doing. She joined the carded wool into her spindle, and soon her distaff was flying again. She smiled up at Calidus, but it was the sad smile of a lonely woman. 'I had too many leggings to knit, I'm afraid. Had a bit of a rush job – the Valeria Victrix had moved up to a dreadful place called Isca. Publius Minor was – and you'll have to excuse the vernacular – freezing his bollocks off.' She grinned like a schoolgirl using a naughty word in public for the first time. 'Or at least, that's what his message said.' Then she was serious again. 'But … Gaius Lucius Nerva was murdered, you say?'

'I believe so, madam,' Calidus said, 'but I'm not sure your husband agrees.'

'Oh, Publius Major can be such an idiot at times. I mean, I adore him, of course, love him to bits, but quite what he's doing in the Senate, I've no idea. He means well, that's about all that can be said. Have you talked to Licinius Glabrio? And his other half, Ulpia?'

'Not yet,' Calidus told her.

'Do,' Virinia said. 'I'm sure they can be more helpful than I. Ah …' the lady of the house looked up as she heard the commotion in the entranceway, 'Publius is home. I'm sure he …'

But Gaius Lucius Calidus had gone.

VIII

The two women faced each other in the bronze mirror. Flavia turned her head this way and that as Paula stood back.

'I'm not sure I like the braid done like this, Paula,' the older woman said, lifting her chin. 'Reminds me too much of the old days. Hold the other mirror up, so I can see the back.'

Paula reached for the other mirror and stepped back, holding it up to the back of her erstwhile mistress's head. The light was dim and the reflections dimmer still, but it showed enough to tell them both that this wasn't Paula's finest work. Flavia poked at the curls at the centre of the back of her head.

'I'm sorry, Paula,' she said. 'It will have to come down. I look like a courtesan who has fallen on hard times.' She half-smiled. 'And Bacchus wouldn't approve.'

Without a word, Paula put down the mirror and set to, pulling out the bronze pins from amongst the greying curls. Usually, she prattled all day long, but today she was silent.

'Are you quite well, Paula?' Flavia asked kindly.

'I am quite well, thank you, Mater Flavia.'

The older woman looked in the mirror and tried to read the girl's expression, but her face was blank, her mouth full of pins.

'Paulina is well?'

'Yes. She's with the women in the kitchen.' She tried a laugh and failed. 'I'll be eating pastry dolls for cena, I'm sure.'

'So …?' Flavia waited. She had had no daughters, and her sons had given her no daughters-in-law before they went to their graves. She was not the mistress of small talk, but this couldn't go on. It was like being waited on by a ghost. Then, an idea occurred to her. 'Are you … are you with child, Paula?'

The girl opened her mouth, and the pins pattered to the ground. She took a deep breath and held it; with luck, she could manage to get out of the room without crying like a child.

Flavia twisted around in her chair. 'Paula? Whatever is it?'

With a great effort, her handmaiden spoke. 'I haven't seen Calidus for … months, Mater Flavia.'

The old woman had got stuck on the idea that a baby was on the way, and her face became stern. 'Well, Paula, I can't say that I approve, but …'

'No, no.' Paula fell to her knees, partly to retrieve the pins, partly to hide her tears. 'No, I am not with child, I am not seeing another man. It's just that …' she sat back on her heels, her tearstained face turned up like a little girl's, 'Calidus doesn't come home. He lives at the Augusta's house, or he is running all over Rome, asking questions … I … there is a woman. Julia Eusabia is her name.'

Flavia blinked slowly, like a lizard. 'Julia Eusabia. I think I remember her.' Then she smiled. 'But really, Paula, I don't think you have to worry. They were little more than children when … and anyway, Gaius Lucius Nerva beat Calidus …' she was saying too much. 'Besides, she is with that tribune now, and if there is one thing that girl knows, it's when she's onto a good thing.'

Paula sniffed and wiped her eyes. 'But … we never see him.'

'Would you like me to send a message? *Insist* that he comes home. There must be business that needs looking after. He *is* my steward, after all.'

'He put Titus in charge. He sees him once a week to tell him …' her mouth turned down again. 'I'm so unhappy, Mater Flavia. Paulina is growing so fast, she misses her father. If he stays away much longer, she won't even remember who he is.'

Flavia shook out her hair and sat back in the chair. 'There are ways, Paula,' she said, softly. 'If you really want him back, there are … people who could help you. Potions. Spells, even. We of the sisterhood …' She closed her eyes. Nerva had given her cause to worry just the once. He would come home, distracted, smelling of musk and infidelity. And she had been to the apothecary and … she didn't dwell on it. That was long ago, and besides, the man was dead. 'Come, child. Pin up my hair and forget about him. There's not a man born worth crying over, take my word for it.'

'But the master …'

'Ha!' Flavia laughed harshly. 'We were in love until the day he died,' she said. 'I am in love still, and I hope that he, wherever he is, loves me too. But … he had his women, of course he did. Everyone does.'

'*Everyone*?'

'Perhaps not everyone. Not Timoteus Aufidius, perhaps. But he does have his … outlets.' Flavia looked in the mirror and saw the girl was beginning a smile, just at the very corners of her mouth.

'And do you remember … oh, what was his name? It doesn't matter. Anyway, he married his goat.'

'I remember that. Was it true?'

'They say so. He moved her out to the country. Apparently, she found Rome a little too crowded.' The women were laughing now.

'And was it true about Licinius Glabrio?' Paula asked.

'Was what true?' Flavia had heard a lot about Glabrio, and she wanted to be sure she was chasing the right hare.

'The twins.'

'Oh, yes! *That's* true. I thought you might mean that enormously fat woman. The one who couldn't get up. Apparently, when he went to her bed, he …' she looked left and right to check little Paulina was not nearby, then beckoned Paula down. She whispered in her ear.

Paula listened, her eyes getting wider and wider. Then, she stood up and leaned back, locking eyes with her mistress in the mirror. 'What? Completely? I didn't know that was possible!'

Flavia shrugged. 'It's what they say,' she said, raising an eyebrow.

Paula laughed until she was doubled over. Flavia knew this hilarity couldn't last, but at least for now, she had forgotten Calidus. And she might manage to put her hair up properly on the second attempt.

But even so … Julia. She would keep an eye on Julia.

*

They walked their horses along the Tiber, as the geese honked high above them, their formation tight against the dying sun.

'Where were we?' Licinius Glabrio was munching an apple from one of his own trees. His orchards ran down a slope from his villa to the banks of a sluggish little stream, but they caught the sun all day, and his apples were the best in Rome.

'The master,' Calidus said. He didn't have an apple. Glabrio was not known for his generosity.

'Ah, yes. The late Gaius Nerva. As I said, in his day, he bowed to no man. I was proud to call him friend.' Glabrio eased himself in the saddle. He was too old for all this, and one day, soon, he promised himself, he'd give it all up and retire to Baiae where the sun always shone, and the grapes were to die for. There again, that was Nero's summer retreat; the retirement plan needed more work. 'I'm not old enough to remember him in Augustus' time, but he was a constant pain in old Tiberius' arse, and don't get me started on Caligula. He was lucky to live through that particular reign, I can tell you that for nothing. Poor Flavia …' he paused. 'Well, I heard she was worried about him. From the wife, you know. Then it was Claudius. Gaius Lucius ran rings around him, but then, who didn't? No, I can see any of those imperial misfits having their knives out for him – or, more likely, some lackey working for them. But now … well, the old reprobate ignored Nero pretty much. Told me many times that the lad was *so* cretinous he wasn't worth getting in a lather about.'

'And what did the emperor think of *him*?' Calidus asked.

'Ah,' Glabrio smiled. 'There's the ten thousand sesterce question, isn't it?' He glanced to left and right and then behind him, for good measure. 'I don't think Nero *thinks* much at all. But that doesn't make him any the less dangerous. No, trust me, Calidus; if you aren't afraid of Nero, you're either mad or dead. Reason tells me you have to be mad, but I suppose only time will tell.'

'Would your wife be able to help?' Calidus asked, 'about the last meal, I mean?'

'Ulpia,' Glabrio scowled. 'I don't see how. Not the most noticing of women, my wife,' he sighed, 'except when it comes to any shortcomings of mine, of course, in which case she has the vision of an eagle and the ears of a bat. Face of a bat, too, more's the pity. But you're welcome to ask her, of course. But if I were you, I'd talk to Locusta.' He suddenly caught sight of a horseman, trotting towards them. 'Ave, Terentius Ablamatus.'

*

The night was warm on the Aventine and the city slept. So did Agrippina's villa, until all hell woke it up. Dogs barked, torches guttered, and a column of cavalry clattered up the hill and halted at the gate, the scorpion standard at their head. There were shouts above the jingle of harness, and a tribune of the Praetorian Guard swung out of his saddle and marched to the portal.

'Io the Augusta!' he called, and frightened heads popped up above the walls. Agrippina's servants muttered among themselves. For months, many of them had dreaded this night. And they knew it *would* be night. Dark deeds are done in darkness. The Praetorians always meant business. And the German Praetorians especially; the uncivilised bastards didn't even speak the language.

'What do you want?' Calidus had strapped a sword on his hip, just in case.

'The emperor's here, lickspittle,' the tribune called. 'Open the gate or we'll break it down.'

Calidus counted at least thirty riders. His own people could match that number easily, but they were no match for these professionals. He crossed the courtyard, and told a slave to slide the bolts. As the gate swung wide, Fabius Quintus tried to push the steward aside. Calidus was faster, however, and the sword gleamed at the tribune's throat.

'Well, well,' Quintus smiled. 'Still here? And whose steward are you today?'

'From the heavies with you,' Calidus smiled back, 'it looks as though the Augusta needs all the friends she can get.'

'What's the trouble here?' One of the Germans slid out of the saddle and joined Quintus. For a German, his Latin was impeccable. 'Ah,' he said, 'the faithful husband.' He pulled off the false wig and beard. 'I'd almost forgotten about you. And your wife.'

Slowly, and without much enthusiasm, all Agrippina's people dropped to their knees. All, that is, except Calidus, who still held his blade at Quintus' throat.

'Nero!' A female voice shattered the tense silence. 'Darling!' The Augusta was hurrying down the steps, a cloak over her nightdress and her hair unbraided.

The emperor smiled at Calidus and gently pushed his blade away from his tribune's neck. 'I've just come for a chat with Mama,' he said.

*

It may have been the middle of the night, but it was not every day that the emperor came calling. In fact, as Agrippina had told Calidus more than once, he had never been to her villa before. She showed her little boy, still wearing his German Praetorian uniform, around the vines in the peristyle, where the most powerful man in the world bent to breathe in the heady scent of the jasmine. She showed him her modest library in the tablinum. He sampled the delights of her kitchen, while slaves and servants, of all degrees, shapes and sizes bobbed and curtseyed. The man they were all afraid of, the man none of them trusted, was just, shorn of the evil gossip of the Forum, a dutiful and affectionate son.

At last, they sat around the waters of the impluvium under the stars, the torches flickering a thousand-fold in the ripples that ran from the fountain that was Neptune's mouth.

'Quintus,' Nero turned to his tribune, 'leave us, will you? Small guard only. Send the others back to barracks.'

Quintus stood up and clicked his sword-hilt before slipping into the shadows.

'And Calidus,' Nero's smile could curdle milk, 'if you wouldn't mind …' the emperor held out his hand, gesturing in the tribune's wake.

'No, darling,' Agrippina said. 'I would like Calidus to stay.'

'Very well,' Nero said, after a pause. He leaned forward towards the steward. 'Whatever you may hear in the next few minutes,' he said, 'I want you to forget.'

'Forget what, Sire?' Calidus asked, straight-faced.

'Good man,' Nero laughed, helping himself to more wine. 'I can see why you chose him to watch your back, Mama,' he said.

'Does it need to be watched, Nero?' she said.

He cleared his throat and put his goblet down on the table between them. 'Yes, Mama,' he said. 'I'm afraid it does.'

'Burrus and Seneca?' she raised an eyebrow. It was good to have these things confirmed.

Nero nodded. 'I think so.'

'Execute them, then,' the Augusta said, cutting to the heart of the matter with a deadliness that had briefly surprised several of her enemies before they died.

'No, no,' Nero frowned, shaking his head. 'That's too easy. You and I both know they're conspirators, plotting against us both; but Rome doesn't know that.'

'Rome?' Agrippina blinked. 'What on earth has Rome to do with it?'

Nero smiled. Perhaps he was more of a statesman than either of his table companions knew. 'Mama,' he said, as though to a child, 'we have to preserve at least the outward show. If I am to remove Burrus, I need the Praetorians with me. Remember the adage – who guards the guards?'

'They're soldiers, darling,' Agrippina dismissed the problem. 'Licentious and brutal. Throw them a bone occasionally, and they'll bark like the dogs they are.'

'They are emperor-makers, Mama. They put Uncle Claudius on the throne, and that was *after* at least three of them hacked Gaius Caligula to pieces in that nasty little passageway behind the palace – somewhere I never go, by the way, even though lightning never strikes twice in the same place. And before you tell me that that was hardly a surprise to anyone, let me remind you they wiped out his wife and child too.' He paused for effect, a catch in his voice and a tear in his eye. 'Poor little Julia Drusilla, her brains dashed out against a wall.'

'All right,' Agrippina conceded, once Nero had blown his nose on a flowing piece of her nightdress. 'I'll grant you, the Praetorians need to be watched. What about Seneca?'

'Darling of the Senate,' Nero shrugged, as though that said it all. 'You know how those charlatans love a philosopher. Makes them think they're bright and that he's one of them.'

She patted his hand. 'But you *rule* the Senate, darling,' she said.

'The Ides of March,' Nero said, his eyes wide, staring into the glittering waters. 'Remember Gaius Julius Caesar.'

'Darling,' Agrippina patted him again, 'that's ancient history. Those were the bad old days. We live in more enlightened times.'

'Lions whelped in the streets.' Nero could feel the hairs standing up on the back of his head – by Jupiter, he was good at this! 'The Tiber ran red with blood.' He shook himself free of the ghastly images whirling in his head. 'No, Mama, if I am to present Burrus and Seneca as the murderous, malevolent shits they are, I have to have facts; evidence. That's why I'm not ready to strike yet. I'm biding my time, giving both of them enough rope to hang themselves.'

'Hanging won't do the business,' Agrippina said, pouring more wine for herself and her boy, 'and their rank precludes them from dying in the arena.'

'Looks like the steps, then,' Nero said, after a pause.

Agrippina's eyes widened, and her face creased into a smile. 'Yes,' she said, clapping at the thought of it. 'Of course, the steps. Er ... you'll garrotte them first?'

Nero frowned, as though pondering a mathematics problem old Seneca might have posed for him not so long ago. 'No,' he said. 'I think not. All the more fun for the mob.'

Calidus knew all about the Gemonia Steps, but he had only ever witnessed it once. He had been a boy at the time, jogging alongside Gaius Nerva's litter on his way to the Curia. Some anonymous miscreant who had upset Claudius was strangled at the top of the steps, the wire cutting into the flesh of his throat and his face turning purple. Then they threw his still-warm body down the steps, bouncing on the stone with his blood spraying. At the bottom, the crowd caught him, roaring like a mad wolf pack, tearing at his clothes, his hair, his flesh. Old Nerva had held the boy's face into the folds of his toga and told the litter bearers to take a side street and go the other way.

Calidus didn't know Seneca, but he'd met Burrus. The old soldier with one useless arm wouldn't go quietly, but he *would* go. And it wouldn't be pretty.

'In the meantime, Mama,' Nero was smiling, crossing the mosaic floor to sit next to his mother, 'let's talk of happier things. You'll be delighted to know that I have made my peace with Octavia.'

'You have?' The Augusta was smiling too. 'Oh, Nero, darling, I am *so* pleased,' and she kissed him full on the lips in a way that Calidus found a little unnerving. Agrippina sat upright. 'What about Poppaea Sabina?'

'Who?' Nero took a swig of his wine.

'That's my boy.' The fond mother patted her son's cheek.

'No,' Nero leaned back, cradling one knee in both hands, 'Poppaea was *so* last week. I shall be nineteen in two weeks, Mama.'

'I know, dear,' she said. 'I was there; remember?'

'Of course you were,' he laughed. 'Silly me. No, I looked in the mirror the other day, and I thought to myself, "It's time you grew up, Nero." That's what the Juvenalia Games are all about, really – proof that I've grown up.'

'Ah,' the Augusta smiled. 'Mothers never think their boys have grown up. You'll have to forgive me. How are the plans coming along, for the new games, I mean.'

'Famously,' Nero said. 'Famously. But first, a lesser spectacle. The Festival of Minerva.'

'The goddess of wisdom,' Agrippina nodded. She knew exactly where this was going.

'Which faculty,' Nero smirked, 'I have recently acquired. I'm not the Augustus for nothing, you know.' Mother and son fell about laughing. Not so much Calidus.

'That's a joke, Calidus,' Nero said. He nudged his mother. 'Face like a poker, that man. What you need, steward, guardian of my mother, is a holiday. So,' he took Agrippina's hands in his, 'I am formally inviting you to Baiae to celebrate the goddess. There'll be banquets, something gladiatorial, I shouldn't wonder.'

'Baiae,' Agrippina smiled. 'How lovely.'

There was something in her tone that made Nero suspicious. 'You already know about this, don't you?' He tapped her playfully on the chin.

'I had heard something,' she admitted. 'A little bird came to my window the other day.'

Nero guffawed. 'What a partnership we make, Mama,' he said. '*And* the best part, and I almost forgot it, I've had a special ship commissioned for you.'

'Really?'

'Anicetus is arranging it as we speak.'

'Anicetus?' Agrippina had forgotten all about him. 'Yes, of course, he's Prefect of the Fleet now, isn't he?'

'Sinecure, really,' Nero said. 'I felt bad about Seneca taking his place as my tutor – oh, I know, you're right, and it was for the best – but now … well. Who knew? Anyway, this ship isn't just to get you to Baiae – it's yours, a present to the finest Mama in the world.'

And they embraced each other, the most powerful man in the world and the woman who had put him there.

*

There was no doubt about it; Agrippina was a changed woman after her reconciliation with Nero. The doubts, if she had ever had any, had vanished. Those double-dyed villains Burrus and Seneca had poisoned the boy's mind against her, but he had seen through them because, against all the odds, he was smarter than they were; and because he was her son.

Calidus tried every trick in the book to make her see reason. Without actually calling the emperor a liar – or worse – all he could do was hint at the danger that Baiae posed. Wouldn't it be safer to stay in Rome? No, because that was where Burrus and Seneca lived. Agrippina had forgotten that she had once told Calidus that, precisely because this *was* Rome, the conspirators wouldn't dare try anything here. But Baiae, Calidus pointed out, was uncharted territory. *He* didn't know it; Agrippina had only been there once. Where was the harm, Agrippina had argued? Her Nero was back in her arms again, back in Octavia's bed, and that bitch Sabina had been shown the door. She was probably servicing gladiators somewhere, lying back and thinking of what might have been. Besides, the Augusta would have the fleet with her; what better protection could there be? She had ended the discussion with the usual raising of her eyebrow and a flare of her nostrils. 'You don't have to come, Calidus,' she said. 'I don't need you.'

And when Nero's mother said that, the sometime steward of the house of Nerva knew exactly where his duty lay.

*

It took Calidus several minutes to realise why Licinius Glabrio had given him his head to talk to his wife; it was the senator's malicious sense of humour.

'Excuse me...' Ulpia Marcia bridled. She had the build of one of Anicetus' warships at Misenum. In fact, Calidus could have sworn he had seen a likeness of her extensive beak on the column in the Old Rostrum, '...but aren't you a steward?'

'I am, madam,' he admitted, not caring for her tone.

'A slave, I heard.' Her voice was like the slamming of a coffin lid.

'Freedman, madam.'

She snorted. Slave. Free. It was all the same to her. 'I don't see why I should talk to you at all.'

'I am trying to solve a murder, madam,' he told her. 'Your husband thought you might be able to help.'

'There are two things wrong with that, young man,' she said, as her maid continued to wrestle with her iron-grey hair, teasing it high above her head. 'First, we have people for that – solving murders, I mean. They're called Urban Prefects,' she spoke loudly and slowly, as though to an idiot, 'and they're paid a small fortune. Second, my husband thinks many things, and hardly any of them are right. A sensible thought in his head would die of loneliness. However, you are not uncomely, and you are polite. So I will allow you to ask me your questions – until you tire me, and then you will go. Understood?'

'Yes, madam.' Calidus was beginning to understand a lot about Licinius Glabrio.

'Go on, then. Time is money, or I expect it is for you. No one in my family has had to earn a living for generations, I am happy to say.' She fetched the girl dressing her hair a nasty one on the leg, with a switch she appeared to have ready for the purpose. 'Careful with the pins, Virginia. It isn't necessary to skewer them in with quite such enthusiasm.'

Above the woman's head, the slave locked eyes with Calidus; sometimes, a cocked eyebrow could speak volumes, and hers could have filled a library.

'I understand—'

'I doubt it.'

'… that you were there the night at the Villa Gellius when Gaius Nerva fell ill.' Calidus had the measure of this woman now. It was vital not to weaken.

'I was. And if you ask me – and I believe you do – it was drink.'

Gaius Calidus had never seen his master drunk in all his twenty-one summers. The vine had not grown that could blur the eye and numb the brain of Gaius Lucius Nerva. 'The drink was poisoned?' Calidus felt, at last, that he was getting somewhere.

'What *is* this obsession with poison?' Ulpia Marcia wanted to know. 'All that stuff and nonsense about Claudius and Britannicus. The latter had the falling sickness, and he merely fell, like you do with the falling sickness. Hence the name, presumably.' She shut her mouth like a trap, opening it again to squeal. She lashed out again with her switch, and Calidus felt the draught as it swung. 'Be careful, you wretched girl,' she snapped. 'I haven't got that much hair to play with.' She turned to Calidus again. 'As to the former, the man was an imbecile. Stuttering and stumbling his way from disaster to disaster. He hadn't so much as run a stable before the Praetorians put him on the throne.' She paused, thinking. 'Can you die because of your own imbecility? Well, Claudius did.'

'The symptoms in the case of Gaius Nerva …' Calidus began.

'Symptoms?' Her voice could have etched glass. 'I thought you said you were a steward.'

'I am, madam.'

'Only doctors talk of symptoms, young man. Doctors deal with diseases. Urban Prefects deal with crimes. Stewards deal with …' she paused. 'I am happy to say I have no idea what stewards deal with. That is why one has them. But one thing is clear to me.' She flicked the switch menacingly. 'You are signally out of your depth. Good morning. I have some Noxii I want to see dispatched in the arena at midday, so you really must be going.' She shook her head, helpfully undoing much of the maid's work over the last half an hour. 'So much to do and so little time.' She looked in the mirror, the ship's prow jutting terrifyingly. 'That's terrible, you slut. Start again.'

Calidus knew a polite goodbye when he heard one, and this had not been one, but he knew it was time to go and bowed. 'One last thing, madam,' he said. 'Your husband mentioned a lady named Locusta but would say no more. Do you know where I might find her?'

'If she's some tart of Licinius' – and the chances are, she is – I haven't the faintest idea. He and I went our separate ways years ago, and one thing he learned early on was that I could be very accommodating, as long as he didn't shit in his own atrium. So don't look for her around these streets. He plays at politics and fondles girls a fraction of his age, while I …' she looked at herself again in the mirror, '… uphold certain standards.'

*

'They look elegant, don't they, on the wheel?' Livia Urraca was smiling up at the slaves who stood there, ropes around their necks and chalk on their feet.

'Is it elegance you're looking for, madam?' Calidus asked. All morning he had been seeking this woman out, and now, here she was, in too exposed a place to ask the questions he intended.

'A slave is a slave,' Livia told him, twirling a horse-tail flywhisk in her hand. Her handmaiden waited behind her and, several paces behind that, a Nubian, muscles glistening in the sun. Livia glanced back at him, smirking. 'But they can have their uses.'

The dealer was in full flight on the wheel, as the huge disc grated round on its axis, and today's offerings rotated slowly before her. 'These men were warriors,' he shouted, tugging on their ropes and tapping them with his whip. 'Fought for Caratacus in the wilds of Britannia. They have a little Latin, enough to get by.'

Nobody seemed much interested. 'Just look at those muscles, ladies and gentlemen. Sawing timber, clearing forests, draining marshes – no problem.' He grinned a gappy smile and leaned towards a gaggle of women in the crowd. 'Then, there's the bedroom, ladies,' he leered and patted the nearest slave on the crotch. 'Built like an aqueduct, hung like a mule. And we've kept them celibate, so they're ready to go as soon as you get them home. Even I, slave-dealer to the stars, cannot find the words.'

The women giggled, nudging each other and covering their mouths.

'Five aurei,' Livia called. 'Five for the one in the tiny subigaculum.'

There was an inrush of breath and sniggers from the crowd.

'I'll do it for less than that, darling,' a pleb grunted, laughing among his friends. The Nubian moved forward, glistening with oil and as svelte and threatening as a panther. Livia held up her hand, and he stood still.

Calidus looked at the slave that Livia was bidding for. He was tall and muscular, with a patchwork cloak thrown back to show off his chest and legs. His hair was the colour of straw, and his eyes looked dead. 'Twelve,' Calidus countered.

The crowd murmured. Livia raised an eyebrow. 'Fifteen,' she said.

The slave-dealer ripped off the Briton's cloak. 'Look at those shoulders, ladies and gentlemen,' he said. He spun the man round with deft licks of the whip. 'Look at that back. Now, don't waste my time. The sun's high, and there's entertainment in the arena later.'

There were whoops and cheers from the crowd. They all knew what that meant. Unsold slaves on the wheel would be led away to the amphitheatre, and they would die as practice targets for the gladiators. They were the Noxii, the damned, bought as a job lot to die as cattle. Only a rich – or a desperate – Roman could save their lives.

'Twenty aurei,' Calidus called.

The dealer laughed. 'I don't mean to be rude, people,' he said, 'but I happen to know that this particular slave killed six of our brave boys before he was taken. Unstoppable, he was.'

'Don't want the murderous shit on *my* estate, then,' a patrician shouted, among laughter and whistles.

'Oh, he's loyal now,' the dealer said. 'Seen the error of his ways. Soon as he saw Rome, he was a convert.' He nudged the slave hard in the solar plexus with the handle of his whip. 'Weren't you, Briton?'

The slave winced, but his dead eyes didn't change, and he kept staring straight ahead.

‘Why do you want him?’ Livia had circled back to Calidus.

‘Why do you?’

She laughed. ‘You heard the dealer. Built like an aqueduct, hung like a mule.’

Calidus smiled and nodded at the Nubian. ‘Haven’t you got one of those already?’ he asked.

She tapped him with her flywhisk. ‘Variety,’ she said. ‘That’s what I like. What about you?’

‘What about me?’ he asked. The dealer was still haggling, and the slave was Calidus’ lot.

‘Thirty aurei,’ Livia shouted. The crowd was enjoying this now. It wasn’t every day that *two* idiots clashed over the wheel. ‘Whose house were you with?’ she asked Calidus.

‘Gaius Lucius Nerva,’ he told her.

‘Nerva,’ she frowned. ‘I know that name.’

‘Perhaps we could discuss it somewhere?’ he suggested. She looked at him in surprise. He was a freedman, she was sure. And there was variety in freedmen as there was in slaves. ‘Don’t you want him?’ Calidus asked. ‘Thirty-five,’ he said to the dealer, who could by now hardly contain his delight.

‘Aha,’ she laughed. ‘You’re slowing up. Forty.’

‘You’ve got him.’ Calidus said, smiling. Livia nodded to the Nubian to handle the transaction, and the Briton was hauled down from the wheel. Here was one, at least, who would not be providing entertainment in the sand under a broiling sun.

‘Can I buy you a drink?’ Calidus asked.

Livia frowned and laughed at the same time. ‘Go to a taberna, do you mean?’ she asked. ‘Do you know who I am?’

‘I know exactly who you are,’ he said. ‘You are Livia Urraca, the friend of Marcus Maxentius.’

‘Marcus Maxentius the senator,’ she nodded. ‘He’d have you for breakfast, freedman.’

‘I’ll take that chance,’ he said.

She shook her head. ‘Not with me, you won’t,’ and turned to go.

‘Tell me how old Nerva died,’ Calidus had no choice now but to get to the point. Heads turned in the slave market. 'You were there. Tell me how he died. Tell me what happened.'

But Livia Urraca and her handmaiden had vanished in the crowd, and the huge Nubian followed them, watching Calidus carefully while dragging a slave behind him.

IX

Calidus had one clue as to the whereabouts of the elusive Locusta, and it wasn't much help. Knowing where someone *didn't* live cut down the options a little but not much. There were fourteen districts in Rome and miles of the latifundia beyond the city walls. He used his common sense as far as he was able. If she was a friend, to use a euphemism, probably, of Licinius Glabrio, then she wouldn't be living in a filthy back street somewhere. He was no prize when it came to looks, but money talks, and he would have had no need of the cheaper end of the mistress market. But then again, Calidus had never heard of her. Mater Flavia was an inveterate gossip, and so if Locusta had been parading on the arm of anyone in her circle, she would surely have had a scurrilous tale or two to tell. So, Locusta was either very, *very* discreet, or she used another name or … Calidus could have slapped himself. Who knew everyone in Rome, on either side of the law?

*

'Piso, are you listening?'

'Hmm?' Piso was using only one sense and that was sight. He was looking, with eyes on stalks, at the dancer on the table in the middle of the room, the room that throbbed to the tabor and the sistrum rattle.

'Are you listening to me?'

'Of course.'

'Well, do you think you might possibly look at me, then?' Calidus had tried everything. He had even jingled some money, and although Piso's eyelid had flickered, he hadn't turned his head. 'I need to ask you something, and then you can go back to … go back to … well, this.'

Piso turned his head as fast as a snake, then his eyes were fixed front and centre. 'There. I looked at you. Is that enough?'

'Piso! Do you want some money or not?'

The purse-lifter chuckled. 'Of course I do. But … whoah! Did you see that then? I didn't even know legs went that way …'

Calidus sighed. The dancer was very limber, it was true, and she didn't have the dead eyes usually found on such girls, in such places. He accepted that he would not have Piso's full attention for quite a while. 'All right. There's no need to look at me, then. I'm looking for Locusta.'

'You are?' Piso did glance in his direction then. 'I wouldn't have said she was your type. But …' he shrugged, 'needs must, I suppose, and she is the best at what she does.'

'You know her?'

'Of course I do.'

'So …' Calidus left a space in the conversation, to see if Piso would fill it in. 'So, where does she live?'

'Live or work?'

'Either. Wherever I'll find her, really.'

'Well, you'll have no trouble. She has a little shop beyond the Porta and lives in the villa on the hill behind it.'

'Thank you.' Calidus pushed himself away from the table, just in time to avoid being trodden on. 'I'll leave you to … it, then.'

'Uh-hmm.'

Piso had to be in love. He hadn't even asked for money, and Calidus, checking, found his purse unbroached. He hoped the thief wasn't sickening for something; summer could be treacherous in Rome.

He was nearly at the door when Piso called him back. The writhing girl cupped her naked breasts and wagged her arse at him but he swerved to avoid her and joined the cut-purse again at his table.

'Are you sure you want Locusta?'

'No,' Calidus said. 'I'm clutching at straws at the moment.'

'It's funny, really. When I first met her, Locusta was doing something like this.' He pointed to the girl.

'Dancing?'

'Yes, but not for men, and not on a table. She was pretty well naked, though, except for a few drags and rags of fur tied round her head.'

'Where was this?'

'The tullianum.'

'The prison?'

'My second home, unfortunately. Some owners of purses are quite malevolent, aren't they, when it comes to prosecuting a poor man trying to make an honest living?'

Calidus raised an eyebrow.

'A living,' Piso corrected himself without a blink.

'What was Locusta in for?'

'She was barking, I'd say. Mad as a snake. Her eyes were rolling in her head, and she was slapping the walls, the bars. I remember her head lolling left and right, and she was tearing her hair under that stupid fur scarf.'

'She was in for dancing?' Calidus knew the laws of Rome were both harsh and strange, but this seemed a little unlikely even so.

'No, no.' Piso was drooling over the girl again, and it was clear his concentration was wandering, but he looked back at Calidus briefly and shrugged. 'She was in for poisoning. That, and biting a guard's ear off.'

*

It wasn't hard to find the little settlement beyond the Porta. Calidus had never visited any of the shops along the road, but he had often ridden past them; apothecaries, seers, soothsayers and any number of premises offering services too delicate to advertise outside. The shop he sought looked very respectable, though, with a large window and a propped-open door. In the gloom inside, he could see bottles, jars and boxes, and through the open door came a scent of chamomile, lavender, wax and other fugitive perfumes he couldn't quite place. Vine leaves curled along shelves and down brackets, golden at the edges with the bloom of the sun. He bent his head and went inside.

An old crone was sitting on a stool, her hands cupped in her lap. She was crooning a lullaby that Calidus didn't recognise and she didn't seem to notice him come in. He waited a moment, then coughed, and the old woman jumped and stopped singing. She looked up at him, eyes milky with cataract. 'Who is it?' she barked. 'You made me jump.'

'I'm sorry,' Calidus said hastily. Surely this couldn't be Locusta? Even Licinius Glabrio could do better than this. 'I'm looking for Locusta.'

'She isn't here.'

'No, I can see that. Could you see your way clear to …' he was suddenly aware that he was using words associated with eyes in every sentence. He felt doomed to keep repeating it. 'Look, if you're busy …' Again? What was the matter with him?

The old woman chuckled and crooned something to the creature she held in her lap. Calidus knew in his bones this was not going to be a kitten or a puppy and steeled himself to look more closely. She suddenly opened her hands and thrust them forward. 'Crapaud,' she said. 'My toad. He's named in honour of a Gaul I knew once.' She ran her hand over the toad's back. 'He had so many warts, you could hardly tell where his bollocks ended and his …'

'Lovely,' murmured Calidus. 'Lovely pet, I'm sure. But … Locusta?'

'Up at the villa. She don't do afternoons these days. A bit too la-di-dah if you ask me. But who am I? Just her mother, that's all. Leaves me here all hours, in charge of the shop. As if I need to make a living. All the money she's got … And don't get me started on the sisterhood, jumped up madams, treating me like the doorkeeper …'

But Calidus had spotted a door in the dim recesses behind the old lady and her warty friend and was through it, as if Cerberus himself was on his heels.

*

The villa was as bright and spacious as the shop was dark and cramped. Sitting up on its hill, it had glimpses of the Tiber, twinkling in the sun, and the city, hazy with smoke; from here, the river looked like a golden pathway, as distance smudged the dead dogs, rats and occasional human floating on its greasy water. The gardens flanking the winding path were fragrant with rosemary, lavender and basil, and the marble atrium had a fountain set in one wall, delivering ice-cold water, diverted from one of the many springs under the city. Snakes were carved into the woodwork, and naked women danced under the stars on the walls. Calidus felt better just walking up into the sunshine; surely, the answer had to be in this calm and magical place?

A slave stepped silently from a niche in the wall; Calidus jumped and tried to hide it.

'I am sorry if I startled you, sir,' the man said, softly and in cultured tones. 'I am Salvius. May I ask your business?'

'I would like to see …' Calidus paused. He realised he only had one name for the woman he sought, and it seemed so gauche, in these elegant surroundings, to say it bluntly.

The slave smiled. He had seen this confusion many times before. 'My mistress has but one name, sir. It is no insult to use it.'

'In that case, I would like to see Locusta.'

'And may I ask your name, sir?'

'Gaius Lucius Calidus, of the house of Nerva.'

The slave bowed and withdrew, walking quickly but silently across the mosaic floor. The picture in the centre cartouche showed a serpent rearing back to strike the heel of a warrior. The man was unaware of the danger he was in and, indeed, seemed to be glorying in his youth, strength and beauty. The snake was black and sneaky, camouflaged amongst the reeds in which it had been lurking. For the first time, Calidus felt a shiver of apprehension.

'I see you are admiring my mosaic,' a musical voice said, from beyond the furthest door. 'Come in, let me see you more clearly.'

Calidus crossed the floor as if pulled on strings. He trod on the head of the serpent as he went and almost felt the thrill of the fangs in his foot.

'It is very … effective,' he said, as he drew nearer.

'Yes, I was fortunate enough to be able to employ one of the mosaic artists from the palace. It is from my own design.'

Calidus didn't doubt it.

'How can I help you, Gaius Lucius Calidus? May I ask – do you come with a recommendation from someone? I usually ask for a letter of introduction, at the very least.'

Calidus felt that tremor of excitement again. He felt he must be near to his answer now. 'A letter? No … I have no letter. Your name was given to me by Licinius Glabrio.'

She turned down the corners of her mouth and shook her head. 'No … I'm sorry. The name means nothing to me.'

Calidus decided to risk offending her. Looking at her in the cool, filtered light of the tablinum, he felt that perhaps he had been wrong. Though by no means unattractive, she didn't dress like any mistress he had ever seen – and he knew he had probably seen even more than he realised. She looked as though she was wearing no make-up, which, Calidus knew, probably meant that her make-up was superbly applied. Her hair was in subtle curls on the back of her head. A gold pin gleamed subtly here and there among the raven's-wing black. Her age was hard to define; she could have been anything from twenty-five to forty; if pinned out over an anthill, Calidus would have guessed the latter. But in every way, from her perfect hair to her delicately sandalled feet, she was clearly well outside the realm of possibility even for Glabrio.

'Let me tell you why he mentioned your name,' Calidus said. It seemed the most sensible way. There was something about this woman that he couldn't quite put his finger on. She was calm, she was softly spoken, her lovely home was cool, scented with herbs and perfectly and tastefully furnished. He felt at home here, and yet … something cold and terrifying seemed to be breathing down the back of his neck. He remembered Piso's memory of her, dancing in frenzy in the hell that was the tullianum and tasting a guard's blood in her mouth. He fought the urge to look behind and sat down on the couch that Locusta indicated with the wave of an elegant hand. In as few words as possible, and trying to fight back the feeling of impending doom gathering behind him, he told her of his hunt for the killer of Nerva. She was perhaps the most intent listener he had ever met. Her eyes didn't flicker all over the place; her breathing wasn't visible even at their close proximity – he felt as though the words were pouring out of his mouth and being swallowed up by her ears and the undoubtedly sharp mind behind them. Finally, he stuttered to a pause, having told her how everyone denied it could be poison, how it was drink, old age. Suicide, even. When he had finished speaking, she leaned back and tapped her lips with a finger, deep in thought.

'Well,' she said at last. 'Clearly, your master … I assume you were freed on his death?'

Calidus nodded.

'Yes, then it is clear to me that the senator was poisoned. I don't believe that anyone has no enemies.'

Calidus drew a breath, and she silenced him with a raised hand. 'No, Gaius Lucius Calidus, hear me out.'

'Please, call me Calidus,' he said. He wasn't yet used to all the names he had so recently taken on.

She smiled, sweetly, and her face was transformed; now, the estimate of forty years old seemed way too high. 'Thank you. I like to keep things simple, too. But believe me when I say that every creature that has ever drawn a breath has at least one enemy. Let me give you an example. Do you have a child?'

'Yes. A daughter. Paulina.'

'I would imagine,' she said, looking him up and down, 'that she is only little yet, but as pretty as the day is long. Am I right?'

He nodded.

'She has enemies. That I can promise you. The woman over the road from where she lives, who is barren. She is her enemy. The woman with the wall-eyed, ill-favoured child who sees your wife walking your pretty daughter in the street; an enemy. The old man she made to stumble as she skipped along the pavement on the way to marketing; an enemy. Do you see?'

Calidus saw the world from a different perspective. Although he had been born into slavery, his had not been a hard life. He had been petted and spoiled by the women of the house when he was just a pretty little boy, getting under their feet in the kitchen. He was indulged by Nerva when he took him under his wing and let him share in the lessons given to the sons of the house. He knew he probably had enemies, but as long as they didn't cross his path, he could manage to forget them. But here was a woman who saw enemies at every turn. And, he didn't doubt, knew how to keep them at bay. He nodded, slowly, as he realised what she was saying. That he was right about Nerva's death; having someone agree with him was a lot to take in.

'I didn't know Gaius Lucius Nerva well, but I have seen him in the Senate. A wise and measured speaker, loved by most, I would say?'

Calidus couldn't argue with that summing up, but he found himself wondering how a woman could have seen the Senate in action. The Curia was a fiercely male preserve.

'But clearly, he wasn't loved by quite everyone. Someone hated him enough to poison him. By the symptoms you relate … were you there with him when he died?'

'No. I was only called … after.'

'That's a shame. With the best will in the world, people sitting by a deathbed are not always the best witnesses. They doze. They imagine. They embroider. But, taking what you tell me to be fairly near what might have happened, I would guess at aconite. There are others but very tricky to prepare. Aconite is easy to get, easy to make from raw materials, easy to administer.'

Calidus was aware that his eyes were growing wider. He was glad he hadn't been offered refreshment, though that omission had taken him by surprise at first.

'Blink, Calidus, for Dis Pater's sake. And close your mouth. You look like a dead cod.'

'You … you know a lot about poisons,' he managed at last.

She threw back her head and laughed. 'Of course I do,' she said. 'That's what I do. Well, not *all* I do. I try to heal as well. After all, a poisoner isn't needed every day of the week, not even in Rome. But, where I am needed, then I *sometimes* will … let's say, guide, shall we? Yes, guide.'

Calidus didn't really know how to phrase his next question. How does one ask a beautiful, self-confessed poisoner if they have indeed poisoned one of one's nearest and dearest? She read his mind.

'But I neither guided, nor aided, nor abetted anyone to poison Nerva,' she reassured him. 'I am only *a* poisoner. Not *the* poisoner.' She smiled at him again, and it looked as though butter wouldn't melt in her mouth. 'This is Rome, Calidus. There are disgruntled wives. There are bored husbands. There are bored mistresses, come to that. Have you considered that Gaius Lucius Nerva was murdered by mistake? He was at a dinner, you say? Well, a goblet can go astray, a portion of food can end up in the wrong mouth.' She ducked her head modestly. 'I can't say I have ever made that error myself, but I understand that it happens all too frequently. Has anyone else at the dinner died since?'

Calidus thought, then shook his head.

'Hmm. That's a pity. Usually, a case of mistaken poisoning is followed up by a successful attempt later. Watch the men at the dinner; if one of them dies soon, you may have your answer.'

The slave materialised at Calidus' back, adding to his sense of unease. Calidus hadn't heard him come in. 'Mistress,' he said in his honeyed tones, 'your next … visitor is here.'

'Thank you, Salvius,' she said, rising like a siren in the waves of her pallium. 'Gaius Lucius Calidus is just leaving.' She moved closer and took his hands in both of hers, pressing them to her bosom. 'Take care, Calidus,' she murmured. 'Take it from me, if there is one thing a poisoner hates, it is to have someone on their trail. And we can strike like the serpent, unseen and unheard. Don't forget that, will you? We are everywhere.' She dropped his hands and gave him a quick kiss on the cheek, as soft as a butterfly's wing. 'But, I promise you, you will always be safe from the kiss of Locusta.' And with that, she turned away.

The slave took his arm. 'This way, sir,' he said, steering him to another door, unseen behind a hanging. As he went out, Calidus saw someone come in, a woman, with head covered. Locusta stood to welcome her. 'I'm glad you've come,' he heard her say. 'We ought to talk.'

*

Calidus took a while to shake off the feeling of someone looking over his shoulder. He would not have been able to explain in words how he had felt in Locusta's house. The nearest he could have come was to say that there was an intangible feeling of dread leaching out of the very stones that made up the villa, as if each one had been laid on another with mortar made from the distilled terror of her victims. She had not made much of her trade. She had not boasted of her conquests, of her kills. But somehow, their ghosts had come back to the place where their deaths had begun, as if they had to weigh the pestle, peer into the mortar that had held the seeds of their destruction.

Riding along the road back towards the city, he began to feel better, as though he was leaving those sad ghosts behind with every hoofbeat. He could hear the frogs croaking from the marshes over the soft thud of his horse's hoofs. The road, built by the legions, ran straight and true ahead, and he could see the Appian Gate, huge and black against the purple of the sky. The horse saw them before he did, twitching ears and nostrils and skittering sideways over the worn stones. Calidus counted three, four, then five, then six. Black shapes that rose out of the graves at the roadside like wraiths; except that these shapes were real enough, clubs in their hands and knives at their hips.

'Io, freedman!' one of them called and Calidus reined in.

'Late to be abroad,' another voice called. 'Past your bedtime, arsehole.'

They had fanned out across the road, blocking it. Beyond them, the torches of the night watch trembled like the tails of fireflies on the great gate. The marshes stretched to right and left, and Calidus knew that his horse would make no headway there; the mud would drag him down, and he'd be helpless. Even so, the horse was his best bet; apart from his knife, his only weapon. He held the reins fast, as the mare swung her head and snorted at the bite of the bit.

'You going to dismount?' the first man called, 'or are we going to make you?'

'What do you want, bum-licker?' Calidus asked.

'You, you prat,' the answer came back with jeers and laughter.

Calidus sighed. 'Oh, all right,' he said and roared a challenge as he drove his heels against the mare's flanks. The animal bolted forward, crashing into the centre of the knot of men. Lashing hoofs cut down one, and he was batted aside. A second collided with the animal's chest and lost his balance.

Calidus swung out as far as he dared without losing his own balance and slapped a third around the head. But the others weren't going so quietly. They jumped up, grabbing Calidus' reins and clawing at his cloak. For a moment, it looked as though he might break free, but the horse had slowed, whinnying in terror and shying at the force on its haunches and back. They dragged Calidus from the saddle, and he rolled across the stones.

A boot hit him in the side of the head, but he was ready for the second one and grabbed it, throwing its owner off his feet. His knife was gleaming in his hand now, but he was still on his knees. Two of them came for him at once, one howling in pain as Calidus' blade ripped the man's forearm, and the blood sprayed. A knee in the face crunched against Calidus' nose, and he couldn't see for the watering of his eyes. There was a crack as a club hit his shoulder, and the knife fell from his grasp. He was surrounded now, bleeding and fighting for breath. The mare had gone, clattering away towards the city, and the little mob closed in for the kill.

He didn't know, as his head sang and buzzed, where the sounds came from. He could hear shouts and running feet. He could see pinpoints of light, growing into flaming torches, carried by running men. The mob around him scattered, muttering and cursing. One of them aimed a final kick, and blackness engulfed Calidus.

'Let them go!' the optio barked to his men, as they watched the assailants vanish into the darkness. 'Check him.' He pointed to Calidus.

One of the night watch rolled him over, feeling the blood on his hair and tunic. 'He'll live,' he said.

'All right,' the optio grunted, retrieving Calidus' knife. 'Bring him. And when he wakes up, he can thank the garrison of Rome for his life.' He looked out across the dark desolation of the marshes. 'Nobody dies on my watch unless I say so,' he muttered.

*

They took Calidus to the valetudinarium behind the Appian Gate. They didn't know who he was, so couldn't take him home; claiming he was a soldier for a while was the only way to find him a bed. The medic checked him over and pronounced that, while badly hurt, he was in no immediate danger. For the look of the thing, he applied a leech or two to the worst of the bruises and prescribed cupping in the morning, if he felt better. Two lots of cupping if he was worse. A dose of valerian in any event. The soldiers of the watch, who had carried him there, went back to their patrols with clear consciences. The treatment he would get there might be rough and ready, but it was certainly better than leaving him by the roadside, which was what the crustier of the two men had initially wanted to do. A career in the watch didn't make men sympathetic.

Calidus moaned, tossed and turned all night, but the leeches stuck fast, doing their ghastly work. Every now and again, a slave would visit his bedside, mop his brow and check that he was still in the land of the living. Between visits, Calidus was aware of other figures coming and going around his bedside, and once, someone went through his clothing very systematically, retiring disappointed. For the next hour, Calidus dreamed of Piso. Eventually, the cocks outside started to crow and day came to the valetudinarium.

'Ave.'

Calidus opened his eyes as best he could for the swelling. Something horrid was clinging near his eye, and as he reached painfully up to touch it, he could hardly stifle a scream. 'What *is* that?' he grated, his throat dry, his lips cracked.

'Just a leech, dearie. Draining the swelling. Nothing to worry about.'

Calidus chuckled but it was like the sound from inside a mausoleum late at night; something to be avoided at all costs. 'I thought it was my eye,' he said, and the chuckle turned to a sob.

'Jocasta,' another voice cut in. 'Just get on with your mopping, will you? I need to chat with this soldier.'

'Soldier?' That was worse news than having an eye hanging out. Had he been pressed while he was sleeping?

'Yes, soldier. Who are you with?' The voice did sound rather martial, now Calidus thought about it. 'You are in the valetudinarium. So you must be a soldier. Praetorian? You were brought in last night, as I understand it. By the men of Cineas Regullus' unit. We had assumed at first you were the worse for drink, but that doesn't seem to be the case. Were you set upon?

Were you fighting?' The voice became stern. 'Because if you were fighting, it will go the worse for you, Praetorian or not.'

'I wasn't fighting,' Calidus managed to grate out. 'And I am *not* a soldier. I am …' he swallowed painfully. 'I am the steward in the house of Nerva. I was returning to Rome, when …' he racked his brain. 'I don't think I can remember quite … I was returning to Rome …'

Through his tortured eyelids, he saw the vague shape at his bedside move away. He could hear a muttered conversation taking place between the martial voice and another, softer, kinder.

'Well,' snapped the martial medic, 'my colleague has suggested that we ask for you at the house of Nerva. I hope, for your sake, they know you there. Otherwise, you will be returned to your unit for punishment for desertion, fighting,' he looked at the pile of clothes on the stool by the bed, 'and impersonating a civilian.'

Calidus let his head fall back on the pillow and closed his eyes. The owner of the gentle voice came nearer. 'Let's tidy you up,' he heard it say, and gentle hands tweaked his bedclothes. 'I'll get rid of these leeches – the night medic does love his leeches. I expect he has also asked for cupping; don't worry, I'll cancel that. What you need is sleep.' Calidus felt a dull pulling sensation on his cheek. 'Don't worry, that's just the leech being removed. You'll not have feeling there for an hour or so, then it will hurt like hell.' The voice chuckled. 'But we find loved ones are a bit squeamish to find their nearest and dearest covered in leeches.' There was another tweak of the covers. 'Sleep now and when you wake up, I'm sure you will find someone you love by your side.' A hand patted his shoulder. 'All will be well. Sleep now. Sleep now.' But Calidus didn't hear anything after 'well'. There was just a certain something in the voice that persuaded him that yes, it would indeed, all be well.

*

'Calidus? Calidus?' From out of the swirling darkness, someone was calling him. But it was warm where he was, warm and soft; he didn't want to go. 'Calidus?' They were very persistent. 'Calidus? It's Paula.' He turned his head as best he could, and his entire back screamed in pain.

'Paula?' He thought he had said it out loud but wasn't certain. He licked his lips and tried again. 'Paula? Is that really you? I'm not a soldier, am I?' Tears sprang to his eyes and made the cuts sting.

'Yes, Calidus,' she whispered. 'It's really me. And of *course* you're not a soldier. Who says you are?'

'Everybody,' he said, on a sob. 'I really hurt, Paula. All over. What happened to me?'

'You were set upon on the road just outside the Appian Gate. Whatever were you doing out there, Calidus?'

'I … I'd been … I can't remember.' Calidus closed his eyes and shook his head, but carefully. 'I just … don't remember. I know I was kicked. I know my horse …' he looked at her as best he could, though his eyes were getting more swollen by the minute. Perhaps the leeches had been a better idea than anyone but the night duty medic had known. 'Did she get home?'

'She came back by herself,' Paula told him. 'They found her in the stable this morning, a bad gash on her side. We were going to go out looking for you when an optio and some men came to tell us you were here. They didn't know your name, just that you were telling them you were from the house of Nerva. Oh, Cal,' she said, burying her head in his sheets, clutching his hand and kissing it over and over, 'we thought you were dead!'

'You and me both,' he said, trying to laugh. 'It is coming back to me but in fits and starts. It's like watching something in a lightning storm, only bits here and there, flashes of faces, fists … but as to who they were or why they did it?' He thought of shrugging, then decided against it.

'Was it because of where you had been, do you think?'

'I don't think so. I didn't know I was going there myself until … I don't know what made me go, but … Paula, can we leave this for now? It's like reading a book with half the scroll missing, in the dark.'

She patted his hand and wiped her eyes. 'I don't mean to badger you, Cal. But …' then the tears came, and with them, all the hurt, worry and anger of the past months. How afraid she had been that he had, to all intents and purposes, left her. How Paulina missed her father. How everyone worried that he was delving into waters best left alone. And now this! It was a wonder he hadn't been killed. Calidus would have loved to have taken her into his arms and tell her how wrong it all was, how he loved her and Paulina more than his own life, but somehow, nothing would work. His arms felt like lead, and his back was screaming with the bruising and the cuts. She looked up and saw his face. And the tears that streamed down his ravaged cheeks were enough. She sat up straight and pulled his blanket straight. 'I'll send for a litter,' she said, in decisive tones. 'I'm taking you home.'

X

The laughter echoed through the groves and lagoons of Baiae that sultry night. Music filled the air, coming and going on the soft breeze from the sea. It was Quinquatria and the Ides of March, engraved on the minds of every political Roman, had come and gone. In the sun-kissed days, the vines were propped in their trenches and pruned, and men and women broke their backs in the fields, sowing the three-month wheat.

All day, the emperor had been on his knees or lying face down in the temple at his villa. He was, after all, Pontifex Maximus, the highest of high priests, and Minerva was the goddess of a thousand works. There were those who dared whisper that she was almost as accomplished a musician as he was. All day, the muffled drums had beat solemnly, and the flowers had fluttered over the great and good of the court. Nero had gazed up, intoning the chanted words over and over, looking at the gilded statue of the goddess, dazzling with candles, her sword point dipped to honour the dead in war, and the owl of wisdom muttering in her ear.

The solemnities over, anyone who was anyone had flocked to the emperor's villa as dusk fell on the warm March night. The wine flowed, and the food was delicious. For Nero, the feast was understated: spring vegetables, garnished whole roast lamb and suckling pig. Instead of elaborate cakes and puddings, fruit was lightly glazed with honey and piled on simple plates. Today, he was in the mood to be spiritual and introspective, the true priest of his goddess; excess would have sat badly with that. And besides, there was always tomorrow. He had a new musical work he wanted to share with his guests, and he didn't want them distracted by the food or by indigestion.

As soon as the platters had been removed and everyone had rinsed their fingers and been given fresh goblets of wine, he struck a chord, and, for want of a better word, the entertainment began. It was debatable which was worse, his voice or his lyre playing. Minerva, many of the guests silently thought, must have been spinning in her universe.

Agrippina was entranced by it all. A shame, she agreed, that Octavia could not have been present. She was unwell, Nero had told her, and the doctors had advised that she should stay in Rome. Could it be, Agrippina had asked, squeezing her little boy's hand, that she was with child? Nero looked coy and lowered his eyelids. 'It is hoped, Mama,' he gushed, 'but I'll say nothing openly.' He pointed skywards and dropped his voice, whispering, 'The gods, you know.'

Agrippina knew. She presided regally over the banquet, her favourite handmaiden, Acceronia, cooing and billing alongside her. When Nero was not performing, he was circling the room as a good host should, leaving his mother to an adoring crowd of his sycophants. They hadn't seen her for *so* long. And how radiant she looked. Was that Indian silk that graced her stola? Simply gorgeous. She had basked in the adulation all night, pleasantly surprised that Nero was behaving himself. He wasn't belching or pinching somebody else's wine or somebody else's wife. In fact, around the ladies, she noticed, he was a perfect gentleman. And above all, there was no sign of that bitch, Poppaea Sabina. Could it be that her little Nero had really grown up at last?

He had wandered away from the festivities as the old day passed and the new one began. He padded down the winding steps that led to the harbour. It was a beautiful night; a bright moon and a million stars twinkling in the heavens. The sea was calm and gentle, and he could see the liburnian, hung with flowers, rocking gently at anchor at the jetty's end.

'Anicetus,' he nodded to the Prefect of the Fleet as the man joined him on the planking.

'Divine Emperor,' the man saluted him.

'Is all ready?'

Anicetus snorted. 'Apart from a night brighter than day and a sea like a millpond, yes, it's all going swimmingly.'

Nero spun round on him. 'Can I remind you, this was *your* idea?' he snapped. 'The mechanics, anyway.'

'What choice did we have?' the prefect asked him, 'with Locusta getting a fit of the consciences? I sensed you were in no mood to let nature take its course.'

'I'm a young man in a hurry, Anicetus,' Nero muttered. 'And,' as a rather sour afterthought, 'I have every faith in you.'

'Don't worry, Sire,' Anicetus said. 'It'll work. Trust me.'

Laughter made both men turn. Torches were flickering down the hill as Agrippina and Acceronia were led to the jetty. Nero dashed up the steps. 'Mama,' he kissed her cheek. 'Are you sure you have to leave so soon?'

She looked up at him, her darling, her purpose in life, the most powerful man in the world. 'I'm not as young as I was, dearest boy,' she said. 'Anyway, Acceronia has one of her heads.'

'That's it,' the woman clucked. 'Blame me. Blame me.'

They all laughed. 'Acceronia,' Nero scolded her gently, 'what would Mama do without you, eh? You will look after her, won't you? The sea …' he looked out at it, 'I do worry …'

Agrippina tapped his arm. 'Don't be silly, Nero,' she said. 'Look at it; it's like a millpond.' She didn't notice the quick glance that the emperor gave to Anicetus. 'Neptune is with us, darling,' she said. Nero took her in his arms.

'Goodbye, Mama,' he said, a tear in his eye. She saw it and used her Indian silk to wipe it away.

'Silly boy,' she crooned, but her eyes were wet too. 'I'll see you back in Rome.'

He said nothing but let his hand trail in hers as Anicetus barked orders, and the crew of the liburnian snapped to attention. The emperor's mother had never stood on the deck of a warship before, and she was a little surprised. The two banks of oars had become one, and everywhere were temporary shelters along the planking, bright with new paint. The murderous bronze beak had gone. She sat on the leather couch amidships and watched with fascination as the crew went about their business, hauling ropes and shuttling oars in their housings.

Anicetus was the last of the emperor's party to take his leave. 'Have no fear, madam,' he said. 'I will be in a boat just behind you, and there are three more; you know, in case of accidents.'

'Accidents?' Acceronia, sitting at Agrippina's feet looked up, alarmed. 'What do you mean, accidents? How often do these ships sink?'

'Er … just the once,' Anicetus beamed, and everybody laughed. The old sailors' joke never failed to amuse.

On the shore, as the anchor chain rattled and the spray flew, Nero took a torch from an attendant and stood, waving, as the liburnian's oars slid outward and the prow glided through the shallows. He waved once, then turned to the stone wall of the little light tower, the small pharos that Nero had had copied from the one in Alexandria. He leaned casually against the rough stone. 'You're witnessing history,' he said softly. 'Come and say goodbye to my mother, as a future daughter-in-law should.'

Poppaea Sabina swayed out from her hiding place, her hair covered with a shawl. 'You're sure about that?' she asked him, running her fingers up his arm and onto his neck.

Nero watched Anicetus' boats follow in the liburnian's wake, like sharks circling for a kill. He passed Poppaea the torch. 'Do the honours, would you?'

She laughed, kissed him deeply and threw the flaming brand into the darkling waters of the sea.

*

Out to sea, Anicetus saw the torch brand tumbling into the millpond, breaking the smoothness and sending smoke-wreathed ripples out from the shore. That was the signal. Now it was up to Neptune. Or, put more accurately, the craftiness of his carpenters. The oar blades struck level over the water's surface, the breeze scarcely shifting the sail. Ropes creaked and the helmsman leaned on the tiller. The liburnian, high in the water, now it was stripped of half its oars and rowers, responded easily, the prow coming round, its garlands of Minerva swinging around the swan's neck and trailing in the waves.

Below the deck, all was darkness. The oarsmen, who had broken their backs against Cilician pirates and driven their ships' bronze-jacketed beaks into the hull timbers of Rome's enemies, were unused to this. They were unshackled – that was usual in peacetime – but the joists around them had a strange amount of give. Water was seeping in at the stern, but the hortator, sitting at the bow and solemnly keeping time with his drum, seemed unaware. The men at the back were calling out to him, in single voices at first, then in a massed shout.

Up on the deck, the Augusta heard them. Acceronia closed to her. 'There's something wrong, madam,' she murmured. It was ill bred to shout, even when things were clearly amiss.

Agrippina looked back to the land. She could still see the lights of the palace, but all sound had faded now, except for the odd bark of a dog scavenging along the quay. The voices of the men shouting and the rush of the wind in the sails filled her ears. She could see Anicetus' rowing boats, but they were losing headway against the speed of the liburnian. The ship was rocking. What should have been a short, smooth trip across the bay was turning into a nightmare. There was a loud crack as the timbers gave way, shorn of their pegs at crucial joints, and the upper deck slewed sideways. The beat of the hortator had stopped, his drum torn from his hand by oarsmen already saving themselves. The masthead broke, almost on cue, and the canvas came down, heavy and hard on the Augusta's couch.

But the women had already gone. The lurch of the ship to starboard had thrown them both into the frothing, foaming sea, as the liburnian rolled like a dying shark, oars splitting against the planking. There were men in the water, shouting for help, spluttering, drowning. Nobody had ever taught Rome's rowers to swim, and they were calling out to the boats.

Agrippina wrenched off the Indian silk stola, heavy now with sea water and tangling with her legs, threatening to take her down to Neptune. Acceronia was with her, both women swimming strongly against the swirl of the waters. The liburnian rose above them, black against the purple of the starry sky as the least likely accident in history played itself out. One by one, as Anicetus' boats came alongside, the oarsmen dragged their terrified comrades out of the sea and rowed in search of the next one.

A spar crashed down into the water, and Agrippina disappeared. Acceronia floundered, trying not to panic, trying to keep herself afloat while, at the same time, looking for her mistress. She took as deep a breath as she could and ducked under the surface. The darkness here was almost total, but she could see and feel legs thrashing all around her. Rough sandals. Tunics. Belts. These were the liburnian's rowers. There was no softness. No shawl. No jewelled feet. She struck upwards to whatever light there was, crashing to the surface in a roar of air that turned to a scream. There was a rowing boat almost on top of her, and she forced her bursting lungs to work. 'The Augusta,' she shouted, waving. 'Over here!'

The rowing boat swung instantly in her direction, heavy with rescued men as it was. She reached up and a sailor caught her. For a second only, she looked into his face. He was young; he was handsome. He had saved her life. And then, with a single swing of an oar, he killed her. Blood spread in the water as the oarsman still gripped the woman's hair.

Anicetus peered over the side and checked her limp wrists in the darkness. 'It's not her,' he said. 'Give her to the fishes.' The sailor let Acceronia go, her lifeless body sliding downwards with the disintegrating timbers of the liburnian. Her hair coiled in the waters and mixed with the blood still oozing from the wound on her head. Her eyes wide, she went down and down, into Neptune's ever-open arms.

*

Agrippina sat bolt upright, eyes wild. Her expensive tiara had long gone. In fact, she had lost that the moment she had hit the water. Her hair, so lovingly braided by Acceronia, was plastered to her head, and she was shivering violently, trying to rationalise what had happened. One moment, she remembered, she was on the jetty, saying goodbye to Nero. The next … she vomited onto the wet sand and sat there, exhausted. She had no clear memory of how she had got this far. She had enjoyed swimming in her private baths as a girl, but this was different. The sea, even when calm as a millpond, was cruel and had given her no advantage.

'She's over here.' A man's voice brought her to, and she looked around helplessly. Her throat was raw from the seawater and the vomit, and she couldn't even croak.

She felt someone lift her head and her wrist as they fumbled for signs of life. She felt fingers tug at the snake bracelet, the one that had always kept her safe, and then heard them say, 'Yes, it's her. It's the Augusta.'

*

'Got away?' Only Nero could put such malevolence into two words. 'Got away, Anicetus?'

'She was rescued, Sire,' the prefect mumbled. It was dawn now, the light of a new day revealing the floating wreckage of the liburnian in the harbour, where the meagre tide had carried it. 'She swam to the shore, and they took her to the house at Bauli.'

'And you didn't think to follow?'

Anicetus took a deep breath. He stepped closer to the emperor, the boy he had once taught to read, the man he now wanted to slap with all his strength. It had been a difficult night, but he had a feeling that the day to come would be worse. Might as well be disembowelled and die in horrible pain for a sheep as a lamb. 'An accident at sea is one thing, Nero,' he said, the stern tutor once again, the sycophancy of the court forgotten. 'Anything else would be pure murder.'

Nero's face was purple, like his pallium. He looked at Poppaea, sitting on the dais next to him. For the briefest of moments, he panicked. He wanted to run to Rome, to see Burrus and Seneca, to ask them what to do; to stick his thumb in his mouth and do as they told him. But Poppaea Sabina was already on her feet, looking at him with contempt.

'You know what you have to do,' she hissed and swept from the room.

Nero recovered himself. He lowered his eyelids, flexed his jaw, then grabbed a sword from the nearest German guard and threw it at Anicetus' feet. 'Pure murder it is, then,' he said. 'I don't want the details.'

Anicetus looked at the madman he had inadvertently helped to create. Then he thrust his arm out straight in salute and turned on his heel. He left the sword where it was. He had one of his own.

*

'Have no fears for me, darling.' Agrippina was dictating to her secretary. Nero had made the house at Bauli available to her so that they could spend the festival of Minerva together. 'Poor Acceronia is no more, I fear. Taken by Neptune. I shall come to see you when I feel stronger.'

She was looking out across the bay, and the sun was high, sparkling on the waters of the Roman Sea. Suddenly, she couldn't hear the scratching of the stylus and turned. The secretary had gone, only the swish of a still-swaying curtain to mark his departure. Instead, the Prefect of the Misenum Fleet stood there. There was a sword in his hand.

'Anicetus,' she nodded, her eyes hard, her voice cold.

'Agrippina.' He nodded back. He realised anew that he had always hated this woman. She was a murderess in her own right – worse, the murderess of an emperor. But most of all, she had fired him, over some trifling nonsense in Nero's tuition; it all seemed so long ago now. But he hadn't forgotten, and he certainly hadn't forgiven. 'I'm sorry it's come to this,' he said, without meaning a word of it. 'Nero's plan – well, mine, actually, but the emperor sanctioned it – was for a little boating accident. Well, it happens all the time off the west coast, doesn't it? Unfortunately, we didn't reckon on how strong a swimmer you are. Surprising that, in a woman of your age and class.'

'What are you talking about?' she snapped. 'I know my son is not responsible.'

Anicetus chuckled, moving forward.

Agrippina stood up to her full height, her voice rising to a shriek. 'He did not order his mother's death.'

'No,' Anicetus growled, 'and I'm a Vestal virgin.'

He brought the flat of his sword blade around in a horizontal slap, sending the Augusta reeling across the room. Dazed, and with blood dripping into her eyes, Agrippina tried to stand. All she could manage was a half-crawl, gripping the furniture as she stumbled backwards. She could feel her heartbeat as she had once felt Nero's inside her. Then her back was to the corner, and there was nowhere else to go. Panic fluttered in her throat, but then she looked down at the snake bracelet, still, as always, on her wrist. She squared her shoulders and looked up, taking her stola in both hands and ripping it open.

'Here, Anicetus,' she whispered. 'Strike here, for this carried Nero.' Her body bucked once as the blade jabbed through skin and flesh, twisting to the left as the prefect wrenched it free. She reached out, clawing at the air as he pulled back to let her fall. Whatever she may have said would never be known because the only sound that came from her was a long, dry rattle. There was a thud as she hit the mosaic, and Anicetus wiped his blade on her stola. Then, as an afterthought, he tore the snake from her wrist.

'There comes a time,' he said to the corpse, 'when even the luckiest of charms runs out.'

*

The candles flooded his eyes, and he pulled the hood back from his carefully pressed curls. The dead woman was ready for the embalmers, her hands clasped over her breasts, a single iris in her hands; her life had not been one of rainbows and sunshine, but a sentimental slave had put the flower there, as if its deep blue, yellow-streaked spears could make this death seem less dreadful.

He had to make sure; if this woman could escape the clutches of the sea, the blue-grey widow-maker, she could escape anything. Her face was calm, her eyes closed, but her lips were still pursed in disapproval of her disloyal son.

On an impulse, Nero grabbed the linen of her shroud and ripped it open, the iris flung aside to be crushed underfoot. Those with him gasped. This was not well done. It was not Roman. He looked at her, naked now with a single black stab wound slightly to the left of her navel. Anicetus' blade had done its work; and in the end, it had all been so simple.

'I didn't know,' he said softly, 'that I had so beautiful a mother,' and he bent to kiss her forehead. Nero straightened and sighed. Then he turned away from the woman who had given him life. 'A letter to the Senate,' he said to his secretary. '*It is with deep regret*, et cetera, et cetera. The usual thing. Then *the emperor is distraught* and so on. Then list her crimes. She murdered the deified Claudius. She had Britannicus killed.' A sudden thought occurred to him. 'She plotted endlessly against me, against my loyal advisers Burrus and Seneca, those fine Romans. I'll leave the language to you, Doryphorus. You gush like a girl. And when it's read out, I don't expect a dry eye in the Curia – understand?'

*

There was something about guard rooms the world over. They all smelled the same, whether it was in Britannia or Armenia, that strange mixture of sweat, ale and salt, with a hint of leather and iron.

Optio Cineas Regullus of the Praetorian Guard had been on the ramparts all night, checking with his subordinates of the night watch. He didn't mind the duty so much at this time of year. The air was balmy and rain was rare. Even so, his back was aching, and he couldn't feel his feet as he trudged into the guard quarters as a new day glowed in the east.

There was a man waiting for him.

'Cineas Regullus?' he asked.

'I might be,' the optio said. 'Who wants to know?' He looked closer. 'Oh, it's you. You're looking a damn sight better than when I saw you last.'

'Thanks to you.' The visitor held out his hand. 'Gaius Lucius Calidus. I owe you my life.' Walking was still difficult, and his neck clicked a little when he turned it to the left.

The optio shook the hand and unbuckled his helmet. 'Dramatic,' he grunted, shaking free what little hair he had, 'but probably true.'

'I don't suppose you saw any of them? My attackers, I mean.'

Regullus shook his head, reaching for the rotgut wine they gave the army these days. 'Like ships in the night,' he said. 'I suppose. Come to think of it, I haven't seen many ships in the night.'

'All right,' Calidus said. 'I just wanted to thank you.'

And he turned to go.

'Let it go.' The optio had eased himself into a chair and was looking around for any remnants of last night's cheese.

'Let what go?'

The optio chuckled. 'I've been in the Praetorians for six years,' he said. 'Eight with the Second Augusta before that. I know men who are marked to die; you're one of them.'

'That's a comforting thought,' Calidus smiled. 'Applies to us all, though, doesn't it?'

Regullus nodded, wiping his mouth with his sleeve. 'Eventually,' he agreed. 'It's all about timing, really.'

'It is,' Calidus nodded. 'Again, thank you,' and he turned to go.

'They were professionals,' Regullus said. 'Bought and paid for, would be my guess, by some nob who's got it in for you.'

Calidus turned back to him. 'What makes you think that?'

Regullus shrugged. 'Think about it,' he said. 'I know my lads and I arrived in the nick of time, but even so … if they were your common or garden thieves, they'd have helped themselves first to your horse, your saddle, your cloak, *then* would have had some fun kicking ten kinds of shit out of you. They didn't. They weren't waiting for *any* passer-by. They were waiting for you.'

Calidus nodded. 'One of them knew I was a freedman,' he remembered.

Regullus spread his arms in vindication. 'Told you,' he said.

'Thanks.' And Calidus turned to the door again. This time his hand was on the latch before the optio spoke.

'They'll still be there, you know.' The soldier was starting on his second cup of wine, stretching his legs out on a bench in front of him. 'Or people like them, anyway.'

'Probably,' said Calidus. He had done a lot of thinking while he healed, and worrying about who lurked around every corner had to stop. 'I'll just have to go around them, then, won't I?'

The optio sat upright. 'You know who it is, don't you?' he asked. 'You know who sent them to beat the shit out of you?'

'Let's say I have a pretty good idea.'

'You'll need this, then.' The optio held up his oak stick, notched and gnarled. It was the badge of his rank, used to crack down on the back of any cowardly soldier wavering at the rear of the cohort. On campaign, he regularly broke half a dozen of them. But the foot-sloggers never learned.

'I'll get my own,' Calidus said.

'I'm not offering you the stick,' Regullus said. 'It goes nowhere without me.'

Calidus paused. 'Are you offering me your services, optio?' he asked.

'Well, yes and no,' Regullus chuckled. 'Look, I'll be honest with you, Calidus. When I joined the Praetorians, I thought: this is it; I've arrived. Actually, it's as boring as shit. Most of my time is spent inspecting tunics and weapons and bloody belt buckles. Haven't had to use the persuader here for months.'

'How much will it cost me?' Calidus said. 'You know I am a freedman – I'm scarcely made of money.'

'Strictly on an as-and-when basis,' Regullus said; he had clearly done this before. 'The good news is that I'll do it for laughs. The lads won't though – it wouldn't be fair to ask them. You'll get all eight of a contubernium too – they'd cut their own grannies' throats for the cost of a flagon or a three-ass girl. They'll be incognito, of course. The emperor wouldn't like it if he thought the Praetorian Guard were prostituting themselves for private hire. You let me know when you need us; I'll do the rest.'

Calidus crossed the room and held out his hand again. 'You've got yourself a deal, Cineas Regullus,' he said. 'I'll be in touch.'

*

'Is it true?' Calidus was staring Licinius Glabrio in the face.

'Is what true?' The senator could have done without an obsessive steward this afternoon. He was poring over parchment in his tablinum, trying to keep cool in the sweltering sun. Summer had come early to Rome, and the shadows of the Villa Glabrio were sharp and gave no real respite from the heat.

'The Augusta.' Calidus had heard the buzz all over Rome. Only in Agrippina's own villa was there silence. Not one of her people was talking, and none of them made eye contact. In the Forum, however, rumours ran in the fountains and bounced off the walls. All that was hot air. Only the Curia would *know*.

'That she's dead or that she plotted against Nero?'

'Either. Both,' Calidus said.

Glabrio sighed and let the parchment scroll itself up. He sat back in his chair and folded his arms. 'Yes, she's dead.'

'Drowned, I've heard.' Calidus wanted confirmation.

'That was probably the plan.'

'What do you mean?' Calidus frowned.

'There *was* an accident. The Augusta's ship went down in the bay at Baiae, but she got out of that somehow and reached land.'

'And?'

'That's where it got a little vague. The message came from Nero via his freedman Doryphorus – limp-wristed arse-licker … and yes, I do mean that literally.'

'We've met,' Calidus said. In the hierarchy that was Rome, he was fish shit to Licinius Glabrio, but death was a leveller, and the senator didn't mind at all when the steward sat down uninvited; gossip was gossip when all was said and done.

'Well, you might know then that he is a slippery bastard – almost as good an actor as that murderous misfit he works for. Had half the Curia in tears. Nero hadn't slept. Nero hadn't eaten. He'd lacerated his breast with his nails. Everybody's taken anything sharp away from him. He'd exhausted himself with crying – you know, the usual.'

'And the other half?'

'We didn't believe a word of it. And yet …'

'And yet?' Calidus didn't like the look on Glabrio's face.

The senator sighed again. 'And yet, we all sanctioned it. Officially, Agrippina was a traitor, an enemy of the state. Her death was inevitable.'

'No one spoke against it?' Calidus couldn't believe his ears.

Glabrio chuckled. 'My old friend Nerva would have,' he said, 'if he had been here.'

'Quite,' Calidus nodded.

'As it was, only one of us left the chamber.'

'Oh? Who?'

'Old Numidius Septimus,' Glabrio told him. 'Just got up, tight-lipped and swept out. Very dramatic. I thought.'

'What did he say?'

'At the time, nothing. But I caught up with him later, and it turns out he wasn't making a heroic stand at all; just needed a piss.'

Both men sat in silence for a while.

'Leaves you in a bit of a spot, Calidus,' Glabrio remarked. 'No mistress. What'll you do? Go back to the Villa Nerva?'

'I hadn't really left,' Calidus pointed out. 'I was just … helping out the Augusta. But I shall go back to Mater Flavia in the short term, at the very least.'

A strange glint shone in the eye of Licinius Glabrio. 'And in the long term?'

Calidus looked up from the mosaic floor he had been staring at. 'In the long term, I have a murderer to catch.'

'Ah, yes.' The senator hadn't forgotten. 'Nerva.'

Calidus stood up. 'And Agrippina,' he said.

'*Two* murderers?' Glabrio chuckled. 'Good luck with that.'

'No.' Calidus made for the door. 'Two murders, certainly. But only one murderer.'

XI

Some things are best done in darkness. That's when dead mothers visit their sons. Agrippina slipped out of the night into the mind of Tiberius Claudius Drusus Germanicus Nero Caesar, and she wouldn't leave. He screamed away the night, clutching Poppaea to him and wetting her belly with his tears. He prayed incessantly at the shrine of Minerva, and he had bulls slaughtered on her altar, washing his hands in their blood as he tried to wash away his mother's. For weeks he couldn't look at a ship, and when the night terrors of one country villa took him by the hair, he roared at his people, and they had to decamp to another.

*

'He wants to come back,' Seneca muttered to Burrus on the Capitol that night. The city below him was closing its shutters, the torches going out. Honest citizens were making their way home; less honest ones were setting out to make a night of it. Some things are best done in darkness.

'Of course he does.' Burrus was feeling his years tonight. His arm ached, and his eyes were tired. 'It's his bloody city, isn't it?'

'Is it?' Seneca the philosopher was in a philosophic mood. 'Or does it belong to Romanus Romae?'

'Romanus Romae!' Burrus guffawed. 'We'll make a republican of you yet, Seneca. We got rid of our kings a long time ago, you know.'

'We did,' Seneca sat back, savouring his Falernian and letting the dark liquid warm his tonsils. 'But who could know that Tarquinius Superbus was a pussycat in comparison with Nero?'

'You give the boy too much credit,' Burrus said. 'As long as I command the Praetorians, we can control him.'

Seneca raised an eyebrow. He was fond of the old soldier with whom he tried to govern Rome, but neither of them was getting any younger, and both of them, at different times and in different ways, had fallen foul of the emperor already. 'Romanus Romae,' he said patiently, 'is a simple fellow. He eats and drinks, he fucks. Anything beyond that is a bonus. But he *does* demand bread and circuses.'

'That's fine, then,' Burrus smiled. 'Nero likes all that too. The last I heard he was still planning those wretched Juvenal Games.'

'And Romanus Romae is a slave to the omens,' Seneca ignored him.

'You've lost me,' the soldier admitted.

'When news of Agrippina's death came,' Seneca said, 'a woman in Nuceria gave birth to a snake. A couple making love was killed by a lightning fork. Three nights ago, you may remember, all fourteen districts were hit by lightning, simultaneously.'

'Yes,' Burrus nodded. 'I do remember. It's called bad weather, Seneca. Live with it.'

'All right,' the philosopher said. 'What about this?' He was holding a leather tag in his hand.

'What is it?'

'It was found around the neck of a baby somebody abandoned in the Forum Boarium yesterday morning.'

Burrus read the badly written message: 'I won't raise you, in case you end up killing your mother.' The soldier shrugged. 'Some poor deranged woman, unable to cope with another mouth to feed,' he said. 'It happens.'

'So do revolutions.' Seneca was half talking to himself. 'Don't you see, Burrus? They *know*. Romanus Romae *knows*, and he's told his wife, his children, his brother-in-law, the cat who runs down his alley. What if they rise up? What if they tear Nero limb from limb? Killing mothers is not what we do.'

Burrus laughed. 'Would that bother you all that much, old friend?' he asked.

'No, it wouldn't,' Seneca said, but he wasn't smiling. 'What bothers me is that, once they've done that, it'll be our turn next.'

*

The Villa Maxentius was in darkness on the slope of the Quirinal, and Livia Urraca couldn't sleep. Tired of the red-haired Briton she had bought in the slave market, she had booted him out of her bed. He only knew one position and seemed reluctant to learn any others, although to be fair, he could go all night and half the next day if she didn't break his concentration. Then there was the language barrier; Livia liked a bit of filth with her passion, but this idiot could only ask the way to places.

She had toyed with going back to Marcus Maxentius' bed because, wrong side of forty though he was, he knew which way was up when it came to women. She was on her way there, crossing the lararium where the flame endlessly burned around the household gods, when she saw it: a flurry of movement in the garden. The moon was not constant; it hid behind the clouds at precisely the wrong moment, and she saw nothing. All that was there was the expensive shrubbery that Maxentius had had imported from Tarraconensis. That, and the fountain spraying over the edge of its basin in the slight breeze. Livia walked on.

No, there it was again. A man, tall, lithe, armed. And another. She saw Phaedo, the villa's toothless old mongrel, waddle out, head low, tail wagging. There was a little squeal, and the dog had been swallowed up by the darkness. A chill ran up her spine, and she quickened her pace. She dashed along the passage in the near-blackness and bounded up the stairs, the stones cold under her bare feet.

Maxentius could snore for Rome when he had had a few, and tonight was no exception. In the half-light from the window, she could see him lying on his back, head flat on the bed, mouth open. She hurried to his side and shook him.

'Marcus,' she hissed. 'Wake up, for Minerva's sake. We're under attack.'

Nothing.

She tried again, and the senator rolled over, thrashing uselessly to shoo her away. In his dreams, he was a boy again, and it was time for his lessons. His mother was urging him. 'Come on, Marcus,' he heard her say. 'You'll thank me later.' He turned again, opening his eyes, trying to focus. He hadn't remembered his mother being so beautiful, and she had *never* appeared before him with her breasts exposed, not even when he was being breastfed; the Maxentii had people for that.

'Marcus!' Livia screamed. 'Jupiter Highest and Best!' She tipped the contents of the chamber pot over him. It wasn't as cold as a jug of water might have been, but it had the same effect. He sat bolt upright, gasping and spluttering with shock and from the pee, which had splashed into his nose and mouth.

'Wha …?'

Livia suddenly realised the danger and clapped her hand over Maxentius' mouth, regretting the move instantly. 'There are thieves,' she hissed in his ear, avoiding the dripping pee with care, 'in the garden.'

Maxentius wiped his face with the bedsheet and staggered over to the windowsill. He tried to focus, but his eyes weren't what they had been, and the Falernian last night had been particularly good, not to mention plentiful. His head was swimming. Then he blinked; not once, but several times. No, he was right. That *was* Phaedo. And Phaedo was waving a paw at him, held upright in the arms of a man who was jerking the dog's leg. The traitorous cur was wagging his tail and licking the man's cheek. The man was holding a dagger tip at the dog's throat.

'No!' Maxentius shouted through the open window. 'Not the dog!'

'The dog is the least of your worries.' A voice in the room made the senator turn.

'Who are you?' Maxentius blurted out, still disoriented but now with his heart in his mouth.

'I am Gaius Lucius Calidus,' the voice said, 'and you and I have some unfinished business, Marcus Maxentius.' He emerged from the shadows and half-bowed to Livia. 'Madam,' he said.

'Don't just stand there, Marcus,' Livia shrieked. 'Fetch somebody!'

Maxentius didn't move. That was partly because he didn't like the look on Calidus' face and partly because there was a second intruder in the room.

'And who are *you*?' the senator asked, trying to be as dignified as a man can be when wearing only a subigaculum and standing, dripping with urine, next to an all but naked mistress.

'I'm with him.' Cineas Regullus pointed to Calidus with a large and very nasty-looking stick. He was not about to give name, rank and serial number to a man who, in the usual scheme of things, held the power of life and death over men like him.

'I shall call my men,' Maxentius warned.

'Bit late,' Regullus beamed. 'I've already called mine.' He crossed to the window and gave a signal. As Maxentius watched, horrified, ten of his biggest, hairiest slaves were hauled out into the courtyard and forced face down on the mosaic. The moon shone to light the scene beautifully. 'Don't worry,' Regullus said. 'They won't hurt the dog. As for the men, well, I can't vouch for that.'

Maxentius leaned over the windowsill, a dangerous thing to do with a steward with a grievance at your back. One of Regullus' boys waved at him, his army boot on the neck of a slave.

Calidus threw Maxentius a pallium. 'Cover yourself, senator,' he said. 'We need to talk. You too, madam,' and he threw Livia's stola at her.

'Spoilsport,' Regullus muttered, and they filed down the stairs to the tablinum, wall to wall with legal books and documents.

'Well?' Maxentius snapped, when he had sat down at his table and at least partially composed himself. 'What do you want?'

'Two things,' Calidus told him. 'First, I want to know what you know about the death of Gaius Nerva.'

The senator spread his arms wide. 'Not that old nonsense again. Don't you know any other songs?'

Calidus drew his dagger, deliberately, slowly. 'A few dirges,' he said. 'What'll it be, senator? Burial or cremation for you?'

'Are you threatening me?' Maxentius was on his feet, decades of pride and tradition at his elbow.

'Er … yes,' Calidus said. How could the man not have noticed? 'So, I'll ask you again. Nerva.'

Marcus Maxentius weighed his options. The fighting members of his household were lying prone in the garden, ruffians' boots on their necks. His pet dog had a knife to his throat. Here he was, in the company of two armed and undoubtedly dangerous men with a slip of a girl for company. All right, he'd made his will years ago, and he silently answered Calidus in his head: *Cremation. But not yet. Not tonight.* 'Very well,' he said, sitting down again. 'Gaius Nerva had his enemies. If you persist in this nonsense that he was murdered ...'

'Murder is a fact of life in Rome, senator,' Calidus said. 'Even the emperor's mother was a victim.'

'The emperor's mother,' Maxentius said, 'was a traitor. She deserved all she got.'

'That's debatable,' Calidus said, 'and we're not in the Curia now, with Greek rules of conversation. I know Nerva had enemies. What I want are the enemies who were with him at the Villa Gellius on the night he was taken ill. Taken ill with aconite.'

'What?' Maxentius looked confused.

'Wolfsbane,' Calidus told him. 'It goes by many names.'

'You'll have to ask Gellius' cooks,' the senator shrugged. 'They had access to his wine, his food.'

'They had access to *everybody's* wine and food,' Calidus pointed out. 'Yours, for instance. And Livia's here. Neither of you, I take it, suffered any ill effects.'

'None whatever.'

'Think back,' Calidus said. 'Who sat beside Nerva that night? Did anybody take him aside? Hold him in conversation?'

'Jupiter Highest and Best, Calidus!' Maxentius exploded. 'Do you have any idea how many dinners I've been to since that one?'

'Poppaea,' Livia said, suddenly remembering.

'Poppaea Sabina?' Calidus checked. Regullus sucked air in sharply through his teeth, giving vent to a soft whistle.

'Don't you remember, Marcus?' the girl went on. 'She was bending the old boy's ear throughout the fish course.'

'Could you hear what they were saying?' Calidus asked.

'Snatches,' Livia said. 'I think the old bugger was flirting with her. He had a twinkle in his eye. I remember he was rude to Julia, Julia Eusabia.'

'Really?' That wasn't like Gaius Nerva. There were many who thought of him as the last gentleman of Rome.

'She leaned across to say something, and he told her, in no uncertain terms, to piss off. I thought Fabius Quintus was going to fell him.'

'There was a scene?'

'There would have been. Quintus told Nerva to apologise. Nerva told him to mind his own business. It could have got ugly, and it was very awkward. Fabius told me afterwards he couldn't have stained his sword with an old man's blood but that he had other plans for that.'

'Did he now?'

'Julia was distraught,' Livia went on. Then she paused. 'You know her, don't you, from way back?'

Maxentius rolled his eyes. Why did these children insist on talking of way back? They didn't *have* a way back, by his reckoning.

'Way back,' Calidus nodded. Julia had a habit of turning up like a bad denarius. Then again, there were times when a denarius kept the wolf from the door. 'And talking of way back,' he turned to Maxentius again, 'I was on my way back from a visit when an incident occurred, which is the second thing I need to talk to you about, senator.'

'Really?' Maxentius arched an eyebrow. 'What's that?'

'Your boys out there,' Calidus waved to the window. 'The ones assiduously examining your mosaics. Were they just out for laughs or were they acting on your orders?'

'I don't know what you're talking about,' the senator maintained, but he was finding it hard to meet Calidus' eye.

'Yes, you do,' Calidus said. 'It would have gone something like this. I tried to speak to Livia Urraca at the slave market, and she didn't want to know. She came home, having paid over the odds for a slave she didn't want and whined to you about an impudent freedman who had accosted her in public. You were already pissed off that I'd been asking questions about Nerva's death all over Rome, and you decided to make an example of me.'

'Well, what if I did?' Maxentius blustered, balancing that fine line between arrogance and shitting himself.

'If you did,' Calidus leaned towards the man and almost pressed his nose to the senator's, 'I'll cut your bollocks off and nail them to the Rostrum. That's after I've let my friend here's lads loose on Livia Urraca, of course. Oh, and burned your house down. Don't worry, though – no one will hurt the dog.'

Maxentius was horrified and couldn't find the words at first. 'You wouldn't dare!' he almost screamed.

'Oh, yes,' Calidus assured him solemnly. 'I would.' He threw his dagger into the air, caught it and slid it back into his sheath. 'Don't leave the city,' he said. 'Rumour is the emperor's coming back from Baiae. He'll want his senators to be here to smother him with kisses and say, "There! There!"' He made for the door. 'Madam,' he half-bowed to Livia again. 'Don't get up, senator. We can see ourselves out.'

As they reached the courtyard, Cineas Regullus gave his lads the signal and they relaxed. All ten of Maxentius' roughs were hog-tied, their feet roped to their wrists behind their backs.

'Good doggie.' One of the Praetorians kissed Phaedo on the nose and put him down at his feet. The dog wagged his tail furiously and, choosing with care, solemnly cocked his leg against one of the men lying on the ground before pattering off back to his kennel.

'Nice doing business with you, Cineas Regullus,' Calidus held out his hand. There was a heavy purse in it.

'Likewise, Gaius Calidus,' the optio said. 'Come on, lads. The last one back to the barracks gets 'em in.'

And they filed off, nodding in turn to Calidus as they passed. He couldn't help noticing that each man was carrying something rather delicious and expensive from Maxentius' kitchen.

*

There were some who maintained that Rome never slept, and as a romantic idea, it fed the styli of many poets. But Rome did sleep, in the manner of a large animal; fitfully and with one eye open because although the city was currently the one all others feared, even wolves, tigers and bears know that eventually, there will come along someone bigger and stronger, with sharper teeth. But on this night, at this hour, Rome slept, not even twitching a shoulder as the man, no bigger to the city than a little flea on a slumbering lion's back, ran through its streets, running with purpose, with a bulky load on his back. His feet made no sound on the cobbles, and he cut corners as he ran – he hadn't much time to do what he had to do and get back into the safety of his home. Like any nocturnal animal, his eyes were wide, to pick up any light they could. The moon was waning, and the darkness in the lee of the buildings was almost total, but the man's eyes were used to it now, and anyway, he knew these streets like the back of his hand.

Soon, he felt rather than saw the huge open space ahead of him. The smell of the fetid, sleeping streets was less, the breeze from the Tiber cooler on his cheek, and he knew he was almost there. He listened, straining his ears to check whether there were patrolling sentries. He knew that usually the piazza was unguarded but what with the events tomorrow and the prevailing mood, who could tell? But there was no one out and about that night, except him, on his own business. He scuttled across the open space, and he was at his target, the statue under the archway. A little scuffling, grunting, and one heart-stopping slide, and the deed was done. Crouching in the shadows, he checked again then retraced his steps. Soon he was slipping back into bed, beside his sleeping wife.

But, like Rome, she slept on, hardly noticing that he was there.

*

The rays of dawn crept over the columns of the emperor's palace on the Palatine, gilding once again the gods that held the sky aloft along the spina of the Circus Maximus. The crowds were there already, jostling, laughing, helping themselves to the free wine their generous emperor had provided for them. Only the garrison of Rome had to stay sober today, and Cineas Regullus' lads let him know their views on the matter.

'Stop grumbling, you arseholes,' the optio commanded, knowing that no soldier could ever obey an order like that. They were standing on the ramparts of the Porta Appia, facing south, and they could see his outriders already, Praetorian cavalry walking their horses ahead of the emperor's column, the eyes of an army, watchful, ready.

'Tighten that belt, Dandalus,' Regullus barked. 'Where do you think you are, man?' The legionary did as he was told. Free wine for the plebs was one thing, but reputations were made on days like this. All the emperor had to do was to glance in his direction, and it could mean promotion for a well-turned-out soldier. There again, it could be decimation, with your mates' clubs spattering your brains all over the Campus Martius. Best accept the fact that the optio knew best.

'Optio!' another voice rang from the shadows below the gate.

Regullus clicked to attention. The tribune Fabius Quintus was wheeling his bay in the circle below the archway. 'Sir,' he saluted.

'All well up there? What do you see?'

'Cavalry, sir,' the optio reported. 'Outriders.'

'How long, do you think?'

Regullus shrugged. 'It's the elephants, sir,' he called down. 'You never know with elephants.'

Quintus hauled on his rein. He should have known better than to expect a simple answer from a veteran like Regullus; stupid bastard.

Regullus watched him go, all doeskin boots and scarlet cloak and horse-hair plume; somebody's little boy who'd got the job before he'd finished shitting yellow. Stupid bastard.

Quintus walked his gelding between the buildings that cluttered the Via Appia. The guard at the roadside saluted him as he passed, but they were watching their backs too. Behind them, the mob was in festive mood. The old remembered ovations like this and full triumphs too, when conquering generals had been allowed to march their legions into Rome, carrying the war booty of strange and alien places, dragging sullen, beaten captives with them, the red dust of the road matted in their hair, the look of despair filling their eyes. The Divine Julius had passed this way, the sun glinting on his bald head, in the mystic past that none of them had witnessed but which they somehow all remembered, part of the web of story, woven by grandparent upon grandparent until it was part of the city's skin. Great Pompey too had ridden in style, his hair combed like Alexander, his piggy eyes bright with the crowd's adoration. There had, in the whispered history of things passed down through the generations, been Vercingetorix the Gaul, strangled on the Capitol for the delight of the mob. There was Caratacus the Briton, who had marvelled at the marble that was Rome. The one who had got away - Cleopatra, the Egyptian slut who had made a woman out of Marcus Antonius. There had been thousands in Rome ready to tear her apart had she been dragged through the Appian Gate. As it was, a snake had done the job for them, in a land far away.

The younger members of the crowd had been fed all this since birth, but that didn't matter. That was *so* then, and this was now. They wore their tribal clothes today, hung with garlands, and petals already fluttered to the cobbles and stuck to clothes and hair. It was a holiday, and if there was no campaign to cheer, no war booty and no chained captives, what did that matter? They could look upon the face of the Divine Nero today, drink themselves into the gutter with his cheap, watered wine and fight each other to get a seat in the Circus for the day's entertainment.

But Fabius Quintus had his mind on other things. For the last four days, every statue of the Augusta had been hauled down, her name chiselled out of offending stone, her likeness on wooden shutters painted over. Quintus reined in his horse with a start. They'd missed one! Jupiter Highest and Best! How could you miss a twelve-foot-high statue, even if it was in the shadow of the Slaves' Wall? He snarled orders to the nearest guards. 'Get me an optio with half a brain!' he bellowed. 'And the aedile. Anybody with a sack. Canvas. Something!' He looked up at the bronze face of the Augusta, smiling serenely as he remembered her. 'Cover her face,' he said softly; then, louder, for the crowd, 'We must not upset the emperor today.'

*

That wasn't Piso's intention either. Yes, the mad bastard roared away the nights with his drinking mates, smashing property and fucking anything that moved, and quite often things that didn't. Oh, and he'd probably had his mother killed, too. But what was that to a man like Piso, whose veins ran with the waters of the Tiber and to whom another man's loss was his gain? He, too, was dressed for the occasion. Since he had no idea who his father was, the ancient tribe he hailed from was a bit of a mystery, but if anybody asked, he told them Suburina. Tomorrow, it might veer towards the Collina, but for now, the green and red of the Suburina would do the business. You had to blend. If you wanted to make the most of situations like these and to honour your emperor, you had to blend.

'Ave!' Piso called breezily, as he collided and jostled with the other Suburnians around him. 'Oops, sorry. One too many there.'

'Watch out!' one of them grunted.

'No, no,' Piso laughed. 'My fault entirely. Clumsiest man in Rome, my missus calls me. Sorry. Oops. Ave. Ave.'

There was no missus Piso, though when he was younger there had been a few very near misses. Three-ass girls up back alleys were good enough for a man who helped himself to other people's purses for a living. Not for Piso the warm comforts of a good woman to share his old age; people like him didn't have an old age. He patted his cloak, the heavy one with the stitched-in loops. He'd got three purses already, and the sun wasn't over the Capitol yet. Even so, he knew without checking that his profit margin would not be impressive in this quarter. The Via Appia, when all was said and done, ran through the First District, where even the rats didn't stay around for long. He made his way through the mob towards the Circus – *that* was where the real money would be.

*

Piso had read the Greek name on the door as he edged past it, but it meant nothing to him. It did to Fabius Quintus, though, as the tribune wheeled his horse around the corner. *Orestes* it read, and the paint was fresh. Orestes, in Greek legend, had killed his mother. Quintus turned in the saddle. Nothing but laughing, happy faces all around him, except the garrison, grim and professional under their helmet rims.

'You men,' he pointed at the nearest two who peeled off the column. 'Find out who lives there. Wipe that off the door. Better, get the occupiers to do it. Then, take them to the tullianum. I'll sort them out later.'

He turned again as his men doubled up to batter on the timbers with their javelin butts. There was rebellion in the wind. And the tribune Fabius Quintus didn't like it.

*

Septimus Numidius had brought his cushion with him, hugging it as his litter bearers jogged their way towards the Circus. The old man wasn't surprised at the size of the crowd. The unwashed would turn out, shutting their shops and downing their tools at the drop of an aitch, and yet again, they'd proved him right. The Praetorians were about their business, clearing the entrance to the Circus with shoves, curses and javelin butts. Numidius had never really been a military man, but he realised anew why the legions carried those rectangular, curved shields – they were perfect for shovelling the shit that was the people of Rome. He declined the offer of wine from a passing seller. He needed to keep his bladder empty today – who knew how long it would be before whatshisname turned up. The emperor.

XII

'Jupiter Highest and Best.' Publius Varro was tangled up in his toga. 'We won't see anything from here.' The senators and their wives were ranged on either side of the imperial box, draped with purple and gold, that looked out onto the sand of the track. The mistresses were subtly separated from the wives, but along the invisible line that delineated the two factions, the air crackled with tension and could be cut with a knife. There was a noticeable difference in the beauty of the two sides; the occasional wife shone like a good deed in a naughty world, but there were few who could come close to Julia Eusabia or Livia Urraca for looks. For days, the shit that was the people of Rome had been re-gilding statuary, polishing marble, raking the Circus floor so that it looked like a mosaic under the climbing sun. 'Don't fret, Publius,' Virinia said. 'It will be wonderful. I'm sure we'll all have a splendid view.'

Varro looked at the little woman he sometimes shared his life with. He was surprised she hadn't brought her knitting with her. The woman was obsessed. Then something caught his eye. 'Oh, no,' he muttered. Ulpia Marcia was in full cry along the row from them. All morning, she had been haranguing the hapless Licinius Glabrio about how he was to behave and what he was to wear. The man looked a shadow of his former self as he half stumbled across to Varro.

'Ave, Varro,' he murmured. 'Virinia.'

'Ave, Licinius,' Virinia raised her hand for him to kiss. 'Ulpia looks adorable.'

Glabrio glanced back. 'Ulpia' and 'adorable' were not words he often heard in the same sentence. In the same year, in fact. 'She would if her hair were her own,' he grunted. 'Can I have a word, Varro?'

They all squeezed up so that he could sit down, the shuffling effect causing old Numidius more than a little discomfort as he slipped off his cushion onto his piles.

'What's your take on all this?' Glabrio made a wild gesture to encompass as much of Rome as he could.

'All what?' Varro could be as obtuse as the next senator when the mood took him.

Glabrio checked from left to right. In their white togas and senatorial finery, they were Nero men all. 'The fact,' Glabrio dropped his voice, 'that half Rome thinks that the emperor murdered his mother.'

'And the other half doesn't,' Varro said. He could be relied upon to see the cup half full. 'Isn't that so, Maxentius?'

Marcus Maxentius wasn't listening. If truth be told, the arrival of Calidus in the night-time had rattled him, and he wasn't *quite* the man he used to be. He had taken to peering around corners and looking behind him at the sound of phantom footsteps. It didn't help to glance to the right and see Livia Urraca flirting with that sad old bastard Pomponius Secundus. 'What?' was the best that the senator could manage.

'Trouble,' Glabrio précised the conversation for him. 'It's coming.'

'Trouble?' Maxentius looked around, eyes wide.

Varro leaned forward. 'Calm down, Maxentius,' he counselled. 'You're looking like a man haunted these days. Glabrio worries that the riff-raff are looking to make trouble.'

'Riff-raff?' He looked at Glabrio. '*Are* the riff-raff going to make trouble?' Even in his nervous state, Maxentius wondered why he was asking Glabrio anything. The man had the brainpower of a chicken.

'Well, they're the ballista-fodder, certainly. Look at them funny and they'll tear up the floor, but it goes deeper than that. Know what I saw painted on a wall in the Sixth District earlier?'

'No.'

'Alcmeon.'

'Who?' Varro and Maxentius looked at each other and shrugged.

Glabrio looked askance. 'Who was your tutor, for Jupiter's sake? Alcmeon, the Greek. You know – seven against Thebes.' He looked at Virinia, hoping for some reaction, but she looked back at him with her imperturbable knitter's eyes, and he got nothing there. 'Killed his mother. Went mad as a result.'

'Didn't they all?' Maxentius had always refused to be impressed by the Greeks.

'I suppose you could say,' Glabrio comforted himself, 'that's not going to happen to Nero. He's there already.'

Maxentius frowned at him. 'I don't care for your tone, Glabrio,' he said. 'Agrippina tried to murder the emperor. She'd already killed the deified Claudius *and* Britannicus. We voted in his support, remember?'

Glabrio did. And the memory of it tasted like ashes in his mouth. He shook his head. He glanced along the row, where senators' widows sat in their black weeds. He saw the quiet, dignified face of Flavia and wished again, as he had so often, that Gaius Lucius Nerva was still here.

*

'It's so good of you to let us sit here with you, Mater Flavia,' Paula said, hugging Paulina to her side and squeezing her mistress' arm.

Flavia smiled at the woman who was looking down into the Circus with shining eyes. Sometimes it was good to look at things from someone else's perspective. To see just the glitter, to hear just the trumpets, not see the ashes and hear the tread of Mors as he followed behind, ready to gather her soul to him. The widows were allowed to bring slaves with them; many were old and infirm and needed help, but for those who were still sound in wind and limb, they could give their slaves' seats to family. Flavia had no one but Paula and Calidus, so they had been her natural choice. Paulina was standing on her seat, leaning against her mother, going up on tiptoe to see better, though at the moment there was little to watch. But when you have just turned two, it doesn't take much to create a spectacle.

Calidus was sitting on the end of the row. For one thing, it gave him more room to stretch his long legs, but also it gave him a feeling of security. If things started to get out of hand, from the end of the row, he could better save his family, better protect them, get them out of the way of harm. Because things were going to get out of hand, of that he was sure. There was a prickly edge to the air, as if the crowd were a thunderhead, clashing together and making sparks which, in the right hands, could coalesce and make a lightning fork which could strike and kill them all.

But for now, he sat back in his hard seat and stroked his daughter's hair, as they all waited for the spectacle, that was even now wending its way through the streets of Rome, to begin. Underneath the hum of the mob, trumpets could be heard in the distance, the cries of the optios and, beneath all that, a vibrating, rhythmic thump and deep cries that had not been heard in Rome for many a long year.

*

The outriders had long ago reached the Appian Gate, and the procession was in plain sight now, glittering in the morning sun. At the head rode Burrus with the cavalry of the Praetorians, his arm stiffly at his side, his helmet white-plumed. At his back and fanning out to the wings, the aquilifers in their lion skins marched in line abreast, the eagles dancing at their standard heads. For the occasion, all the images of past emperors riveted to the poles had been altered to that of Nero; his face was everywhere.

Next, with braying horns and deafening drums to announce their arrival, the emperor's hand-picked German bodyguard from the tribes called the Chauci and the Marcmanni in the wild lands north of the Rhenus. Barbarian they may have been but they marched now in the civilised Roman style, shields locked to their arms, javelins pointing skywards. Their army boots shook the earth.

But, when all was said and done, the crowd had seen all this before. There was nothing like soldiers and a band to whip the enthusiasm of the mob, but it was what came next that stunned the watchers at the roadside into silence, at least for a while.

Two great elephants, their tusks blunted and bound with brass, their dusty grey hide draped with gold-encrusted cloth, lumbered along the Via Appia like asses on their way to market. Their great, flat feet struck the cobbles in unison as they swayed together to the cry of their drivers, sitting on the neck of each one, perched high above the crowd, their goads flashing in the sunlight. Long chains hung from the beasts and dragged on the stones of the road, sending up sparks. At the end of the chains, the gilded chariot of the emperor and, waving to the crowd with a silly, self-satisfied grin on his face, the man they had all come to see – the most powerful man in the world; the man who had killed his mother.

Nero wore the resplendent gold cuirass of Augustus, carved with its gods and goddesses, along with a purple cloak, hanging in exaggerated folds from each shoulder. On his head, around the carefully pressed locks, the laurel wreath of victory announced the fact that he had survived treachery and death. The charioteer, a professional who often raced in the great Circus, wasn't used to elephants. Give him four horses, any four in the world, and half a day, and he could drive for the gods. But elephants were another matter. He didn't like their size. He didn't like their colour. He didn't like the fact that their drivers were really the men in charge; he wasn't used to being just there for the look of the thing. He didn't like their smell; he *really* didn't like their smell. Whatever did they feed these things? But most of all, he didn't like the particular duty he was called upon to perform every Roman half-mile all the way from Baiae. Whether Nero was swigging wine or picking his nose or scratching his arse, the charioteer's message was the same. 'Remember you are mortal, Nero. Look behind. Look behind.'

He was delivering the traditional warning as they reached the Appian Gate, and the whole procession stopped. It was unfortunate that the brief silence coincided with Nero finally losing his temper. 'Shut the piss up, essedarius!' he snapped. 'I get the message.'

Then the cornicens blasted again, and Regullus' boys were on the gate, hauling on the weights and timbers and dragging the huge doors back.

'Ave, Imperator!' Regullus bellowed, and the whole gate company thundered their response, 'Longa vita!' Swords flew clear of scabbards, and the Praetorians beat a clattering tattoo on their shields with their blades.

Fabius Quintus trotted under the archway, the way to the Circus as clear as he could make it. He saluted Burrus, sitting his grey in the shadows and swung his horse into position behind him. The column moved off, Burrus calling the orders for the unit to advance. Men knew the drill. Horses did too, used to the drums and the horns. Elephants, not so much. The beasts swayed uneasily, confused by the roar of the crowd. As the cavalry manoeuvred to negotiate the narrowness of the gate, one of them trumpeted. The crowd froze. It had never heard a noise like that before. Then the crowd laughed, and the elephants moved forward again, jabbed from above by their drivers. In the torrent of noise that reverberated around the gateway, it is doubtful that Nero heard the single shout of, 'Murderer!' that broke from the throat of a pleb standing to his left.

Fabius Quintus had hung back. He had ridden in his rightful place as the emperor's cohort actually entered Rome, but that was for show. Today he was watching Nero's back, and this was the moment he feared. He drew his sword and waved the blade backwards and forwards in the air. Regullus saw the silent order, and he grabbed the miscreant by the hair, throwing him bodily against the rough stones of the wall. If he had chosen the wrong man, so be it. This wasn't for punishment; this was simply to encourage the others to take pains not to go down this path. People scattered to get out of the way; they had seen the Praetorians in action before. The man was babbling hysterically, but he seemed to be unarmed, and he seemed to be alone. In his saddle, Quintus mimed a sword blade across his throat, and Regullus complied for real. The heavy-pommelled gladius was in his hand, and its edge drew a crimson line across the man's neck in seconds. He gargled, hands flapping uselessly towards his neck, and Regullus' boys dragged him away. The smell of blood tainted the air; horses wrinkled their nostrils and stepped lively. The elephants waved their trunks in the air and rolled their eyes in distress.

The tribune couldn't chance any more breaches like that. He sheathed his sword and forced his horse across the column, across the face of the litters that came next in the emperor's cortege.

'Was that Fabius Quintus?' Poppaea stuck her head out through a gap in the thin veil that shielded her and her attendant from the sun and prying eyes. 'Remind me, Bella, when I see the emperor next, to reprimand that man. He rode ahead of us like some uncouth lout.'

And Bella just knew that the 'us' didn't include her.

*

As Burrus and his cavalry clattered around the turn into the Circus, the whole crowd there was on its feet. Senators, their wives, their mistresses, the ordo, the tribal leaders, anybody who was anybody who had got themselves a seat on the terraces, stood and cheered until they were hoarse. Calidus didn't find it difficult to mime his enthusiasm. All around him, people were making so much noise that his mutely open mouth could pass muster, and he looked as though he was cheering Nero to the heavens.

*

Thank Minerva for terraces, thought Piso, not for the first time. Whoever had invented that style of seating had left steps in the aisles from which a passing, cheering fan of the emperor could reach up and help himself to purses various when the crowd was on its feet. Thank you, Minerva. Thank you, thank you.

*

The elephants' drivers were looking at each other anxiously. They knew that they were the lowest of the low, only allowed to wear sumptuous robes and ride like princes because they were the only ones who understood their enormous steeds. They had had to tell the idiot in the chariot not once but many times not to use his whip, not to flick his reins. He was just a passenger, they were in charge today. And all was not well. The two huge creatures, usually so placid, walked in step, always. They swayed to the left, then the right, as they plodded along, and this meant they didn't knock into each other and get annoyed. This was important because an elephant in a temper was not something anyone would want to meet, let alone be sitting astride, legs tucked down behind the leathery ears being the only way of staying on. But back in the gateway, those idiots with horns and drums had unsettled them, Bos, the mighty male on the left in particular. His mate in their compound many miles away was in heat, and Bos had not wanted to leave her. Her desolate trumpeting had rung in their ears for hours as they made their way towards Rome. Luca, the younger male on the right-hand side, was used to taking his mark from Bos, and he was now out of step and as lost as though he had been turned loose, alone on the marshes. His pace was wrong, and every step or so, his shoulder collided with Bos, and the big bull tossed his head in anger. His driver was hanging on for grim death, and his hooked goad was buried deep behind the animal's ear, irritating him and making him even more angry. The driver called to Luca's handler to try and keep the youngster in step, but it was useless. They would be lucky if they made it into the Circus without a disaster.

*

In the Circus, everyone was craning forward to see the procession approach. For once, the glories of the Praetorian Guard were almost ignored. Almost no one gathered to welcome Nero had ever seen an elephant, and they were the stars of the show, no matter what the emperor had intended. Paulina was almost out of her seat with excitement, and Calidus had to hold on tight to the back of her shift to stop her tumbling down the rows in front.

'Papa!' she screamed. 'I can see the efunts.'

Faces in front of her turned round, smiling to hear her excitement. The widows of the senators had soft hearts for little ones, and Calidus shone with pride at his little girl.

'Efunts!' she chanted, bouncing up and down, testing the strength of her mother's stitching. 'Efunts. Efunts!' The child had never seen anything so enormous moving on its own. Only boats on the Tiber were as huge, but these creatures were here, on the land and would soon be almost near enough to touch. 'Pina stroke the efunts, Papa?' she asked, turning trusting eyes to him. Papa could do anything.

*

Finally, the elephants were back in step and Bos' driver relaxed his death grip with his knees. Luca's driver sent a smile of relief across the grey heads, scattered with sparse hair, harsh as knife blades under their knees. Not far now and they would be able to uncouple their animals and lead them somewhere away from the noise, the smells, the rabble.

Then, it happened. Bos was not the first to see the abomination, but he was certainly the first to react. The bloated, carrion-smelling thing swayed in the hand of the statue of Nero at the entrance to the Circus. White and hairy, the goatskin hung grotesquely, moving in the breeze of the elephant's passing. Bos showed the whites of his eyes and threw back his head, trumpeting his fear. His driver fell to the ground, where he lay, writhing from the pain of his broken back. But he didn't writhe for long. Freed from the hook of the goad and the weight of the driver, Bos reared and came down on the man's head, and he writhed no more. Now, in addition to the swaying goatskin, there was fresh blood in the air. Luca's driver hunkered down behind his enormous beast's head and hung on for his life to one of the flapping ears. All he could do was wait for the inevitable death and hope it was as quick as Bos' handler's had been.

For once, acting in concert, the elephants stormed into the Circus, Nero's chariot bouncing behind. The Praetorians scattered in front of them, and the emperor clung to the charioteer, his eyes shut, and his fists closed tight on the man's girdle. The crowd gasped as the giant creatures rampaged into the Circus, trunks flying, ears flapping and making an unearthly noise, as though Vulcan himself were bursting through the floor. The harness holding them together snapped like thread, and suddenly, all was still. Without the pull of the other elephant, they both calmed down, and although they were still stamping and rolling their eyes, they were no longer careering along the sand. The emperor's chariot rocked to a halt, and Nero slowly unfolded himself from his crouched position against the charioteer's chest.

Burrus recovered first, with a cheer. Soon, the crowd was on its feet, cheering their emperor, but softly. Until the elephants were led away, they would do nothing to make them panic. Only Paulina looked at them with eyes shining with wonder.

'Papa,' she whispered, pulling Calidus ear down to her mouth. 'Mama never told me efunts could do that.' Then, she was bouncing again. 'Make efunts do 'gen, Papa. 'Gen. 'Gen. 'Gen.' Calidus swept her up and kissed her neck. He wasn't sure what had made them panic like that. But he had a very good idea.

*

The most powerful man in the world stayed in his chariot, waving to his people until his knees stopped knocking. The charioteer stood unmoving beside him, drying the emperor's pee from his leg; the leather straps of his pteruge could wait. For now, he was waiting until his heart descended from his throat. He had had some scary times in the Circus – what charioteer hadn't? – but he had always been in control. Being hauled along behind thirty thousand libra – and rising – of enraged bull elephant was a different story. His uncle had been asking him for years to join him in his bakery in Padua, and as soon as he could gather up his bits and traps from his lodgings, he was on his way. Sometimes, messages from the gods are subtle; sometimes they weigh thirty thousand libra and rising.

Burrus, Anicetus, Lepidus and a whole host of grovelling senators and other worthies gathered at the rear of the chariot and all but carried Nero shoulder-high to the imperial seating, under an awning specially made, featuring his likeness, his initials and as much gold as the fabric could support. The seats there didn't need cushions – they were thick with fleeces and pillows covered with cloth of gold. Slaves stood at strategic points with ostrich feather fans. Chosen guests from among the senators, wives and mistresses filed in from the rear, making a backdrop of vivid colours to Nero and his bodyguard. The crowd was roaring, now that the elephants had been led safely away. Their forlorn trumpeting from the pens beyond the Circus was drowned by the sound of thousands of feet stamping, thousands of hands clapping, thousands of throats opening to roar one thing. *Nero! Nero! Nero!*

The emperor lay back for a moment on his cushions and felt for the hand of Poppaea. He clutched it, and she felt him trembling. She'd long been a mistress of keeping her counsel, and she did it now. If they had been alone, she would have told him he was a coward, a child, a lily-livered craven thing not worthy of her love. He would have kissed her feet and begged her forgiveness. She could keep it going for hours, hardly taking any notice of him until she finally lay back and let him take her. It wasn't to her taste, but he seemed to like it, and, after all, he was the most powerful man in the world. But in public, he was above everything. She kept her eyes downcast, her gown low-cut and herself safe, for now, from those who set themselves up as his guardians. She patted his hand and whispered to him to bear up, to have a sip of wine and address his people. He nodded and kissed her, took a deep breath and stood up.

'People of Rome,' he shouted.

'Speak up,' muttered Piso, fat with purses, lounging in the riff-raff section. 'We can't hear you at the back.'

Burrus leaned forward. 'Let the cornicens announce you, Sire,' he said. 'The crowd is excitable, let them calm down for a moment.'

Nero nodded and gestured to the ewer bearer to bring wine. He then waved an arm at the cornicen players, and they drew deep breaths and blew. The horns brayed across the hot sand of the Circus, and the crowd stopped shouting, stamping and clapping. All eyes turned to the emperor, who was standing waiting, cup in hand.

'Not now, Sire,' Burrus muttered from the corner of his mouth. 'When you have spoken, you may drink then to the health of your people. It doesn't look very ... imperial ... to step forward to speak with a ring of wine above your mouth like a common drunkard.'

Had Nero not been dragged behind some enraged elephants he might have had Burrus run through for his temerity, but he was still feeling a little fragile and willing to let small things go for once. He put down his goblet and stepped up onto the table so that his adoring people could see him more clearly.

'People of Rome,' he called.

'That's better,' Piso said, helping himself to a passing purse. 'Now just keep it short and we can all go home.'

An outraged matron sitting in front of him turned round and shushed him.

Piso shrugged. 'What?' he asked, all innocent.

'Be quiet,' she hissed. 'The Divine Nero is speaking.'

Piso smiled to himself. He already knew it was possible to fool most of the people some of the time, and here it was in action, right here in the Circus Maximus.

Under the golden awning, Nero was getting into his stride. 'Romans,' he began, trying to keep his voice strong and steady. 'From the bottom of our hearts, we thank you.'

Piso nodded to himself. So *that* was how you got to be Emperor of Rome – you had to have two hearts.

'Know that we have recently escaped certain death.'

Only the charioteer and the elephant handler knew that.

'It grieves me to have to tell you that my mother …' he paused, letting his voice waver and reaching out to Poppaea to steady him, '… my mother was a snake in the grass. I have *proof!*' and he yelled the word loudly, pointing a defiant finger to the heavens, '*proof!*' once more for effect, 'that she tried to have me killed. As surely as she killed the deified Claudius.' There were howls of, *Shame! Shame!* all around the Circus.

'No,' Piso mumbled, on the lookout for anything gold and shiny. 'Tell us it isn't so.' His eyes suddenly focused, and as quick as a wink, he pulled out a gold pin glinting in the hair of the shushing woman.

'And the man who was my brother …' again, a masterly pause and a choking sob, 'my Britannicus …'

More cries of, *Shame!* – interlaced with *Boo!* Some of the women, especially those with children, were crying. Paula was not.

'And I cannot express our gratitude that you have all come to pay your respects to us today. And to allow us to bask in the warmth of your love.'

Piso toyed with throwing up in the corner, but somebody like him would have to clean it up and so, in an unusual rush of solidarity with the people of Rome, he thought better of it.

The crowd went wild. They were in a mood to applaud anything, but Nero, when he got it right, could have them eating out of his hand, and this was one of those days. It had been close, once or twice, in the days since Agrippina's sad accident, but he had won them back, his people. He grinned and stepped back down from the table, helped by many willing hands. His guests had known better than to drink while he was speaking, although a lucky few had managed to get in a deep draught before he began. Lepidus and Anicetus, hidden more or less behind the great man's legs, had managed even more than that and had even topped up their cups, surreptitiously. It would take more than a speech to keep a sailor from his wine.

'Well done, Sire,' Anicetus told him. He was a natural liar; it had kept him alive for many a long year, and he hadn't lost his touch. But this time, he could speak the truth; Nero really had snatched triumph from the jaws of disaster. Even Seneca, who usually wrote this stuff, was impressed. The prefect raised his goblet and his voice. 'Everyone; drink to the health of the emperor!' Nero grabbed for a goblet, the nearest to him and knocked it back in one.

Lepidus raised a hand, but Anicetus stopped him. 'It's not worth it,' he whispered. 'If it isn't your drink, it's your woman. Just drink his – some people think it's an honour. Hang onto the cup – you'll be able to flog it later in the Forum Boarium.'

Lepidus didn't know his emperor as well as Anicetus did and wouldn't have risked it, but if Nero's ex-tutor said it was acceptable, then who was he to argue? 'The emperor!' he said and clicked his goblet against that of Julia Eusabia.

'The emperor!' she smiled, looking up at the man as he stood there, legs apart, shoulders back, trying not to look like a spotty youth who had pissed himself with fear not twenty minutes before.

Lepidus felt ten feet tall, as any red-blooded man did after Julia had smiled at him. He tossed back the wine and slammed the goblet down on the table.

'Well done, Lepidus,' Anicetus said. 'See, the emperor's wine is just like any other man's.' He looked into his goblet and swirled the contents round, dubiously. 'By that, of course, I mean half full of Tiber water, with just a hint of rat's pee.' He smacked his lips. 'A nice little aftertaste, though, like a cheap whore's …'

Lepidus sank slowly to the floor, holding his throat, retching.

'Very funny, Lepidus,' the prefect said, nudging him with his foot. 'But that's taking my little joke too far.' He grinned desperately at the emperor, who was looking down at Lepidus in amazement. 'Get up, get *up*, for the love of Jupiter. You'll have us both disembowelled, man.'

Nero bent to look closer. 'Is he all right?' he asked of the crowd in general.

Burrus knelt next to Lepidus, who, after a few half-hearted kicks with his legs, lay still. He lifted an eyelid, felt under his robe for his heart, looked carefully at the man's neck for the telltale throb of life. Then, with difficulty, he levered himself upright, using the table. He took a deep breath and looked at the emperor solemnly. 'Not really, Sire,' he said. 'It would appear that this man is dead.'

Anicetus swallowed hard. 'Dead?' he asked, as if it were possible to have misheard the word. 'Really dead?'

Burrus looked at him with a little sympathy but not much. This man was supposed to be Prefect of the Misenum Fleet; surely, he had seen dead people before. And it was not Burrus' way to become fond of anyone he worked with; that way sadness lies. 'Is there a reason to suppose he is shamming, in some way?' he asked.

Anicetus was caught, like a rat in a trap. If he suggested that he had been criticising the emperor's wine and that he thought that Lepidus was pretending to be poisoned – that probably wouldn't go too well. So he just shrugged.

From the back, someone was making their way to where Lepidus lay, awkwardly trapped between the couch and the table. Papirius Longinus finally elbowed Anicetus out of the way and looked down at Lepidus. The man lay awkwardly, one hand to his throat, the other reaching out, with clawed fingers. There was a faint drool of wine running from the corner of his mouth and his eyes were closed to slits. He had not died painlessly, but it had the advantage of having clearly been quick.

'I am a doctor,' Papirius said. 'And I can categorically say that this man is dead.'

'Not shamming?' Anicetus still could hardly believe it.

'No.' Papirius looked at him searchingly. 'You're in shock. Come with me, and I can give you something to settle your nerves. The rest of you …' It was pointless to say, 'Give him air,' – the man had clearly drawn his last breath ever. 'Perhaps you might like to move elsewhere so that someone can move this poor man to somewhere more appropriate. Oh, and perhaps you would like to change the wine.'

'Change the wine?' Burrus asked. 'Why?'

Papirius shrugged. 'It's up to you, naturally, but I would imagine that this man died by poison. A fast acting poison. And so, unless there are some venomous snakes hiding around here,' everyone skittered their feet and looked around them, 'I would guess that it was in the wine.'

Nero gripped Poppaea with one hand and his own snake bracelet with the other. Beyond the emperor's canopy, nobody had noticed the kerfuffle. The elephants' performance was still the talk of the moment, and brightly caparisoned horsemen were trotting around the Circus, announcing the festivities which were to follow. There were to be chariot races, acrobats, clowns, gladiators and music. The emperor himself was to perform. What was one dead man against all that?

XIII

There were only two men left, who had dined with the late Gaius Lucius Nerva at the Villa Gellius, that Calidus had not spoken to. One was in Lusitania, a sea voyage and ten days' ride away. The other was Fabius Quintus, and he was a hard man to find. Calidus knew exactly where he was. When he was not on duty at the palace, he was in his quarters beyond the Esquiline, in the huge rectangular camp that was the Praetorian headquarters. Its walls bristled with guards, their javelins across their shoulders as though on the march, their eyes watching the people of Rome as much as they watched the marshes outside. The eternal city was, as always, a haystack in summer, dry and brittle and in need of just one spark to set it alight.

That spark might have been the steward of the house of Nerva, who came to see the tribune Fabius Quintus. He had tried each of the four camp gates and had been turned away from them all. The tribune was a very busy man. The tribune was away. The tribune never saw anyone without a senatorial pass. Calidus knew it was pointless to make a scene. He needed these city guardians with him, not against him, if he was to make any headway with his enquiries. And always, at the back of his mind, was the old question – who guards the guards? They had hacked Caligula to pieces because he had laughed at the squeaky voice of one of their commanders. And Caligula had been their emperor; what would they do to a steward who was, until recently, a slave?

All day, Calidus watched the city gate, the scorpion standards shifting in the breeze over the walls. He toyed with strong-arming Piso to lift the pass of some senator. He toyed with bending the ear of Cineas Regullus to lend him a lorica and helmet and slip him through the gates as a guard detachment. Nothing like that was going to work, so Gaius Lucius Calidus went home. There was work to be done, a villa to organise, and he had left Mater Flavia to her own devices for long enough.

*

'Suicide.' Publius Varro was lying in the tepidarium of his favourite baths that night. His eyes were closed, and his hands were clasped around the stem of a goblet resting on his stomach. The room was half hidden in the steam, and he was vaguely aware of muttered conversations in dark corners. Welcome to Rome.

'Suicide?' Fabius Quintus was lying down too, the sweat running in rivulets down his back, but he sat up at that. 'Bit public, wasn't it?'

Varro shrugged, not an easy move when you're lying down balancing a good wine on yourself. 'Some people like to impress,' he murmured, half asleep. 'Go out with a final flourish.' He sighed. 'It's how I'd like to go.'

'Is it?' Quintus propped himself up on one elbow and looked at the man. That was odd; he'd got Publius Varro down as a snivelling coward. Varro looked at him out of one eye. No, not really, he answered in his head; he had no intention of going at all, but he wasn't getting into a philosophical debate on the question of life after death. He'd done that with Seneca more than once and had lost the debate every time. True, a tribune of the Praetorians was no match for Seneca, but then, who was?

Quintus had moved on. 'I always had Lepidus down for a good man.'

'Yes,' Varro conceded. 'I'd heard that.'

'Knew one end of a ship from another.' Quintus lay back down again. 'Unlike Anicetus, who doesn't.'

Varro glanced across at the man. What was Quintus? Thirty perhaps? A young man in a hurry, no doubt. But how did he sit with Nero? How, in trying to cope with that madman's antics, did any of them sit? Time perhaps to change the subject.

'Has Calidus been to see you yet?' he asked.

'Calidus?' Quintus couldn't place the name.

'Gaius Nerva's steward. Mad as a tree. He's got it into his head that the old boy was murdered and that one of us was responsible.'

'One of us?' Quintus was up on his elbow again.

'One of us at Gellius' villa the night the old codger was taken funny. Thinks one of us poisoned him.'

Quintus frowned. 'Does he, now?'

'Well, I told him it's nonsense.' Varro struggled to lift his head and lower the cup at the same time, found it impossible and gave up. 'In fact, I've told him several times. He wants you next.'

'Yes,' the tribune said. 'The man's a pain in the arse. I remember him now.'

'Well, it's rubbish, of course,' Varro went on. 'I mean, the idea of a tribune of the Praetorian Guard being involved in murder! Whatever next?'

'Yes,' Quintus said, but he wasn't smiling. 'What indeed?'

*

It was raining hard later, one of those freak summer storms that comes out of nowhere and hits Rome with the fury of Jupiter's bolts. The litter bearers stood dripping in the forecourt of the Villa Nerva, having carried their master as near to the door as they could.

'Io, Nerva!' Publius Varro called out, hauling aside his litter curtain and peering through the downpour. There was a clatter of bolts and timbers, and torches flickered between the gateposts.

'Calidus,' Varro nodded. 'Beastly night.'

'Sir,' Calidus half-bowed. 'I'm afraid the mistress has retired.'

''Course she has,' Varro said, reaching behind him for more of the grapes he had been munching all the way from the baths. 'Long overdue. But it's not her I want, it's you. Grape?'

'No, thank you.' Calidus was confused. 'You want *me*?'

Varro gave the steward a rather old-fashioned look. 'Not you per se,' he said. 'Don't build up your part. I happened to bump into a friend of yours earlier, in the baths.'

'Oh? Who?'

'The tribune Fabius Quintus.'

‘Really?’ Calidus was all ears.

Varro checked the wet streets as far as he could in all directions without falling out of the litter. ‘I happened to mention dear old Gaius Lucius.’

‘And?’

‘Let’s just say I believe he may have something to hide. I haven’t been a senator for half my life without picking up the scent when a man is lying.’

‘What did he say?’

‘Ask him yourself,’ Varro said.

‘How?’ Calidus opened his arms, the rain bouncing off them, ‘I can’t get to him.’

‘This might help.’ Varro thrust a vellum scroll at the steward. ‘It’ll get you past those morons who guard the gates at the Castra Praetoria. It also gets you into the Temples of Minerva, Mars Ultor and six free seats for the season at the Circus, but I hope you’ll use those with discretion.’ He tapped the side of his nose and winked solemnly.

‘I can’t thank you enough,’ Calidus said.

‘Yes, you can,’ Varro leaned nearer. ‘That business with the wolf; it’s over, all right? We’re even now.’

‘We’re even,’ Calidus smiled. Even though he had his fingers crossed behind his back.

*

This time, the guards on the Praetorian gate offered no resistance. Tangling with somebody’s steward was one thing – getting up the nose of somebody who carried a pass from the Curia was a very different proposition. Calidus took the shortest route to the Principia, the unit’s headquarters, with its sacred shrine to the scorpion standards and Burrus’s private chambers. No, Fabius Quintus wasn’t there. Had the visitor with the senatorial pass tried the First Cohort? The tribune would be there.

He wasn’t. What about the valetudinarium? There were always malingerers in any outfit. A good tribune would be there, kicking the arse of the layabouts. He wasn’t.

‘Who wants to see him?’ An old crone stood at the door of the tribune’s house, like the rest of the camp, in solid red brick, with porticoes and columns fanning out to left and right.

'*I* do!' Calidus' patience wasn't endless, and he was surprised to find a female in this preserve of all that was masculine.

'Who might you be?'

'I might be Dis Pater,' Calidus said, peering around the timber at her. 'Come to collect you.'

She spat volubly onto the flagstones. 'That's an 'orrible thing to say to somebody what's staring death in the face,' the old girl whined but still made no move to open the door any further.

'Is the tribune in?' Calidus felt he should move the conversation on before Mors or Dis Pater beat him to it.

'What is it, Tullia?' a voice called from inside.

'Some civilian,' she scowled, as though the word was painful to her.

Fabius Quintus towered over the stooped old woman.

'I am Gaius Licinius Calidus,' the steward announced himself. 'I'd like a word with you, tribune.'

Quintus nodded. Varro had, after all, warned him of this. He had no idea, however, how easy Varro had made the meeting itself.

'Thank you, Tullia.' Quintus took the old crone by the shoulders and showed her the way back along the gallery. 'I'll deal with this now. I understand that Marcellus Acronius' laundry is ready for you – if you wouldn't mind?'

He gave her his best smile, but the old girl wasn't pleased. ''T'ain't right, sir,' she slurped, a martyr to wobbly teeth. 'Folks pesterin' folks all hours of the day. An' you bein' a proper soldier an' everythin'.' And she was still muttering as she shuffled off to wrestle with Marcellus Acronius' laundry.

'She's my Cerberus,' Quintus said. 'Guards us all as if we were her babies. Won't you come in, Gaius Licinius Calidus?'

He ushered the steward into an elegant atrium, complete with comfortable couches and a low table littered with maps. As Calidus turned to be told where to sit, he found himself facing a drawn sword, the tip at his throat. The man at the other end of it had made no sound, and his charming smile had gone.

'Now,' Quintus said, 'All bullshit apart, arsehole. What are you doing here?'

'If I may sit ...?' Calidus waved his hand, slowly, towards a couch.

'Of course,' Quintus said, 'but first, the knife.'

Calidus was impressed. The weapon was carefully hidden in the folds of his tunic skirt, but the tribune had spotted it. '*Left* hand,' the tribune insisted, and the steward did the honours. Quintus took the knife and threw it onto the table between them; then he slowly lowered his blade. The plumed finery of Nero's entry to the city had gone, and today Quintus wore his undress tunic, plain linen, edged with leather.

'All right,' he said. 'Now that we have the formalities out of the way, what is it, exactly, that you want?'

'Gaius Lucius Nerva,' Calidus said. 'How did he die?'

'I really have no idea,' the tribune said. 'I wasn't there.'

'You were there when he was taken ill at the Villa Gellius.'

'Yes,' Quintus agreed. 'I was.'

'I understand you had words.'

'Words?' the tribune repeated. 'Who told you that?'

'Does it matter?' Calidus was giving nothing away that he didn't have to. Men like Fabius Quintus were used to walking tightropes, like the acrobats in the arena. You didn't get to be a Praetorian tribune by telling the truth.

'I suppose not,' Quintus said. 'Yes, I had what you might call a difference of opinion with Nerva.'

'What about?'

'Does it matter?' The tribune had yet to meet a steward he couldn't out-quip.

'It does to me,' Calidus said, leaning forward and looking into his eyes.

'Very well,' Quintus folded his arms. 'If you must know, he insulted the lady I was with.'

'Ah, yes,' Calidus half-smiled. 'Julia.'

For a moment, Quintus frowned, then he remembered. 'That's right. You knew her, didn't you? Back in the day? She did say something about it.'

'In what way did Nerva insult Julia?'

'I think he told her to "piss off",' Quintus said. 'Not the sort of thing you expect a senator, however gaga, to say to a lady over dinner.'

'He must have had his reasons.' Calidus knew the old man too well.

'If you say so,' the tribune said. 'You'll really have to ask Julia. She isn't here at the moment.'

'Fabius Quintus,' Calidus stood up, slowly, so as not to alarm the man with the still-naked sword. 'Did you kill Gaius Nerva?'

Quintus looked up at him. He'd never seen a man so single-minded in his life. 'I'll answer that,' he said, 'when you tell me what happened to the Augusta.'

'I have no idea.'

'You were *her* Cerberus, weren't you?' Quintus said. 'From the night I took you to her villa?'

'I wasn't there,' Calidus said. And he would regret that for the rest of his life. 'I was unavoidably detained here in Rome. All I know is what the world knows – the gossip of the Forum.'

Quintus searched the man's face for a moment, then he stood up too, lifting the sword and slamming it home into its scabbard. 'That's a pity,' he said. 'I liked her. We all did.' He flicked up Calidus' knife and threw it into his hand. The steward saw himself out.

*

She was waiting for him in the garden as the day gilded into dusk. Titus, who had filled in for Calidus while he was at the Augusta's beck and call, had not known quite who she was, but he recognised the scorpion sign catching the dying rays of the sun above her litter and knew that she was a woman of importance.

Calidus hadn't expected this. Fabius Quintus had suggested he talk to her, but the steward assumed he would have to seek an audience, wait at doorways, hope to catch her eye. But here she was, trailing her fingers through the fronds of Nerva's grapes coiling above the cool expanse of the pond.

'It's been a while,' she said, smiling at him, and she held out both her hands.

He took them, in spite of himself. On the far side of the house, the wife he loved was settling the daughter he adored to sleep, crooning lullabies and stroking her hair. In front of him stood a woman he once loved. They had no babies together; had had little time together. But the memories were there: the lost days when they had laughed together in the sun, the long nights when they had lain in each other's arms. He had been a slave then, still a boy. She had been a freedwoman, older than him by three summers. And those three summers had given Julia Eusabia a world of experience. She was his first love, before Paula had taken her place. And by then, Julia Eusabia had become something untouchable, a fading dream. The touch of her fingers tonight brought it all tumbling back: the fumblings in the darkness, the softness of her lips on his, the swell of her breasts under his hands.

Even then, there had been pain. He remembered Gaius Nerva when he had found them together at Terracia, looking for truffles. 'You are a slave,' the old man had growled at the boy, shaking him roughly by the shoulders. 'She is a freedwoman. More than that …' but he had said no more before his slap had rocked the boy, spinning his head. He remembered Julia snatching up her clothes, tears of shame trickling down her face. Then he remembered the beating, the cat with its bone tips bouncing off his shoulders and back, cutting into his flesh. He could have expected nothing less. The old man he loved had owned him, body and soul. Punishment lay in his gnarled hands. Short of murder, Gaius Lucius Nerva could do as he liked.

'I'd forgotten how lovely this place was,' she said, watching the sun, a crimson ember on the water. 'It hasn't changed.'

'Nor have you,' he said, letting her hands slip slowly out of his, lingering on the fingertips for just a few seconds longer.

She laughed, the magical, musical sound he had once loved so much. 'Yes, I have,' she said. 'At least, I hope I have.'

And she was right. Julia Eusabia had always been beautiful, but now she was a lady of the court, the woman of a tribune of the Praetorians. She wore a ring of Fabius Quintus' on her right hand and a scorpion bracelet at her wrist. Her hair was braided high with gold pins and pearls, and azure lines ringed her dark eyes. Gold vine leaves glittered on her ears. Calidus found himself smiling. He knew that Paula was his love now; would be his love forever. But she could never compete with this.

'You came to see Fabius,' she said.

He ushered her to a couch beside the pool, and they sat side by side as one of the slaves brought wine, bowed and left. 'I did,' he said. 'He suggested I talk to you.'

'And here I am,' she said, as he poured two cups of Flavia's Falernian.

'Old Nerva,' Calidus said, raising his cup.

She chuckled again. 'Is that a toast, or an enquiry?' she asked.

'A little of both,' he said. 'You remember the old man – how he used to sit here, on this very couch and watch the stars come out.'

'I remember how he screamed at us at Terracia. I think that was the last time I saw him.'

'Until the dinner at the Villa Gellius.'

She nodded again, sipping her wine. 'Fabius tells me you believe he was murdered.'

'That's right,' Calidus said. 'I do.'

Julia put her wine down and looked into the eyes of the man she had loved and left. 'Very well,' she said. 'One murder deserves another. Tell me about Agrippina.'

'The Augusta?' Calidus raised an eyebrow. Whether Fabius Quintus and Julia Eusabia were meant to be together for always or whether they were not, they certainly spoke as one. 'What was she to you?'

'A friend,' Julia said. 'A very dear friend. After I left here, she took me under her wing, taught me to read and write, to dance and play the lyre. I wouldn't presume to claim that I was the daughter she never had, but she was like a mother to me.'

Calidus remembered. 'You didn't know your real mother, did you?' he said. 'Any more than I knew mine. We're orphans of the storm, Julia, you and I.'

'The storm,' she nodded. 'The storm off Baiae that night. Tell me about that.'

'You're listening to the wrong gossip,' he said. 'There was no storm that night. The sea was calm, the moon bright. The stars …' he glanced up through the tangle of vines overhead, '… as they are tonight.'

A mischievous smile flitted across Julia's face. 'A moon … stars …' she said. 'Are you flirting with me, Gaius Lucius Calidus?'

He was suddenly serious, her words jolting him back to the present, to the here and now. The past, after all, was a foreign country, where things were done differently, by a boy and a girl looking for someone to love. 'No,' he said, firmly. 'I'm not.'

'Well, that's a pity,' she said softly. 'No storm.'

Calidus cleared his throat. 'No,' he said. 'I wasn't there, but I have spoken to men who were. There was no storm. The Augusta's ship simply … fell apart.'

'Fell apart?' she repeated, blinking. 'I'm no expert, though there was a sailor once …' she gave herself a little shake and smiled a secret smile, 'but how in Minerva's name can that happen?'

'I've seen it done at the theatre,' Calidus told her. 'There, it's all a matter of concealed hinges, trick joists, wires, smoke and mirrors. In real life, it could be missing pegs, inadequate caulking, a careless carpenter … or a calculated killer.'

'So, the Augusta drowned?'

'No,' the steward shook his head. 'They say she swam to the shore.'

Julia nodded. That made sense to her. 'She always was a strong swimmer,' she said.

'Somebody killed her later. Who and how, I don't know.'

'I do,' Julia sat upright, her statuesque body lit now by the rising moon. 'Nero.'

Calidus looked at her. There was sadness in that dark, beautiful face, but there was hatred there too. He was nodding. 'Now, *that's* the gossip I've heard,' he said.

'It all makes sense.' Julia half-turned from him and was staring into the pool, her own reflection shimmering in the ripples of the water. 'The emperor is as mad as the snake that guards his wrist. He's a mummy's boy who woke up one morning and decided he didn't want to be one anymore. He's grown up. Whereas most boys put off the toga praetexta and on with the toga virilis, Nero decided he'd kill the woman who gave him life as his move from boy to man. Ungrateful bastard!'

'There are quite a few who'd agree with you there,' Calidus said. 'But there's no proof.'

'Do we need proof?' she asked, turning to him suddenly.

'We?' he asked.

'Like I said, Cal,' she smiled. 'One murder deserves another. What about Lepidus? Was he at Baiae? Involved in the collapsing ship, all the other things we can't explain?'

'Ravenna, the gossip says. With the Second Fleet there.'

'The gossip!' Julia sneered. 'Do you follow nothing but the prattle of the gutter?'

Calidus chuckled and patted the side of his nose. 'Romanus Romae,' he said. 'The average pleb doesn't miss much, and his nose is often pressed to the grindstone of the great and not so good. Any idea how much the average slave overhears on any given day? How much he sees of things done in the dark? Watch.' Calidus raised his head, and his voice and said, 'Titus?'

The slave stepped forward. 'Sir?'

'Nothing. Just checking you were there.'

'I am always here, sir.' The man was imperturbable and, as it so happened, totally trustworthy and discreet. But the point had been made and made well.

Julia laughed. 'You've become quite the philosopher, haven't you?' she said. 'Since the good old days.'

'Perhaps,' he shrugged. 'But in the old days, I didn't need to be a philosopher. Life was simpler. Like Titus, I waited in the shadows. I watched. I listened. But still I have no idea who killed my master.'

'Life was simpler,' she agreed. 'But none of this solves my problem. And who killed Lepidus?'

'Not who,' Calidus said. 'What? And the answer to that is easy; bad wine.'

She snorted in derision. 'Don't tell me the man who sees murder in every shadow believes that a third-rate Falernian killed the Vice-Prefect of the Misenium Fleet. I've had some wines that made me think my teeth would drop out of my head then and there, but I didn't *die*. You don't drop like a stone from bad wine, Cal. I don't believe in coincidences, and neither do you.'

'You were there, weren't you?' he asked.

'There?'

'In the emperor's canopy when Lepidus died.'

'I was there, yes,' she told him, 'if you count being at the back, trying to avoid being groped by some senile senator being there. I couldn't see anything from where I was standing. One moment it was drinks all round and nauseating hypocrisy from the prat in purple, then poor Lepidus just keeled over. I saw him fall, and some doctor came out of nowhere. Come to think of it, he looked familiar.'

'Papirius Longinus, old Nerva's physician.'

'Of course,' she said. 'I knew I'd seen the face somewhere before.'

'He diagnosed poison.'

Julia nodded. 'Did he know what sort?'

'Wolfsbane, according to—'

'—Romanus Romae,' she butted in. 'Yes, I know. The gossip of the Forum. Be careful, Cal,' she said more softly. 'Such rumours can get you killed. I don't know a great deal about poisons, but surely, it can't *always* be wolfsbane, whatever that is. And anyway, who would want to kill Lepidus?'

Calidus laughed. 'I thought we were talking about two murders,' he said, 'Nerva's and the Augusta's. Do we have room for a third?'

'We do if the same hand killed all three,' Julia said.

'What?'

'There were eleven guests at the Villa Gellius the night that old Nerva was taken ill, if memory serves; Fabius and me; the senators Glabrio, Varro and Maxentius – oh, and their boring wives. And Nerva himself, of course. Then there was that drinking pal of Nero's, what's his name?'

Calidus shrugged. There were too many drinking pals of Nero's to hazard a guess.

'A real oaf. Oaf … Otho, that's the one. Who haven't I mentioned?'

'Poppaea Sabina,' Calidus said.

Julia was nodding, a strange look on her face. 'Poppaea Sabina,' she said. 'The same Poppaea Sabina who has replaced Agrippina in her son's affections. The same Poppaea Sabina who, if I remember rightly, was *most* affectionate to Gaius Nerva at the Villa Gellius. It was quite embarrassing, to tell you the truth, even though he gave her no encouragement, to be fair to him. Now, if we can just establish what links she had with the late Lepidus …'

'You keep saying "we", Julia,' he reminded her.

The girl stood up, her wine glass empty, her mood changed. 'Figure of speech,' she said. 'We women don't involve ourselves in such things. We leave it to you men. But, Calidus …' she closed to him and kissed him full on the mouth, just like the old days. He felt her sensuous body press against him, and she stepped back. 'For the sake of Gaius Nerva … and for the Augusta, you will get her, won't you? Because behind that scheming, vicious bitch, is the *real* murderer we're after. Nero.'

Before Calidus could answer, she was sweeping out of the door. Titus stepped from the shadows and was only just quick enough to let her out and avoid getting his fingers shut in the catch.

'Is that likely to be all, Calidus?' Titus said, all thoughts of 'sir' gone.

'Who knows?' Calidus said, shrugging. 'We live in interesting times, Titus. Go to bed, if you like. I'll get the door if anyone else comes calling.'

'Thank you,' the slave said. 'I have a … friend … here this evening.'

'That's nice,' Calidus said, absently. He knew that, as steward, he should look further into whoever Titus chose to bring into the house, but his memory was not so short that he had forgotten how sweet a snatched moment could be after a busy day.

'And …' Titus looked awkward, his hands twisting in front of him.

'And?' Calidus looked sharply. Anything might be important, even the murmurings of an embarrassed slave.

'And … your wife …' Titus had lowered his voice, 'she was … umm … listening. Just now.'

Calidus sighed and patted the man on the shoulder. 'Thank you, Titus,' he said. 'That will save me a lot of black looks. I'll nip the sulking in the bud.'

Titus bowed and scurried off, back to his rooms, before his friend went off the boil.

XIV

In their chambers, Paula was sitting close to a candle, sewing. She didn't look up when Calidus went in. The air could be cut with a knife. Paulina was sleeping on a couch, pulled into the shadow of a niche, and apart from the guttering of the wick and the angry stab of the needle through linen, all was silent, the silence of an angry woman biding her time.

Calidus could play this game. 'It's a beautiful evening,' he said smoothly. 'Shall I call someone to watch over Paulina while we go for a walk? Nights on the Esquiline are always lovely.'

'Can't you see I'm doing the mending?' she snapped.

'I can see you're sewing,' he said, sitting in a chair opposite her. 'I can't tell it's mending, though.'

'Well, it is.'

'Just put it down for a minute, Paula; come for a walk with me.'

'I don't *want* to come for a walk.' She was on the verge of tears.

'Any reason? Bad leg? Headache?'

She shook her head and wiped her eyes with the back of her hand, like a child.

'Julia?' He spoke softly and went down on one knee, looking up into her face.

She put down her mending and looked at him, kneeling there with a quizzical look on his face, one eyebrow raised.

'Why should it be?' she said, sniffing.

'Well, you were hiding, listening to us talking by the pool,' he said, in level, conversational tones.

'Talking! Was that what it was?'

'Yes. We were talking about Nerva. The Augusta. Lepidus.'

'And *kissing*.'

He got up. 'Don't be a child, Paula. Julia kissed me goodbye, yes. She's like that. If Titus had been standing where I was standing, she would have kissed him too. It's just her way of … communicating, I suppose you could call it.'

'She wants you,' Paula said, in tones of doom. 'Mater Flavia has said we will always have a home here, Paulina and I, for when you … go.'

'Go? Where would I go? Julia has a tribune of good family to obey her every wish. And, though no one could call me humble, in a looks contest, Fabius Quintus would leave me standing.' Calidus struck an athlete's pose, his fist to his forehead, one leg bent. 'I couldn't fight his shadow. Have you *seen* the muscles on him?'

A smile twitched at the corner of her mouth. 'He has got nice legs,' she conceded.

'So!' He put his hands on his hips. 'You look at men's legs, do you?'

Laughing now, she put her sewing aside. 'I'll call Dorcas,' she said, 'to watch Paulina. Then,why don't we go for that walk?'

He kissed her lightly on the lips and thumbed away a stray tear. 'Let's,' he whispered. 'And you can tell me all about who killed Lepidus.'

'Lepidus was murdered?' Her eyes were wide. 'I thought it was bad wine.'

'There you are, you see,' he said, wagging a finger. 'Gossip. It will bring Rome down, one of these days. The empire will crash in ruins, and all for a spoonful of gossip.'

Her eyes were wider. 'Rome fall? Don't be silly, Cal. Rome will always be here.'

'We thought that about Gaius Nerva,' Calidus said, suddenly very serious. 'Yet that wasn't true, was it?'

And arm in arm, their heads full of their thoughts, they went out into the moonlight, the old graves on the Esquiline their silent company.

*

The scorpion standards circled and writhed under the moon, and the old man, his hair almost gone, his teeth yellow and loose, smiled, then wagged a finger at him. There was darkness over Rome, great black clouds that had been rolling in from the western sky all day. It was night now. A night of darkness, yet a night of moon and stars.

It was the bearded star that Nero was watching. It was larger than the rest, and it trailed a tail of sparks that lit the clouds, now from above, now from below. He could see the Praetorians drawn up in battle order, Burrus at their head, their helmets shining under the meteor. The thunder, when it came, and he knew it would, hurt his ears and he pissed himself. He felt the noise as much as heard it, thumping in his chest and jarring in his head. Then he saw the great doors of the temple of Jupiter Victor crack and fly wide, a swarm of bees, like a hail of death, hurtling out over the Field of Mars. They moved as one, millions of them on the wing in the night air, scything over the stricken city where the Tiber ran sluggish, and the maggots crawled through slime. They swarmed through the tall tenements of the insulae, curling along the twisting lanes where he drank and stole and raped. Then, they were out over the parade ground, driving their stings into the Praetorians who stood there, unflinching, unmoving.

Then the rain came out of that black sky. And the rain was blood.

'Mama!' The voice didn't sound like his own. It sounded like a plump little boy, with two chins and dimples.

'Jupiter Highest and Best!' he heard the woman next to him in bed scream. 'She's dead, Nero. Your mother is dead. Now, for Minerva's sake, go to sleep.'

'Dead?' The most powerful man in the world was sitting bolt upright in the bed, staring ahead into the near-blackness of the room. There was a fumbling of tapers, and a candle burst into light, its flame casting twisting shadows on the walls and ceiling. Nero felt his hair, his naked shoulders. No blood. Just sweat. He felt his arms, his chest. No telltale stings, with their swollen, painful lumps and pulsing bags of poison still embedded in his flesh. No ache that ran through his limbs like lead. He looked into the candlelight. The old man had gone, warning finger and all; old Claudius the cripple had vanished into the flame.

Poppaea Sabina flopped back on her pillow. How many more nights could she put up with this? If it wasn't Claudius, it was Britannicus. And if not him, then Agrippina, hair matted to her forehead with brine, her mouth gaping in silent accusation, her finger pointing at Nero. Poppaea had heard him describe those scenes so often that she could almost see them herself. Were it not for one thing: Poppaea Sabina was sane.

'My mother and my father, both dead,' Nero moaned and dropped his head forward into his hands, sobbing uncontrollably. She slapped his shoulder, then hauled off and slapped him around the head. 'Pull yourself together!' she commanded, and he stopped crying at once, looking at her. For one terrible moment, it was as though Agrippina herself was sitting there, her breasts naked in the candlelight, the halo shining in her hair.

'To begin with, Claudius wasn't your father. Who'd have had that pathetic old drunk in bed with them long enough to conceive a child? As for your mother, *she* had the old bastard slung on a hook to Hades, not you.'

'But it was to make *me* emperor!' He was still fighting the tears, his lip trembling.

'And now you are,' she said. She looked at the snivelling wretch. If Rome could see him now, the imperious bastard who threw his weight around the Palatine, who whored and drank with the best of them, who ordered men to kill other men and then themselves. And, at the bottom of it all, he was just a lost little boy.

She reached out, stroking the shoulder, red from her slap. She took the golden-curled head and cradled it against her breasts. Slowly, hesitantly, he took a nipple in his mouth and sucked it, lost again in his infancy and the loving, hateful clutches of Agrippina.

'They're just dreams, Nero,' she soothed. 'They're meaningless.' She rocked him in the bed, slipping her hand under the covers and stroking his thigh. She had had many men in her short life, and if there was one thing she had learned, kind words and kisses were a poor second to sex when it came to making them forget their troubles. And it was often far less effort. As usual, she was right, and soon she was rubbing him gently, as he squirmed closer. 'There, now,' she whispered in his ear. 'That's better, isn't it?'

He nodded, making little mewling noises and nuzzling her breasts. She speeded up her stroke with expert fingers. 'There's just one little problem left,' she said.

'What's that?' Problems were starting to feel surmountable to him now. She leaned in closer and gripped just that little bit harder.

'Octavia,' she whispered.

*

'Octavia?' The prefect Anicetus looked up. He'd let Nero win once too often today, and the dice held no excitement for him. But this was different.

The emperor nodded. 'Octavia,' he said.

Anicetus had spent the past few days in Rome, but people would talk if he didn't get to Misenum soon. His second in command was dead, and for now, until he could reshuffle various posts, the onus was on him. He may actually have to be an admiral for a change. 'What do you want, sir?' He had already checked that they were alone. 'Locusta or one of her girls?'

Nero looked up too, blinking at him. 'No blood,' he said. 'There's been enough of that. I was thinking … divorce?'

Anicetus breathed a sigh of relief. He didn't suffer Nero's night terrors, but killing a woman had lain uneasily with him. He didn't want another on his conscience. 'Well, that's easy,' he shrugged.

'Is it?' Nero's eyes narrowed. 'Poppaea thinks all I have to do is twizzle round three times, muttering.'

'Bless!' Anicetus chuckled.

'I'll need grounds, I suppose,' Nero said. He'd been thinking this through. 'I thought perhaps … adultery?'

'Hmm,' Anicetus nodded. 'Adultery's good. You've got no actual evidence, I suppose? To keep Seneca and the Senate quiet, I mean?'

'Jupiter, no,' Nero frowned, reaching for his wine. 'Who'd have her? Oh, back in the day, before I knew better, she seemed not such a bad lay. But, well … conventional, you know. No imagination.'

'So …?'

'So, I thought, what about somebody coming forward, confessing. It's treason, of course, to shag the emperor's wife – we all know that, but I'll make it worthwhile for this somebody. No action taken, a rather large villa and estates in Campagnia somewhere. Tax free. For life.'

'Generous,' Anicetus said. 'Anybody in mind?'

'Yes,' Nero smiled. 'You.'

'Ah.'

*

'I've heard some rather disquieting news, gentlemen.' Licinius Glabrio disliked the palace. It was too sprawling, too brash. He didn't object to the naked men, painted in terracotta on the walls. He actually quite approved of the naked women. But it was all so *in one's face*. Not, all in all, the sort of place one would bring the children.

Sitting on chairs at the end of the huge atrium, the emperor's guardians assumed the stoic look they'd adopted years ago, when Nero was still actually a boy, and everybody agreed that Claudius had to go.

'Oh?' Seneca raised an eyebrow. You didn't get to be the right hand of the most powerful man in the world without choice and clever phrases like that.

'Games,' Glabrio said.

'Bread and circuses, Glabrio,' Burrus placated him. 'Bread and circuses. You know how the populi love them.'

'I do,' the senator nodded. 'And if they love the games, they'll love the man who gives them. Is that not how it works?'

Seneca chuckled. 'We'll make a philosopher of you yet, Licinius Glabrio,' he said.

'I don't want to be a philosopher,' Glabrio snapped back. 'I want to be a senator. The disquieting news I've heard is that we senators – and our wives – are to take a personal part in this nonsense.'

'I should have thought that wife of yours could give any gladiator a run for his money,' Burrus laughed. Even Seneca smiled.

'That's offensive, Burrus,' Glabrio said, 'and unworthy of a commander of the Praetorian Guard. Has that madman so debased you all?'

Burrus got up slowly and without menace. He came down from the dais and stood toe to toe with Glabrio. 'I'd be very careful, senator,' he said, 'about comments like that. Even the Augusta wasn't, as it turned out, safe. Things happen to people, on dark nights, on lonely roads.'

'Is that some sort of threat, Burrus?' Glabrio stood his ground. He and Afranius Burrus went way back and came from the same stock; it was just that the one-armed crawler had got his knees well and truly under Nero's table and Glabrio had not.

'Just saying,' Burrus shrugged.

'There's no threat implied.' Seneca became conciliatory and came down from his chair too. He clapped a friendly hand on Glabrio's shoulder. 'Come on, Licinius,' he said. 'How bad can it be? Nero'll be doing all the work. He'll win a few chariot races, sing the odd song—'

'Very odd,' Glabrio interrupted him.

'And we'll all have a marvellous time. There'll be the usual sacrifices and devotions. Everybody'll be happy, except the Christians, of course.'

'Yes,' Burrus cut in, 'and who gives a flying fart about them?'

'You don't have to take part if you don't want to,' Seneca said as though to a child. 'But Burrus is right – I can see Ulpia Marcia having a whale of a time.'

'Can you?' Glabrio was not placated. He looked at them both. 'You do *know* he's insane, don't you?' he said.

Seneca held the man by the shoulders, looking solemnly into his face. 'Which of us, if we're totally honest, is not?' he asked.

Glabrio broke away and turned on his heel. Then he turned back. 'Think back,' he said, 'to Nero's triumphal entry into Rome. There were things daubed on walls, implications, mutterings. The bag – the goatskin that so terrified the elephants.'

'What of it?' Burrus asked.

'Come off it, Afranius,' Glabrio said. 'You know as well as I do the symbolism of that. In the great days of the Republic – days when men like us actually *ran* Rome – a certain kind of criminal was trussed inside such a bag with a dog and a poisonous snake. He was then thrown into the Tiber. Whether the snake bit him or the terror-struck dog tore his throat out or the water filled his lungs, however it went, it was a death sentence.'

'So?' There was no one as obtuse as Afranius Burrus when he was in a certain mood.

'So, that certain kind of criminal was a parricide, a murderer of his parent.'

This time, Burrus *did* lean over the senator. 'That's a road best left untravelled, Glabrio,' he said. 'Believe me.'

Glabrio's jaw flexed, and he held his temper, barely. 'There's trouble in the wind,' he said, 'and these games will only hasten Nero's end. If he makes it to the nones, I'll be amazed.'

*

Imperial business irritated Poppaea Sabina. Unfortunately, it went with the territory. When she had been in the bed of Rufrius Crispinus, the Praetorian prefect, she had been a soldier's wife. When she had married Marcus Otho, she climbed another rung of the ladder of life as the consort of a patrician, albeit an often pissed one. Now that Otho was mouldering somewhere foreign, Poppaea virtually wore the purple herself. She enjoyed that, even if it meant pandering to the increasingly neurotic Nero.

Today he was playing soldiers, inspecting the Praetorians with Burrus on the Field of Mars. There'd be hard drinking, tall stories, a lot of hearty back-slapping and a few promotions. Little boys enjoying themselves. Here at the palace, it was business as usual; petitioners, as far as the eye could see. They had been forming an orderly and patient queue around the corner to the Circus Maximus since early morning, long before Poppaea had had her women apply her make-up and thicken her eyebrows. She wouldn't be seen dead on the imperial dais without all that.

She was grateful to take a much-needed break mid-morning and told the remaining supplicants to wait. The German guard crossed the front of the dais, forming an armed wall between the crowd and the imperial presence. Just to make a point. Just because they could.

She walked with her women into the anteroom. Here, on a table, sat a model of a palace, lovingly crafted in miniature by the finest carpenters. She smiled down at it, as she did most days. The architects were tearing their hair out. First, the atrium was too small. Then the baths were all wrong. Why wasn't the master bedroom facing south-west? The list of Poppaea's complaints went on and on.

'Ah.' She caught sight of the man waiting in the corner. 'You're the muralist?' she asked, 'with the designs for the triclinium?'

Calidus stepped forward. 'No, madam,' he said. 'I have other matters to discuss.'

Poppaea looked at her attendants and frowned, confused. 'Oh, you're with the botanists, are you? The garden? It has to be cherry trees. I just love the blossom.'

'No, madam,' Calidus said. 'I am not a gardener.'

Poppaea's blue eyes flashed, and she put her hands on her hips. 'Have you *anything* to do with my palace plans for Oplontis or is this ludicrous guessing game going to go on all day?'

'I am Gaius Lucius Calidus, the steward of the house of Nerva.'

'*Are* you?' she frowned. 'Well, how did you get in?'

'Shall I call the guard, my lady?' an attendant asked.

Poppaea looked Calidus up and down. He seemed harmless enough, a few years younger than her and not at all bad-looking. 'No, it's all right,' she said. 'Perhaps the steward of the house of Nerva will tell us, eventually, what he wants.'

'It *is* rather personal, madam,' he said.

'Is it?' a smile played around her lips. 'How exciting. Tell me, Gaius Lucius …'

'Calidus.'

'Calidus. Are you armed?'

'No, madam.' Calidus spread his arms.

Poppaea was half tempted to search him herself. His muscles stood out nicely across his shoulders, and his skin was clear and honey coloured. She had grown used to Nero's plump, damp, acned skin; it was a price she thought worth paying. But to run her hands across such perfection … no; there were, after all, standards in front of one's servants, and who could tell just who could be trusted implicitly, in these trying times? She nodded to a slave, who proceeded to pat down Calidus' tunic, checking sleeves, armpits and …

'I don't think you need to delve there, Porcia,' Poppaea smiled. 'If a man can hide a knife in his subigaculum, there must be something seriously wrong with him. Wait outside, all of you. And close the door.' She circled

Calidus, smiling and nodding. 'How do you like my little palace?' she asked.

He glanced down. 'Very nice,' he said, realising he sounded a lot like Piso.

'I'm going to have it built near Pompeii. That's my home town, you know.'

Calidus didn't. 'If I may come to the point, madam?' he asked.

'I wish you would,' she sighed and deftly removed half a load-bearing wall with a flick of her finger.

'The death of my master, Gaius Lucius Nerva.'

'Really?' She didn't look up from the model, closing one eye to check the angles of the colonnade. 'There's so much death these days, isn't there? I find it difficult to keep up.'

'He became unwell at the Villa Gellius on the Ides of December last year. You were there with Marcus Salvius Otho.'

Poppaea straightened and looked at the man. She wondered now, whether she had been right to admit him so freely to her presence. 'If you say so,' she said.

'He became unwell, and you were kind to him.'

'Was I?' she smiled. 'Well, I'm that kind of person.'

'You were very attentive.' Calidus was like a dog with a bone.

'Who told you this?' she asked.

'Oh, a little bird,' he smiled back.

'You are impudent, steward,' she said. 'I take it you are a freedman?'

'I am, madam.'

'Well, I don't really know how these things work, but I'm sure that can be reversed. I'm sure my Nero could work something out; have you back in the dog tags again. How would you like to be sold on the wheel, freedman, or perhaps you'd care to try your luck in the arena?'

In one sentence, the woman had turned into Livia Urraca, Agrippina and the madman who ran Rome all in one. But Calidus was too far along this road to pause for breath now. 'I believe that Gaius Nerva was poisoned,' he said, looking Poppaea in the face. 'Did you see anyone pass him a drink? Offer him some food, perhaps?'

Poppaea narrowed her eyes. 'No,' she said. 'No one. If I'm to be frank, the old shit bored me rigid. The Senate this, the Senate that. I only talked to him to make Otho jealous. I like my men younger.' She closed to him, looking up into his face. Then she ran her fingers along the neck of his tunic and let her tongue slide over her lips. She moved even closer so that he could smell the sweet, honeyed scent of her breath. Then, she broke away, laughing. 'I also like patricians,' she said. 'Was there anything else?' She was already studying the model palace again.

'What was Marcus Otho to Nerva?' he asked her, the last stone upturned at last.

Poppaea stood up, blinking. The thought had obviously never occurred to her. 'As brick to marble, I should think,' she said. 'I don't recall Otho ever mentioning the old bugger. But then,' she was walking towards the door, beyond which her attendants were gathered anxiously, 'I don't remember much of what Otho mentioned, ever. He was *so* last year. You clearly found your way in, freedman. Find your way out.'

And she was gone, back to the throne room where the line of petitioners and supplicants had grown even longer.

*

'Do I have your full attention this time, Piso?' Calidus sat with his back to the wall, his hand on his purse, both sensible precautions in this part of the city.

'As if you'd got my right bollock in one hand and my left in the other, sir,' the cut-purse said.

Calidus didn't know where Piso had got the bottles of Setian from, and it felt rude to ask. Even so, it was a very fine wine. 'I've talked to them all now, everybody who was at the Villa Gellius the night that Nerva died – all except Otho.'

'Oh, he's the bald one, isn't he? How cruel is nature, eh? Bald at twenty-five.'

'It must be a bitch.' Calidus found it difficult to feel sorry for a man who was governor of Lusitania. On the other hand, he had been virtually exiled by Nero and the man's old drinking pal was now between the sheets with his wife.

'I thought your money was on Locusta,' Piso frowned, chugging the Setian as if it were Tiber water.

'So did I,' Calidus said, 'until I met her. She may have *made* the potion that killed the old man, but she didn't administer it. Somebody else did that – one of the eleven who sat down to dine.'

'You're excluding Gellius himself, I suppose?'

'I am,' Calidus said. 'Shit and doorsteps – you know the saying?'

'I do.'

'I can't help thinking about Poppaea Sabina.' The steward swirled the wine in his cup. Come to think about it, the cup itself was rather above the pretentions of a man from the Via Flumena, Insula IV, as well as the wine.

Piso wagged a finger at him. 'Well, of course, I've never got that close, but she *is* a cracker. Ten-ass girl, I shouldn't wonder. Dangerous, though, sir, bearing in mind who's giving her one every night.'

'I don't mean in that way, Piso; do try and keep up. You know what they're saying in the Forum about her?'

'That she's behind the death of the Augusta. Yeah, I'd heard that. Horrible how spiteful people can be, isn't it? I mean, how's a nice, honest girl supposed to get by in this world of men, eh? Other than by lying flat on her back or adopting one of the stranger positions from the east? Oh, and slipping something fatal into some poor old sod's drink, of course.'

'What would be her motive?' Calidus had already asked himself that question many times over.

'Where's she from?' Piso asked.

'Pompeii, I think. Why?'

'No reason.' He was thinking around the problem. 'She's been around the insulae a few times, hasn't she?'

'Married twice – soon to be three, if Nero does the decent thing.'

Piso snorted. 'He wouldn't know a decent thing if it fell on him,' he said. 'Could that be it, then? Who was husband number one?'

'Er ... Rufrius Crispinus, Praetorian prefect.'

'Never!' Piso was half out of his seat.

'You know the man?' This didn't seem likely.

'I know what other name he went by,' the cut-purse chortled, 'and so do you, I shouldn't wonder.'

'Who?' Calidus was lost.

'Felix Salinator.'

'The senator?' Calidus could place him now. 'Jupiter, he must have been years older than Poppaea.'

'That's Rome for you,' Piso shrugged. 'Natural progression of things, isn't it – soldier to politician? What do the nobs call it? Cursus Honorum? Way of honour, my arse! You'd know more about this than me, but didn't the Senate kick him out? Financial irregularities? He killed himself, I heard.'

*

'You heard right.' Licinius Glabrio was sitting in the barber's chair the next day, lather all over his face. 'Sword, apparently. Why do you want to know?'

'What part did Gaius Nerva play in that?'

'Nerva?' Glabrio frowned, his voice distorted as the barber tweaked his nose to one side and scraped his jawline. 'Steady, tonsor; only got one throat, you know.'

The barber bobbed an apology.

'Well – oh, you probably don't remember; you'd only have been a boy. Gaius couldn't stand the Praetorians, and here was one who'd resigned his commission and was pretending to be one of us. Well, Nerva wasn't having any of it. It transpired that the man was up to his pteruges in fraud; helping himself to every fund going, apparently. Nerva denounced him. There was quite a scandal.'

'That must have upset his wife,' Calidus remarked, trying to keep his tone casual.

'Wife?'

'Poppaea Sabina.'

'Jupiter, yes; I'd forgotten that. Oh, she was the merest slip of a girl then, of course. What? Fourteen? Fifteen at the very outside. It must have been more like losing a father than a husband. Why do you ask? Calidus? Calidus?'

But the man had gone, and Licinius Glabrio settled back again for his shave.

XV

The two people he loved most in the world were lying together, a fitful moon lending its silver light through the open window. A cool breeze was wafting over the Esquiline, and it would be dawn soon. He bent to kiss his little girl, a smile on her face as she dreamed her dreams, and he could never know what those dreams were. Was she lining up her dolls and giving them orders, as her papa did with the slaves of the house? Was she combing her mama's hair and winding flowers into it with her still-chubby fingers? Or was she riding the great grey beasts before a huge crowd that gasped in wonder at Paulina of the Efunts? Her hair and skin smelt like all the scents of his own childhood, and it was hard to pull away.

Paula was dreaming too, and Calidus couldn't even begin to guess what. The woman he had loved and nearly lost, the woman who had borne his child; he half toyed with waking her. Then he knew he couldn't. His was a journey that he must make alone. He trailed his fingers over her hair and kissed her forehead. She murmured something in her sleep, but he couldn't catch it. Then he laid the covers gently over them both and turned away.

The household gods, carved in bronze and glowing in the oil lamp's light, watched him as he crossed the lararium where they were worshipped. He turned briefly and bowed his head. These gods had watched over the house of Nerva all his life. They had kept out the wind of change as far as such a thing was possible, until the greater gods had intervened, taking away the sons of the house and now the father.

He saw the moon shining on the water in the impluvium, and old Apollonius, the cat, raised his ancient head. Calidus wasn't sure the animal could actually see him anymore, but the twitching whiskers were proof that he could smell him. The steward smiled and crouched to stroke him.

'Goodbye, old friend,' he whispered. Then he straightened. Mater Flavia was standing beyond the pool, like a ghost in the predawn light. She carried no lamp and no candle because she knew every stone of this old house, every tessera of the mosaics, every fold of the curtains.

'You're leaving us again, Calidus,' she said.

'I hope I'm not,' he said, 'but I may have no choice.'

'You're leaving,' Flavia repeated, 'and not saying goodbye.'

He crossed the space between them. 'I couldn't find the words, Mater Flavia,' he said.

'Only to Apollonius,' she said, smiling. 'He has heard a lot of my troubles over the years, and he always understands. Where are you going?'

He hesitated for a moment. 'I must talk to Poppaea Sabina again,' he said.

Flavia arched an eyebrow. 'And Poppaea Sabina means Nero, doesn't it? You've faced him down before, I suppose.'

'I haven't accused his mistress of murder before,' he said.

'Murder?' Flavia frowned. 'Whose?'

'The master's,' he said.

'Gaius?' Flavia's eyes were wide. She didn't sleep well these nights and often wandered the house in the early hours. If she were truthful, she would admit that she was only half awake in these ramblings, remembering her years with Gaius, their talks in the tablinum, their laughter at the table and on the couches, his warmth alongside her at night. Their joy when their sons were born; their insupportable sorrow when they died. But now, she was fully awake. Now she had to face the truth; face it because it might save a man's life.

Calidus nodded. 'Do you remember,' he asked her, 'a senator called Felix Salinator?'

'The happy salt-maker?' Flavia snorted. 'Yes, I do. An objectionable reptile. He represented everything that was vile about the imperium. Gaius had him thrown out of the Curia.'

'And that's what killed him,' Calidus said.

'No, no.' Flavia frowned, not quite taking this in. 'Salinator killed himself, I'm sure.'

'Yes, but that, I suspect, is not how his wife sees it.'

'Wife?'

'Poppaea Sabina.'

Flavia opened her mouth to say something, then snapped it shut. She took his arm. 'Come with me,' she said firmly. 'We need to talk.' She led him into the tablinum and lit the lamps herself. 'Sit down, Calidus,' she said. 'I have a story to tell you. Somewhere in these tomes of Gaius' are the letters of the consuls Quintus Marcus and Spurius Postumia, from generations ago. Those narrow-minded prurient bastards were obsessed with repressing certain rites. It was long before your time and mine, but some things never die. What is Bacchus to you?'

'The god of wine.' He had no idea where this conversation was going.

She smiled and nodded. 'A drunken oaf. You've seen his statues here and there in various houses, I'm sure, his paintings on walls. He's a fat little man in his cups, a harmless, if rather annoying, pet.'

Calidus nodded.

'Well, he was once Dionysus of the Greeks, a god of fertility, of birth and life. That was what those old frauds of the Senate hated about him. The hypocrites. They permitted all sorts of debauchery in the alleyways of Rome, but the worship of a god who gloried in things of the flesh – that, they pretended, was too much. The rites of Bacchus were outlawed on pain of death. Seven thousand people, they say, were butchered, right here in Rome, on the orders of the Senate. Blood ran in the streets.'

'I don't see …'

Flavia held up her hand. 'The women of the cult were placed under house arrest. Their own families were expected to kill them. Such was the humanity of the Senate in the good old days. Of course, it didn't work.'

'It didn't?'

'No. Some families refused such a cruel order. They didn't murder their wives, mothers and daughters. My family, for instance. And the Augusta's.'

Calidus blinked. 'You mean …?'

'I mean that the Bacchantes survived, the worshippers of Dionysus. It all began as a female rite anyway; men weren't allowed – which, I admit, does seem a little pointless when the cult was all about procreation.' She was smiling and crossed the room to a cupboard that Calidus did not remember ever seeing open. She rummaged inside it and pulled out a wand, a vine stick, carved and lacquered.

'This,' she chuckled, 'is my thyrsis. Why I've kept it, I've no idea. My cymbals and my fox skin disappeared long ago.' She looked at her steward, still a young man trying to cope in a world he only partly understood. She twirled away from him, swaying, humming a strange tune he had never heard before. Flavia ended up laughing, covering her mouth with her hand and flopping into Gaius Nerva's chair. 'It all seems so silly now,' she said, 'the music, the frenzied dancing, the nights on bare mountains. What were we thinking?'

Her smile faded. 'I gave it all up when I married Gaius. He never knew; wouldn't, I suspect, have understood. Don't misunderstand me, Calidus. He was a wonderful man, a husband such as other women can only dream of. But he could be a little ... old-fashioned.' She looked at him, an indulgent smile on her face. 'And I suspect, deep down, there isn't a man in Rome who would not be the same. But with Agrippina, it was different.'

'She still believed?' Calidus asked.

'I hadn't clapped eyes on the woman for years,' Flavia said. 'So I've no idea what she believed. With a son like hers, I doubt she had time for the old pastimes. The Bacchanalia!' She was laughing again, but her eyes were far away, the cymbals still clashing in her head. 'It all seems so unreal.'

'And you gave it up for Gaius' sake?'

'Not completely,' she said. 'I gave it up because the Bacchantes were not what they had been. There had always been a dangerous element, come to think of it, back in the bad old days of repression. It was survival, I suppose. The legend is that we tore beasts apart with our bare hands, drinking the blood; that we danced with snakes coiling over our fox pelts, that we poisoned people ...'

Her voice had trailed away.

'Poisoned people?' Calidus repeated in the stillness of the dawn. He realised that his throat had become dry, his lips parched as if the maligned god of wine had sucked the moisture from the very air.

'The cult of Dionysus has been stolen by women like Locusta.'

Calidus nodded. It was all beginning to fall into place. The carvings in the woman's shop, the mosaics at her villa – snakes, vine leaves, the trappings of Dionysus Bacchus for all to see; if only you knew where to look. And now Calidus knew exactly where to look.

'I wanted no part of that,' Flavia said. 'What began as a ritual to celebrate love and life had become a secret society of murderesses, a cult of death.'

'Poppaea Sabina,' Calidus said.

'No,' Flavia checked him. 'That's precisely why I'm telling you all this. Agrippina was our high priestess as befits the Augusta. Locusta is among our number, and there are others … their names don't concern you. But not Poppaea. She isn't one of us. Or what I used to be.'

Calidus took the woman's hands in his own. 'Mater Flavia,' he said, 'perhaps you're right. It puts all the rumours in perspective. If Agrippina had Claudius murdered. And Britannicus; whether Locusta actually did the work herself or not – all that fits. But what about the master? Why would the Bacchantes kill a harmless old man who had never crossed them? Who, if you're right, didn't even know that they existed.' He stood up. 'I still have to talk to Poppaea, Bacchante or not.'

He bowed to her and kissed her hand. Panic rose in Flavia's breast, thumping against her ribcage and tightening her throat. 'There's one thing more, Calidus,' she said. 'I have told you things tonight I have never shared with another man, and you must let me tell you the rest. There is one more thing you need to know.' She hadn't risen from her seat but sat stoically, as widows must, her hands in her lap, her back straight, her eyes clear. 'Gaius loved you like a son,' she said.

'I know,' the steward said. 'And I will always be grateful for that.'

'That, Calidus, is because you *are* his son. Gaius Lucius Nerva was your father.' And, with a hand raised against questions, she turned and walked into the darkness, disappearing like a ghost.

*

The son of Gaius Lucius Nerva sat all morning in the Forum. Around him, the greatest city in the world burst into life with its bustling stallholders, its vigiles of the watch trading insults with them, its litter bearers, its builders, its freedmen and its slaves. Little boys raced each other on their way to their schools; old men snarled at them and cuffed them round their ears for their impudence. Senators, fat and lazy with years of inactivity, rolled up for their day's business, among them Publius Varro.

'You're like a bad denarius, Calidus,' he said, as his people helped him out of his litter. 'Always turning up when not wanted. Are you still chasing shadows?'

'Still looking for a murderer, yes.'

Varro looked up at the august columns of the Curia. 'Well, you'll find any number in there,' he chuckled, gathering up his toga.

'I'm only interested in one,' Calidus said, 'and actually, he isn't there anymore.'

Varro frowned at the man. Insane freedmen who talked in riddles, he could do without. 'You'll have to explain that,' he said. 'And please do it quickly; there's an important vote on the Claudian aqueduct later and I don't want to miss that.'

'Felix Salinator,' Calidus said.

'Jupiter Highest and Best,' Varro laughed. He was already making his ponderous way up the steps. 'That's a name I haven't heard in a while.'

'Ten years, to be precise.'

'That long? Fortuna guide us!'

'He was married,' Calidus said.

Varro paused. The man was beginning to irritate him beyond measure. Keeping up with him was like trying to herd cats. 'I'm sure he was. At the moment, there's no law against it. Although,' he nudged Calidus, 'I'll wager Licinius Glabro wishes there were, eh?'

'His wife was Poppaea Sabina.'

Varro's grin vanished. 'Yes,' he frowned, his voice dropped to not much more than a whisper. 'Yes, I suppose she was. Slip of a thing back then, of course. I forget whose daughter she was. Anyway,' the voice lifted again, 'tempus fugit, you know.'

'Time isn't all that flies, senator.' Calidus held onto the man's toga. He hadn't finished yet by a long way. 'Rumours do, too.'

'Er … true,' Varro said. It was like talking to Seneca in one of his more cryptic moments. 'How do you mean?'

'The late Felix Salinator was made late, men say, by the stand taken by Gaius Nerva.'

Varro stood there, mouth open in disbelief. This man really had no other topic of conversation. Senators were hurrying past him; the Curia would come to order in a minute, and he'd be late; though not, he hoped, as late as Felix Salinator.

'The same Gaius Nerva,' Calidus was filling in the gaps for him, 'who was poisoned at the Villa Gellius. The same villa at which the widow of the said Salinator was present. Do you see a pattern emerging here, Varro?'

Varro? Varro felt even more uneasy. Not only was this lunatic pointing a finger at the emperor's newest love, he was addressing a senator by his surname. The world had truly gone mad. 'I'm not sure that I ...'

'The wolf,' Calidus whispered in his ear, 'remember the wolf.'

'Now, we agreed,' Varro almost shouted. Heads turned, and he waved a cheery greeting to passers-by. 'Ave, ave.'

'*You* agreed,' Calidus said. 'I didn't.'

Varro closed to the man and hissed in his ear. 'What do you *want*?'

'The itinerary of Poppaea Sabina.'

'What? Are you mad?'

'I've got into the palace once, by subterfuge. It won't work again.'

'Well,' Varro spread his flabby arms, 'I've really no idea.'

'Yes, you have, Varro,' Calidus said. 'It's in the court papers deposited with the Senate. Find out where she's going to be this afternoon.'

Varro looked serious. This man wasn't just mad; he seemed bent on self-destruction. 'If you go after Poppaea Sabina for crimes real or imaginary, Calidus, they'll kill you.'

Calidus nodded. 'I'll take my chances,' he said.

Varro spun on his heel and climbed the rest of the steps. This was no way for a man to start the day, and he could feel his heart flutter a warning.

'I'll give you an hour,' Calidus said. 'If you're not back with the information I want, you'll find me over there on the Rostrum, delivering another oration; telling the world about the senator who didn't cry "wolf"!'

*

Calidus knew exactly how to get into the palace – the same way he had come the day before. It was via that nasty little alley where men said the Emperor Caligula was hacked to death by his Praetorians, the place where Nero never went. There was one guard on duty, half dozing, and he was built like an aqueduct. Calidus had slid round the corner.

'Excuse me.' Piso had done this sort of thing before. 'Ave.' And he waved at the man.

The Praetorian scowled at him. It irked him to be woken up as much as it irked him to be caught asleep and he could smell Piso from where he stood. Yesterday, he had let in some pillock who claimed to be an architect or a gardener or something like that. That had bothered the Praetorian; the man had had no pass, and he shouldn't have let him in. He wouldn't do anything so stupid again.

'What?' was his cheery greeting.

'Is this the place, then?'

'Is this what place?' the Praetorian snarled, looking the smelly pleb up and down.

'The place where it all happened, back in the day. Caligula.' Piso made some chopping motions with his hands and waited, expectantly.

'What are you talking about?'

'I'm from Asculum,' Piso lied.

'Well,' the guard grunted, 'life certainly is a bitch, ain't it?'

'In the city for a few days, and everybody said to me, "You've got to visit the spot where the emperor got his." Caligula, that is. Little boots. Is this it?'

'It might be,' the Praetorian said, 'for a consideration.'

'Oh, of course,' Piso grinned. 'What was I thinking?' and he lifted a purse from under his cloak that he had lifted from under somebody else's cloak earlier that morning. Easy come, easy go. Anything to help a friend.

The Praetorian weighed it and stuffed it into his belt. Tourists, eh? One born every minute, and it seemed to be true; people from Asculum really were one brick short of a wall. 'Well, it was all before my time, of course,' he said, leading Piso conveniently away from the door, 'but it was here.'

'Where?'

'Down there.' The guard pointed to the stones of the wall nearest the ground.

'Midget, was he?' Piso asked.

The Praetorian ignored him. 'Look,' he said, with a suitable air of mystery, 'the blood's still there. We can't get rid of it.'

'Really?' Piso was craning his neck this way and that. 'I can't see anything.'

'Yes, look.' The Praetorian tutted. The man wasn't only as stupid as everyone else in Asculum, he was also blind. He knew that the bloodstain had been touched up by one of the guard with an artistic bent only the day before; if you had to have a reputation as emperor-murderers, it was only fair to make a bit of money out of it, should the gullible pass your way. Both men knelt down to look for the blood of a maniac, and while they did, Calidus slid silently through the door with the briefest of waves to Piso.

*

There was never a time when the emperor's palace was deserted. There wasn't even a time when it was quiet, but now, shortly after the noonday, it was as peaceful as it was likely to be. The revels of the night were still hours away, and Nero himself was out on the marshes, hunting with the sycophants who rarely left his side.

Calidus had found the throne room yesterday, the main atrium and one of the six triclinia. But he had no idea where Poppaea was, and so it all had to be done by trial and error. If he ran into her attendants first and any of them recognised him, he could expect a rapid exit, but it would be on the point of a javelin or sword, and he wouldn't reach the street. He doubled back more than once and turned corners sharply as slaves hurried past on their various duties. What wouldn't the steward have given for a quarter of their number at the Villa Nerva?

He suddenly heard squeals of laughter from an impluvium. It was smaller than the one he'd passed already, and through the curtain, he could see three girls, swimming naked in the pool and splashing each other. One of them was Poppaea Sabina. Calidus knew that this was his one opportunity; he might not get another, and he steeled himself to step out into the open. It was then that he felt it – the prick of iron just behind his left ear; iron that drew blood as he instinctively tried to dodge away.

'I wouldn't do that,' a kindly voice said. 'I'm not very good with one of these and I might slip.'

The man at the other end of the dagger was immaculately dressed in an expensive pallium, and he had a world-weary look about him. He nudged Calidus into the open, and all three girls squealed. They made absolutely no attempt to cover their modesty and splashed about in the water, laughing hysterically.

'Seneca, you dirty old bastard,' Poppaea said. 'Brought a friend to spy on us too?' Her voice changed down the octaves, and she tucked in her chin to look pompous. 'The emperor shall hear of this!'

Seneca smiled. 'Best Burrus impression I've heard in a while, my lady.'

'You old flatterer,' she said. 'It's not as though he's hard to do.' She clicked her fingers, and the two other women climbed out of the water, dripping on the marble and found a large robe which they wrapped around Poppaea. 'Better cover up, ladies,' she giggled. 'Seneca's gone a funny colour.'

The philosopher's blade was still pricking Calidus' neck, and the steward of the house of Nerva thought it best to play along for now. Poppaea focused on him. 'I remember you,' she said, as the attendants wrapped themselves and began to towel her hair dry. She sprawled on a couch. 'You're Gaius Lucius … somebody or other.'

'Nerva,' Calidus said.

Seneca gave him an odd look.

'Really?' Poppaea blinked. 'Oh, all right. If you say so. What's going on, Seneca?'

'I don't know, my lady,' the man said. 'I was passing, and our friend here was spying on you. I'll call the guard.'

'No,' she said quickly. 'No, don't do that. Yesterday, this man was called Calidus. Now he's called Nerva. He's either very forgetful or there's something deliciously mysterious going on.'

'Madam …' Seneca began.

'I said *no*, Seneca.' Her voice was as hard as her eyes, now without her make-up. 'Keep your knife on him by all means, although …' she looked

Calidus up and down, smiling, 'I expect he could take it from you whenever he liked. So … Calidus Nerva or whatever your name is. What do you want today?'

She let her gown fall open just a little, in playful mood as she was. Her ladies were busying themselves with combs, pins and mirrors.

'The truth,' Calidus told her.

'Now, *that's* a rarity in this place, isn't it, Seneca?' The philosopher said nothing. 'What particular truth had you in mind?'

'Why you waited ten years to kill the man you held responsible for your husband's death.'

Poppaea's mouth and eyes opened wide. Seneca's blade wavered. Neither of them had any idea what Calidus was talking about.

'You'll have to explain that,' Poppaea said. 'I fear some of the water must have got into my brain.'

'Your first husband,' Calidus said, watching her closely. 'Rufrius Crispinus, who took the name Felix Salinator.'

'Yes,' she laughed. 'Silly name, wasn't it? Actually – and don't mock, Seneca – I chose it myself. When Rufrius decided on his change of career. From soldier to senator. Not much of a leap, really – all part of the cursus honorum, after all.' She frowned at Calidus. 'What about him?'

'He committed suicide.' The steward didn't really feel he had to remind her.

'He did,' Poppaea sighed. 'Silly old sod. I still don't see …'

'His career was ruined – you might say he died – because of opposition in the Curia, led by Gaius Lucius Nerva; my father.'

'Your father?' Seneca had all but forgotten the knife in his hand. It was lucky for Calidus that Seneca was not Burrus – he would certainly have used it by now.

'Ah, I see.' Poppaea was nodding, her eyes bright, her smile radiant. 'And Gaius Nerva was poisoned, you told me yesterday, at the Villa Gellius. So …' she was frowning, gnawing her lip as though wrestling with one of Seneca's philosophical problems, '… it goes something like this. I was heartbroken by the suicide of a repellent and decidedly dishonest old man, old enough to be my father with some to spare, by the way. *So* heartbroken was I that I waited, as you would, ten years to track down and murder the man responsible. Now, I don't know much about the Senate – and I'm sure that Seneca will put me right if I go wrong – but I suspect that there were several politicians there who couldn't stand old Felix Salinator, almost as much as I couldn't stand him. I think the law says that it would have actually been the censor for that year who showed the old fart the door. What was I going to do, poison them all? No, Calidus,' she was still smiling, shaking her head, 'if anything, old Nerva did me a favour. My marriage to Rufrius was arranged by my father. It was a political thing. Minerva, I'd barely finished playing with my dolls when the dirty old bugger … well,' she laughed. 'I know many women will tell you that their husbands were very understanding, but I am here to tell you that there are exceptions to every rule. I won't paint you a picture, but you catch my drift.'

'I do, madam,' Calidus said. There was a pounding in his brain that may have been his heart. He had got it wrong, just as Mater Flavia told him he had. Either Poppaea Sabina was the best actress in the empire or she had no motive to kill Gaius Lucius Nerva at all.

'So, I'm very sorry to disappoint you, Calidus,' Poppaea said. 'All that remains now is to decide what should become of you.'

'Death, lady,' Seneca said. 'I'll call the guard.'

But Poppaea's hand was in the air. 'Ladies?' she said, turning to her attendants. They both looked Calidus up and down but openly now, rather than from below their eyelashes as they had thus far; they whispered, one in each of Poppaea's ears. She shrieked wildly. 'Impossible!' she said. Then she looked at Calidus again, 'Although, I don't know …'

Suddenly, she was as imperious as he had seen her the day before, with her model palace and her supplicants. She sat upright and alone as her ladies moved a little away. 'We'll say no more about this business,' she said. 'We'll just put it down to the heat of the day and the silliness of the season. *But* if I see you on these premises once more, Gaius Lucius whatever your name is, I'm going to hand you over to my Cuddles. And,' she leaned forward, 'as I'm sure you've noticed, Nero is not as cuddly as all that. See him out, Seneca. You've ogled enough of my body for one day.'

*

The sun was still high on the Esquiline when Calidus got back to the Villa Nerva. Flavia was in the garden, talking to Titus, and she leapt up at Calidus' arrival, suddenly, on an impulse, hugging him to her.

'Thank Minerva,' she whispered, over and over.

'Leave us, Titus,' Calidus said.

The under-steward hesitated for a moment, then, at a word from Flavia, bowed and left. The pair sat down together. 'What happened?' she asked, holding both his hands in hers, as she had when he had somehow displeased the master all those years ago and there was straight talking to be done.

'You were right,' he said, a half-smile on his face. 'It wasn't Poppaea.'

Flavia was too kind to say, 'I told you so.' Not even her face betrayed a little smugness, but she felt it nevertheless. 'I'm just glad you're safe,' she said.

'I may not be,' he told her. 'Poppaea was in a forgiving mood today. She found the whole thing rather amusing, I think.'

'Gaius' death amusing?' Flavia bridled. 'What an utter bitch.'

Calidus nodded. 'And she might, of course, turn around tomorrow and change her mind. Seneca was there.'

'Privy to your conversation?'

Calidus nodded again. He had a question to ask Mater Flavia, and this wasn't getting him even near it.

'I'm sure he's heard worse,' she said. She longed to ask him how he'd put it, how he had asked the whore of the most powerful man in the world whether she had murdered a man. Perhaps these things were best left unasked.

'This morning,' Calidus said, not quite believing where the hours had gone, 'when you talked of the Bacchantes, of Locusta's women, you said there were others.'

Flavia nodded. She knew she had spoken out of turn, but she had half expected at that point never to see Calidus again. She knew that whatever she told him, he would go to see Poppaea anyway because men like him can never give up. Now he was back and had remembered a thrown-away line she would have given her right arm not to have said.

'Who are they?'

'Let it go, Calidus,' she said softly. Cineas Regullus, the optio at the

Appian gate had said that too, urging the steward not to go after the men who had crossed him on the road. He had ignored him just the same.

'I can't.' He looked into the kind, sad eyes. 'I've come too far; you know I can't.'

'I can't really help,' she said. 'I left it all so long ago; there have been new acolytes since then, people I don't know. Others are dead. Don't forget, they were my age or older; you'll find most of them under the stones along the Appian and the Aurelian, lying with their ancestors.' She half chuckled. 'I'll meet them all again soon.'

Calidus wasn't smiling. He took her hands again, firmly, as if he would never let go. 'Who, Mater Flavia?' he asked, the voice trembling and not his own. 'They aren't all dead, and they aren't all new. Whose name are you not giving me?'

He saw the woman gnaw her lip, felt her hands flap in a useless bid to escape his; it wasn't going to work. Her eyes brimmed with tears, and she shook her head. 'It can't be,' she said, when she felt sure enough of her words. 'I promised.'

'Who is it?' Calidus asked again. There was no tremble in his voice now, just harshness, and his eyes burned into hers.

'There was one girl,' she said, 'one acolyte I introduced myself. When I told you I gave it all up when I married Gaius, that wasn't quite true. I stopped going to their Bacchanalias – it didn't seem right for a respectable married woman, somehow. But I did stay in touch. I introduced this girl to Locusta, and she, in turn, introduced her to the Augusta. But she didn't learn the black arts, Calidus,' she said, her words rushing out of her like a torrent. 'Not poison. Nothing like that. I took her out of it as soon as I could. I couldn't live with myself.'

Calidus closed to the women, his face so near hers she could feel the fan of his lashes. 'Who is it, Mater Flavia?' he asked again, his voice barely audible now.

For what seemed like an eternity, Flavia sat beneath the pomegranate trees of her garden, the house quiet around them and Rome on the far side of the moon. 'It's Paula, Calidus,' she whispered. 'Your Paula.'

XVI

Paula wasn't hard to find. All Calidus had to do was to listen for his daughter's excited screams and the splashing, and there she was, bending over the bath as Paulina played in the fragranced water.

Paula turned a flushed face to him as he went into the room, brushing a lock of hair back from her forehead with a wet hand. 'Just in time,' she said, smiling. 'As always, your daughter is keen enough to get into the bath, not so keen to get out.'

Calidus knelt on the tiles alongside the sunken bath and reached for the child, as slippery as an eel. His longer arms caught her with ease, and he hauled her, sparkling with water as she kicked her legs and arched her back, into the air, to be caught in a towel and wrapped firmly. 'Why is she having a bath now?' he asked. 'Isn't it usually something that happens before bed?'

'As a rule,' Paula said, subduing her wriggling child by swaddling the linen around her. 'But not when she has been digging.'

'Digging?'

'Yes. Mater Flavia told her that where the rainbow ends, there is gold. And then Titus, who happened to be passing, told her he had seen a rainbow's end just that very morning in the old onion bed. And that was enough. When I caught her, only her head was visible. She digs like a mole.' She pulled out a reluctant hand from the wrapping. It was like a pink starfish, perfect and soft, without a trace of grime. 'It's taken us this long just to get her nails clean.' She squashed the girl to her and kissed the top of her curly head.

Paulina struggled free of the towel and spoke up for herself. 'I wanted some gold to buy an efunt, Papa,' she said. She had always found him eminently reasonable if she could come up with a good enough excuse. And what could be better than having your very own efunt?

He took her onto his lap, absently rubbing her legs dry. 'I don't think rainbow gold is good for efunts,' he said. 'You need a different sort.'

'What sort?'

'Umm … the sort only the emperor has. It's special.'

She looked rebellious, and for a moment, tears threatened. Then, as was her way, the mood passed. 'Efunts probably eat too much anyway. Can I go and play, Papa?'

He gave her a squeeze. 'Yes, darling. Are you dry now?'

The child nodded.

'Even between the toes?'

She nodded again and wriggled down, running off in her perfect pink skin to find someone to put her clothes on. Calidus watched her go, envying the years of perfect trust that could never last for long.

Paula folded the towel on her lap and looked at her husband. 'I assume you didn't come to help me bathe Paulina,' she said and waited. Her stillness had been the first thing to attract Calidus to his wife, once he had stopped marvelling at her beauty. She could wait without a fidget or a twitch and certainly without harsh words. She waited now.

He knew there were ways to ask the questions he must ask, carefully judged ways that would not bruise a relationship, still a little fragile after recent events. But he had no time for finesse. 'You're a Bacchante,' he said and set his lips firmly. He would brook no denial, yet still longed to hear one.

She took a deep breath and smoothed the towel. Then she looked up at him and smiled. 'Yes,' she said. 'I was, I'm not now.'

He blinked. He had expected her to hedge at least a little. 'One of Locusta's women.'

She kept the smile on her face, but it didn't reach her eyes. 'You make that sound like … an insult, Calidus. What exactly do you think being one of Locusta's women means?'

'Dancing,' he said, aware that his tone was becoming truculent. 'Drinking.' He lowered his eyes. 'Procreation.'

She laughed. 'That's a very splendid word when I assume you mean unbridled sex with men in the woods. Well, that isn't part of it, don't you fret. And, before you say anything else, neither is poison. Some Bacchantes have gone on to be mistresses of that art, but not me. Not most of us, I would think. But …' she held up her hand, '… since we rarely met one another, I wouldn't know. I even have to visit Locusta to get a simple love philtre. I thought I would mention that, as we bumped into each other nearly when you were at her villa. Fancy you not knowing your own wife, just because I had a scarf over my head!'

Calidus hardly remembered the woman he had seen. His beating on the road had removed much of the detail of the whole day. 'That was *you*?'

She bowed her head.

'And you were there for …?'

'A love potion, yes. I thought I might be losing my husband.' She looked him in the face. 'I think it still.'

'No!' He grabbed her hands. 'No. Never.'

She pulled away, but gently. 'I used to worry it was Julia who had stolen you from me. I know she could easily do it if she wanted to; it's her way. But now I know it isn't Julia. It's a dead man, and until you can let him rest easily in his grave, Calidus, he will always be between us. I'm sorry I am not the poisoner; how much simpler life would be if I were. You could kill me now, and we'd be done. But your search must go on, my beloved husband. You can't stop now.'

'No,' he agreed. 'And especially not now that I know I am Nerva's son.'

'He always loved you …'

'No, I mean I *am* his son, his flesh and blood. Mater Flavia told me last night.'

Paula was stopped in her tracks. 'Has she known all this time?'

Calidus shrugged. 'I don't know,' he admitted. 'She didn't say.'

Paula laughed, her previous mood forgotten. 'How like a man,' she said, tapping him on the chest. 'Perhaps she was waiting for you to ask. Have you thought of that?'

'I will ask,' he said. 'When there's more time.'

'Time,' Paula said, getting up and heading towards the sounds of her daughter choosing her clothes, never a very quiet process. 'I hope we all have enough, Calidus.'

He let her go, but as she reached the door, thought of something. 'Did you use the potion?'

She turned and smiled. 'I'll leave you wondering on that one, Cal, if you don't mind,' she said and closed the door quietly behind her.

Then, another thing struck him. How was it that Paula knew so much about Julia and her ways?

*

'We have to talk.' Julia Eusabia hurried past Calidus as he stood in the atrium. Outside, the Roman night was wild, rain battering the shutters and bouncing off the pantiles. Every street in the insulae had turned into a miniature version of the Cloaca Maxima, the great sewer that belched into the Tiber. Only the most resolute drunk was still wandering the streets in search of a half-dry taberna to slake his thirst. Jupiter forbid that he just throw his head back and open his mouth.

Calidus glanced at the litter bearers, drenched to the skin. There was no Praetorian scorpion now; Julia Eusabia had come alone and unarmed.

'Never mind them,' she snapped. 'Slaves have got wet before.' The house of Nerva had retired for the night, and Calidus, who liked to check these things for himself, was locking and bolting against the storm.

'Can I offer you some wine?' he asked her. Paula was on the far side of the house now, fast asleep, if there was any sanity left in the world.

She shook her head. 'You were there, weren't you?' she said, striding past the lares, without so much as a glance. She threw herself down on a couch, throwing back her hood and splaying out her damp cloak. Her sandals were caked in Roman mud and she was trembling.

'Are you all right?' he asked her.

She looked at him, her lips pursed, her eyes angry. 'No,' she said. 'No, I am not all right, Calidus, since you ask me. I thought we had an understanding.'

'An understanding?'

'Poppaea. And through her to get to Nero.'

He sat down on the couch opposite. This was a Julia Eusabia he had never seen before, a woman with vengeance on her mind. 'You expected me to kill Poppaea?'

'You could have slapped the bitch around, raped her, done whatever you liked. *Anything* to hurt that vicious bastard she lives with. I'm sure of it now, Calidus. Poppaea worked her wiles on Nero to kill Agrippina. And Agrippina was my friend. You actually went to the palace and talked to her. Just *talked* to her!'

'I did.' He nodded. 'Twice.'

'*Twice*?'

'I didn't ask the right questions the first time. Come to think of it, I didn't ask them the second time either.'

'Riddles!' Julia scoffed. 'He gives me riddles.' She sat upright, her face and her voice softening. 'I thought you loved me once, Cal,' she said.

'I did,' he told her.

'Then …'

'You expected me to put my life at risk because you've heard rumours about Poppaea? My life doesn't just belong to me, Julia – I have Paula and the little one to consider.'

'They aren't rumours,' she said, sulkily. 'It's the truth.'

'How did you know I had been to the palace?'

'Fabius,' she said. 'The gossip machine of the emperor is nearly as all-embracing as the Forum. Apparently, Seneca shot his mouth off – he might as well have made a speech on the Rostrum.'

'So, Poppaea didn't say anything?'

Julia shrugged. 'Who knows? She and I aren't exactly sisters under the skin. I've given up trying to guess what game that one's playing – except to become empress, of course, the new Augusta. That's obvious.'

'I told you, Julia,' he said, quietly. 'I am looking for the one who killed Gaius Nerva – nothing else.'

She sat there, shaking her head. Then she stood up. 'I heard another rumour the other day,' she said, 'about this house. Nero wants it.'

'I know,' Calidus said, although he had hoped that the emperor had more pressing problems on his mind.

'Do you know he has been closeted with his architects for the last two days?'

'Poppaea's palace at Oplontis, I expect.'

'Poppaea's palace be buggered!' she snorted. 'He's back on the Golden House nonsense. And this little place,' she looked at the painted wall, where brave Horatius kept the bridge, 'would fit very neatly in the auxiliaries' stables.' She got up and stepped close to him, sorry for her anger, resigned to finding another way. 'Don't let him, Cal,' she said. 'The man steals other men's women and other men's wine; don't let him take the house of Nerva too.' And she kissed him, featherlight, nothing that any wife could object to, and was gone.

*

'A dinner?' Licinius Glabrio slipped the towel off his face, 'at the Villa Nerva?' He looked at Titus with the eye that wasn't sticky with sweat. 'Don't tell me old Flavia's decided to enjoy her widowhood after all?'

If he expected even a smile from Titus, he was talking to the wrong man. Titus hadn't laughed since Tiberius was emperor.

'Er ... I don't think we need trouble my wife with this one. No disrespect to your erstwhile master, but he was one of several dozen people that Ulpia Marcia couldn't stand. I expect she will have passed that on to his wife; she's like that.' And he covered his face again, soaking up all the indulgences of the baths of Suranae.

*

'Flavia?' Julia Eusabia frowned. 'I barely know the woman.'

'I thought you spent time in her household, back in the day?' Fabius Quintus was drawing up plans for the next Praetorian field day; they seemed to come around more often than ever.

'Oh, yes,' she said, reading the letter. 'But back in the day is right. I was only a girl then. She tried to encourage us to call her *Mater* Flavia. I didn't want to know. No, it was her old man I was more fond of.'

Fabius Quintus didn't look up. He didn't want Julia to read in his face that

that surprised him not at all. 'Well, perhaps we should go. That annoying prat'll be there, of course.'

'Which annoying prat in particular?' Julia Eusabia could think of half a dozen who would fit that description, without even pausing for breath.

'Calidus, the steward.'

'I thought you liked him these days,' she smiled. Calidus had let her down badly, but Quintus didn't know that.

'Let's say he's growing on me,' the tribune said. 'But he does tend to have only one question to ask whenever we meet.'

'Well, you don't have to talk to him,' Julia reminded him, leaning her cheek fondly on the top of his curly head. 'He *is* a servant when all's said and done. I'll tell Flavia's man.'

*

'An invitation from the house of Nerva?' Nero blinked. '*To* the house of Nerva. Brilliant!'

'You'll go?' Poppaea was lying naked on the bed. Doryphorus was too, but Nero kicked him unceremoniously out of the way and sat re-reading Flavia's letter.

'Of course not,' the emperor said. 'Don't sulk, husband, dear,' he said, tossing the remark over his shoulder to the youth, still spreadeagled inelegantly on the floor. 'It makes your eyes piggy. Fetch Seneca, will you? I've got some games to organise.'

The slave clambered to his feet and snatched up his tunic before blowing Poppaea a kiss.

'Incorrigible,' Nero sighed. 'He'll have to go, you know. Ideas *far* above his station.'

'Don't be silly, Cuddles,' she laughed, 'he has his uses.' She sniggered to herself. 'And he *adores* you, you know that.'

'Yes, yes. No, I couldn't possibly go to a commoner's house; emperors don't. Oh, I know Caligula did, but he was barking. Handy though, isn't it?'

'What is?'

'The Villa Nerva. All part of my master plan for the Golden House. You go.'

'Me?' Poppaea rolled over and sat up, pulling some pillows into the small of her back so her stomach and breasts jutted invitingly.

Nero ignored it. 'You don't know as much about architecture as me, I'll grant you, but you're no slouch. Take a couple of architects with you if you like; they won't mind dressing as attendants just this once. And take a length of knotted twine; you can wind it round your waist, pretend it's the latest fashion in girdles. You can do a bit of measuring up.'

Poppaea looked at him indulgently. One good thing that could be said about Nero, amongst all the bad, was that he only ever had one thought in his head at once. And at the moment, happily for her, it was building. She enjoyed fun and games as much – if not considerably more – than the next woman, but a rest now and then was always welcome. She clicked her tongue. 'And you say Doryphorus is incorrigible,' she said. 'Do you have any idea as to how I can unravel my girdle and start pacing out the villa without anyone noticing?'

But Nero just flapped a hand at her – the details were for other people; he, after all, was the most powerful man in the world and didn't need to bother with the trifles.

*

The litters moved up the Esquiline as dusk fell, the bearers taking the strain as they always did, bracing backs and squaring shoulders.

Licinius Glabrio was first, but he was swept aside by Ulpia Marcia like a bireme at ramming speed. 'Flavia, darling,' she gushed, kissing the air some way from her hostess's cheeks. 'How well you're looking, all things considered. Licinius "forgot" to tell me about this until the last minute, so you'll have to excuse the frightful frump.' She leaned in closer, but not so close that her elaborate coiffure would tangle with Flavia's simpler tresses. 'I think he may be beginning to go the way of his mother, I don't know if you remember her?'

Flavia shook her head, flattened by the onslaught.

'Mad as a house from the age of about thirty, so I suppose we've had a few more goodish years from Glabrio than we might have expected.' And she swept on.

Flavia smiled. It had clearly taken Ulpia hours and several maids to achieve the statuesque elegance that was now haughtily surveying the décor of the Villa Nerva. Her hair was piled so high at the front that she loomed over her husband, who was ruing more than ever now, that he had let slip the fact of this evening in a casual conversation. Why, oh, why had he not shut up? He kissed Flavia's hand and made a beeline for the appetisers, laid out on simple dishes in the triclinum. It was nice to see food you could recognise, not all tarted up to go with the host's clothes, as always happened at the palace.

Marcus Maxentius was next. He had never set foot in the Villa Nerva before, largely because he loathed its late owner. But the man had been dead for months now, and it seemed churlish to refuse the invitation.

'Madam,' he kissed Flavia's hand, 'I trust widowhood is agreeing with you.'

'Oh, yes,' she smiled, acidly. 'Loving every minute of it.'

'Er …' it took a lot to discomfit Marcus Maxentius, but Flavia had managed it. '… you know …'

'Livia.' The beautiful girl on his arm thought she ought to step in; clearly, the senator was having a senior moment. 'Livia Urraca.'

'Welcome, my dear.' Flavia ushered the pair towards the food. There were grunted 'Aves' in the next room, as two senators collided.

'Flavia, darling!' Virinia Metella's greeting was the first genuine one she'd received so far. She hugged her hostess and stepped back, holding her hands. 'It's been too long. How *are* you?'

'I'm well, Virinia, thank you. What news of your boy?'

'Britannia's cold, he says,' the beaming mother told her. 'The men all have to wear leggings. Can you imagine that here in Rome?'

'Unbearable,' a voice said, a little behind her. 'I'd have to resign.'

The women turned to see the handsome face of Fabius Quintus. He was wearing his undress uniform of the Praetorians, and he saluted them both. The two women smiled fondly; it didn't matter how old you got, the look between them said it was still nice to see a well-turned leg.

'Julia,' Flavia reached out a hand, and the girl took it. 'It's been a long time.'

'It has,' she said; there was something in her tone that said that Julia was rather glad of that.

'Ave!' Publius Varro broke in, rather annoyed. It was all very well for his wife and the hostess to get on like a house on fire, but when some upstart from the Praetorians butted in front of a senator, that was a bit much.

'Publius!' Flavia extended her hand. 'I'm so sorry. I didn't see you there.'

Considering that Publius Varro was the fattest man in the room, *and* he was wearing his toga, that was rather unlikely, but he let it go. He kissed Flavia's fingers and nodded at Quintus, who nodded back. Flavia sighed to herself. Her worst fears were confirmed, and no one had so much as touched the wine yet. Why had she agreed to Calidus' request to call these people together for one last time, as he put it? What did he hope to achieve? He hadn't said.

There was a fanfare of trumpets beyond the courtyard, and an imperial litter, fringed purple and gold, appeared in the gateway. Outriders of the German guard reined in their horses and waited while everyone rushed from the house to bow before the emperor's mistress. Poppaea Sabina undulated from the litter, a snake bracelet dangling gaudily from her wrist. Every woman already there hated her on sight, not for what she was or what she may or may not have done to get where she was but because of her appearance.

'Close your mouth, Licinius,' Ulpia Marcia hissed at her husband, wobbling, as she was at full curtsey. The senator complied.

'We are honoured, my lady.' Flavia rose first.

'Yes,' Poppaea said. 'Of course you are. Sorry Cuddles couldn't make it. Protocol, you understand? So, this is the Villa Nerva.' She swept around the atrium as guests and servants bobbed around her. 'How sweet. Flavia, you must show me round.'

Her hostess looked a little taken aback.

'Now.' And the whole entourage followed on a tour of the place.

'I like what she's done in here,' Virinia Metella whispered to a startled Fabius Quintus in Flavia's private quarters. 'I wonder where she gets that fabric.'

Calidus had not yet shown himself. He had watched, hidden by the vines, as they come from the shadows of the impluvium. Now he crossed the courtyard. The Germans had dismounted and were tethering their horses under Titus' directions by the stables, muttering to each other in their outlandish guttural language. Calidus saw a solitary figure in a broad sun hat tottering towards the front door.

'Ave, Septimus Numidius,' he called.

The old man stopped, listening. Then, assuming it had been a trick of his hearing, he staggered on.

'Sir!' Calidus thought he'd better raise the volume.

'No need to shout, young man,' Numidius said. 'I'm not deaf … er … this is the right place, is it? Villa Nerva?'

'Indeed, sir.'

Numidius frowned at him and swept off his hat, which was flopping in his eyes. 'I know you, don't I?' The old man thought he could place the face, but the toga looked a little odd.

'Gaius Lucius Calidus, sir. Nerva's steward.'

'Yes.' Numidius clicked his fingers and winced as his knuckles cracked painfully. 'Yes, of course.'

'Do you have a litter, sir?' Calidus couldn't see one.

'Probably,' the ex-senator said. 'Thought I'd walk up the hill, though. Got to keep active, eh?' He nudged Calidus in the ribs. 'Got any Falernian?' The steward showed the old man into the triclinium, and finally the wine began to flow.

*

When Poppaea had finished her tour of inspection, gathering enough information for Nero to tell him the only solution was to tear the entire place down, they all returned and waited to be seated.

Titus waited for the nod from Calidus, then he bounced the butt of his staff on the mosaiced floor, and the buzz of conversation died away.

'Ladies and gentlemen,' he said. 'Your host for this evening, Gaius Lucius Nerva.'

There was a stunned silence as Calidus swept into the room, Paula on his arm. Flavia's hand instinctively fluttered to her lips. Calidus was wearing her late husband's clothes. His hair was combed in the senatorial style, and his face was as hard and cold as she'd ever seen it.

'Is this some sort of joke?' Maxentius was the first to break the silence.

'No joke, I assure you,' Calidus said, 'but I hope you'll indulge me. I have been pestering all of you of late with what happened at the Villa Gellius the night my father was taken ill.'

'Father?' echoed Varro. 'Is that a euphemism for master?'

'No, Varro,' Calidus told him flatly. 'It's a fact. I don't suppose you can remember where you all sat. For now, I shall play, not Nerva, but Gellius. I shall sit in the host's traditional place, with my wife,' he patted the couch, 'beside me.'

Paula played along. She had been no more happy about this than Flavia, but unlike her mistress, Paula knew exactly what Calidus had in mind, and it frightened her.

'This is ridiculous!' Maxentius snorted, hauling up his toga, 'I'm not playing some nonsensical charade.'

'Yes, you are,' Calidus told him. 'You all are.' He pointed to the atrium through the archway. 'The doors are locked, and no one is leaving until I say so.'

'Outrageous!' Maxentius sat down hurriedly.

'Look, Calidus ...' Glabrio thought it time to intervene.

'This is *fun*!' Poppaea Sabina clapped her hands. 'Wait until I tell Nero. Here's a game he hasn't thought of. It could catch on. Gaius Calidus Nerva,' she smiled at him, sitting alongside Maxentius, 'if you need any help in keeping people where you want them, just say the word. I have ten rather large German soldiers outside.' She looked at Maxentius, blowing him a kiss, 'if you catch my drift.'

One by one, the imprisoned guests took their places on the couches, and Flavia's servants moved among them, offering wine and titbits.

'No, you weren't sitting there,' Varro said to Glabrio.

'What?' The man was embarking on his first, much-needed, drink.

'At the Villa Gellius. You were over there, with Otho.'

'Sorry about him,' Poppaea said. 'He's been called away, I'm afraid. Lusitania is *rather* a long way away to nip back for a dinner party. But I *was* sitting here, wasn't I, Maxi?' She fluttered her eyelashes at Maxentius.

'Appalling!' Ulpia Marcia moved away, and the triclinium shook. Poppaea pulled a face and laughed. Glabrio winced – he'd pay for all this later.

'This is dreadful, Fabius,' Julia hissed in the Praetorian's ear. 'Disrespectful and not a little sick. Can't you *do* something?'

The tribune weighed his options. Getting through a locked door was never easy, although he was carrying his dagger and knew that the blade tip at the throat of the keyholder, worked wonders. On the other hand, the whore of his ultimate boss seemed to be going along with things. He shrugged. 'Let's make the most of it,' he said. 'It may get amusing later.'

Julia scowled at him, clicking her fingers for more wine. If she had to endure this nonsense, at least she wouldn't do it sober. Calidus had given his people careful instructions – plenty of Falernian, keep the cups topped up. Nothing like liquor for loosening tongues and revealing the beast within.

'There *is* a law against this, isn't there?' Maxentius murmured in Varro's ear.

'Against what?'

'Against what?' The man's voice rose more than he had intended, and he leaned in closer. 'Against kidnapping people. Holding them against their will.'

'Er ... yes,' Varro frowned. 'Yes, I'm pretty sure it's in the Twelve Tables somewhere.'

'Not to mention dressing up in a dead man's clothes and an ex-slave wearing the toga virilis. I mean, I'm as enlightened as the next man ...' since the next man was Septimus Numidius, smiling serenely as the Falernian got to him, that was debatable. 'Wait a minute. Didn't I see you drinking with old Nerva quite a bit that night? I'd forgotten until now.'

'Well, forget again, Maxentius. You've misremembered it anyway. The one who was all over him was ...'

'Ave, my dear.' Numidius was leaning across a corner of the table, no mean feat in somebody of his years. 'I haven't seen you for a while.'

Julia's smile was acid. What was the old idiot rambling about now?

'Not since the demise of your dear father, in fact. Please accept my deepest condolences.' He clawed for her hand. She pulled away, suddenly aware that Quintus had heard the old man.

'Thank you,' she muttered.

'Father?' Quintus frowned. 'What's he talking about?'

Julia shrugged. 'Don't know,' she said. 'He's got me confused with somebody else.'

'No, I haven't!' Various people lying around the table had never heard Septimus Numidius shout before. They were all too young to remember the firebrand who had once roared in the Curia when the deified Augustus reigned. 'Your father was Gaius Nerva. He told me so himself.'

A goblet thudded to the floor, dropped from the hand of the hostess.

'Septimus,' she said, disbelief and horror on her face. 'What are you saying?'

The old man sat up. Everybody was looking at him, and the room had fallen silent. 'I was just being polite, Flavia,' he said, 'passing on my condolences. I'm sorry if I've caused offence.'

'You haven't,' Calidus said. 'Tell us what you mean.'

'Er ... well,' Numidius said, feeling all eyes on him. 'I don't know what more I can say. I'm sorry, Flavia; I thought you would have known. Gaius sowed a few wild oats in his day – we all did, eh, lads?' He flashed a toothless grin at his fellow senators. Ulpia Marcis snorted, and Poppaea giggled. 'I remember him telling me how proud he was of his children, his boys. He also told me and, yes, he was in his cups at the time, that he had two other children that he knew of – a boy and a girl. You were one, Calidus, the boy I mean. And the other was you, Julia.'

The silence was deafening.

Numidius broke it, chuckling. 'Jupiter Highest and Best,' he said. 'I'm not *that* out of touch, am I? Masters sleep with their slaves all the time. The result is children, unless I've misunderstood the process all these years.'

'Is that why you killed him, Julia?' Calidus asked, looking at her across the room.

She was on her feet. 'I don't have to listen to this garbage,' she said, her voice deep in her throat, and not like her own at all. 'Fabius. We're leaving.'

'No,' he said, still sitting. 'Calidus, you'd better explain yourself.'

Julia spun on him and tried to slap his face, but the Praetorian caught her arm and held her off with ease. 'The old man's gaga,' Julia shouted. 'And drunk.'

Numidius sat upright. 'Madam,' he said. 'I have not been drunk since the first year of Claudius.'

'Mater Flavia,' Calidus turned to her. She sat bolt upright, elegant and somehow detached from everything. The storm could come later, but for now, she had guests and couldn't weaken. 'Did you know about this?'

'No.' Flavia shook her head slightly, and her pearl earrings swung, tapping against her neck; in the silence, it was almost audible. 'I had no idea.'

'That was why the master thrashed me so soundly at Terracia that time,' Calidus said, talking to Julia, 'when he caught us. We are half-brother and sister. The master – my father … our father – was always a traditionalist. That kind of thing would never do.'

'You're dreaming, Calidus,' she said. 'Talking rubbish.'

'I've heard nothing that makes any sense,' Quintus agreed.

'When you left the house of Nerva,' Calidus was still talking to Julia, but he had the rest of the room in the palm of his hand, 'where did you go?'

'Here and there,' she told him, sitting down now and sipping her wine as if this were just any dinner, at any time, in any place.

'And you ended up with Locusta.'

There were a few gasps in the room, not least from Flavia.

'Oh-oh.' Poppaea giggled, eyes sparkling. That was a name that she and Nero had often whispered in their pillow talk, especially recently.

'I don't know who that is,' Julia insisted. 'Am I supposed to know every miscreant in Rome?'

Calidus smiled. Even if he hadn't been sure of his ground, Julia had slipped up – who but a few would know that Locusta was anything other than a rich, idle woman, living in luxury along the road through the marshes. 'Yes, you do,' he said. 'She's a Bacchante, like the late Augusta …'

It was Poppaea's turn to snort, and she put Ulpia Marcia to shame.

'… like … others,' Calidus was careful not to look at Flavia or Paula, 'who use the dark arts.'

'Bacchantes,' Numidius frowned, then grinned in toothless recollection. 'There's a word I haven't heard for years. Quite a night for revelations, isn't it?'

'Shut up, old man!' Julia hissed, on her feet again. 'Haven't you said enough for one night?'

'He may have,' Calidus said, 'but I haven't. Let me entertain you, ladies and gentlemen, with a little story. It has taken me a while to piece it together, but I think I have it now.'

Quintus reached up and took Julia's arm and pulled her gently back onto her couch.

'There was once a girl,' Calidus began, 'a wild child, if memory serves. A child I fell in love with when I was only a child myself.' He felt Paula tense slightly beside him. 'The girl fell into bad ways. She joined a cult, a cult that had come to use murder as its chief purpose. The dancing, the fox skins, the shrine of Bacchus, all that was on the surface. Underneath, the cult had become subverted. It had become a cult of killers. Locusta taught you, Julia; taught you how to poison people.'

'This is preposterous,' Julia said. 'Tell him, Fabius.'

But Fabius Quintus said nothing, his handsome face as still as something painted on a wall.

'At the Villa Gellius,' Calidus spoke to him for the first time, 'you were furious with Nerva, weren't you, tribune? Why was that?'

'I told you,' the Praetorian said. 'He insulted Julia.'

'But it was *why* he insulted her that mattered to Julia, wasn't it? When had you confronted him?' he asked her. 'Was it that night or before? When did you remind him who you were? That, old man as he was, he had to make provision for you in his will.'

'As a point of law,' Varro said, 'he didn't actually have to …' and his voice tailed away as they all stared at him. Even in the Curia, he'd never seen an opposition so hostile.

'Julia wasn't interested in the law, were you, Julia?' Calidus asked. 'Just revenge. In this little story of mine, when Nerva rejected you, no doubt quoting the law that Varro is talking about, you wanted to lash out, didn't you? You weren't going to get a bronze denarius from the Nerva estate, so you decided to put an end to the old man.'

'That's right!' Julia screamed, slamming down the cup she'd been cradling for the last few minutes. 'Yes, Calidus, smart-arse, you're absolutely right.' She looked around the table; everyone's face had the same expression of stunned amazement. Even Ulpia Marcia was lost for words, an event that was rarer than lions whelping in the streets. 'Look at you,' she snarled. 'You bunch of hypocrites. You crawling senators, patting each other on the back and treating your slaves like shit. And you, their bossy, prissy wives, only where you are because of your men.'

Virinia Metella's lip quivered. That was just so *unfair*.

She ignored Fabius entirely. 'You, Flavia. You were of our sisterhood once, weren't you? A Bacchante. But you didn't know I was, did you? And you didn't know how your husband was sowing his seed in any old receptacle along the way. Yes,' she was looking at Calidus again, 'yes, I killed Nerva. And I'm glad I did. He had it coming.'

'How long did you know?' Flavia asked. 'Who told you?'

Julia sneered. 'I don't know why you ask that,' she said. 'If this old fool,' she tossed her head at Septimus Numidius, 'knows, then surely all Rome must know. He rambles in his cups to any girl desperate enough to let him squeeze her tits.'

The old ex-senator looked outraged, hitched his toga on his shoulders and generally sat on his dignity.

'Yes, yes, we all know about you and your sad little habits,' Julia said. 'And so that's how I found out about the inheritance.' Numidius had the grace to look a little crestfallen. 'You recognised me tonight, didn't you, you horrible old man, but not a year or so ago when you had one hand down my stola and the other …'

Virinia Metella passed out with a well-bred little shriek. Her husband absently fanned her with the edge of his toga.

Calidus felt Paula shift again at his side. He needed to move this on, if only for Mater Flavia's sake. 'What about Lepidus?' he asked.

'Ah,' Julia half-smiled. 'That was a mistake.'

Calidus nodded. 'Your target there was the emperor, wasn't it? Except that he steals other people's wine like he steals their wives.' He glanced at Poppaea, whose smile was frozen on her lips. 'He grabbed Lepidus' glass and left the vice-prefect his as the only alternative with which to drink a toast.'

'You absolute bitch, Julia,' Poppaea sneered.

'It takes one to know one, whore!' Julia snapped. 'Hypocrite doesn't begin to describe you all,' she said. 'You're all sitting here, so high and mighty, pointing a finger at me, when there's a far guiltier woman in this very room.' She pointed at Poppaea and pitched her voice a note or two higher. 'Kill her for me, Cuddles, kill her.' It was a very good Poppaea impression and would have got a round of spontaneous applause in any other setting. 'I could never be happy with a mother-in-law like that.' Her own voice returned, bitter, harsh. 'I don't know who actually killed the Augusta, but you orchestrated it, you and that snivelling madman who wears the purple. Look at her, all of you. She's wearing Agrippina's bracelet, the snake that kept her and Nero safe for all those years.' There were tears in her eyes. 'I loved that woman,' she said. 'The leader of our order, the empress of our rites.' She looked across at Flavia. 'I loved her as much as I once loved you, Mater Flavia,' she said, the tears trickling down both cheeks.

There was a silence. Then someone clapped, slowly, with a perceptible pause between each sound. All eyes turned to Poppaea. 'Very good, Calidus,' she said. 'Marvellous entertainment. And all for free, too – quite remarkable. The question arises, though, doesn't it – what are we to do with her?'

Eyes swivelled left and right. No one wanted to be the one to take up this baton and run with it, unless it was far and fast and without looking behind.

'The magistrates.' Glabrio spoke for the first time. 'Hand her over to the law. Surely, we don't have any choice.'

'The law is an ass, senator,' Poppaea said, dismissing it. 'I favour the Gemonia steps.'

'No,' Quintus spoke up. 'That's not going to happen.' He had a restraining arm around Julia's waist but whether to hold her back or to keep her safe, probably not even the man himself knew for sure.

'Perhaps,' Ulpia Marcia mused, 'something tasteful in the arena.'

There were groans of disapproval all round, not least from Glabrio, not caring now what price he would have to pay later. 'Exile,' he said. That she was wicked was clear, mad almost certainly, but he never could resist a pretty face.

'Standard practice,' Varro concurred, nodding wisely, wishing he had said it first.

'Not for murder, surely?' Maxentius was having none of it. And besides, Livia had never really liked her.

'Exile's too good for her,' Ulpia said, silently furious that not only had

Glabrio spoken without checking with her first but that people appeared to be actually *listening* to the man.

'Calidus,' Flavia said, turning to him. 'You are sitting there in the place of Gaius Lucius Nerva. You have tracked down his murderer. The choice is yours. What shall be done?'

Calidus looked at the woman he had always looked on as his mother; the woman who, in other circumstances, another alignment of the planets, could have *been* his mother. He looked at Paula, her face a mask of pain. She, too, had been a Bacchante, a sister under the skin, and that sisterhood had killed an old man she had always looked on as a father too.

He stood up and raised his wine cup in time-honoured tradition. 'Ladies and gentlemen,' he said. 'In the matter of the murder of the late Gaius Lucius Nerva, I hereby exile his killer, Julia Eusabia, to the furthest part of the empire. She will go to Britannia ...'

An involuntary sob broke from the throat of Virinia Metella, whose little boy was serving with the legions there. She was still feeling a little dizzy from her faint, and her husband rather brusquely shoved her head between her knees.

'... unable to return on pain of death.'

'Shouldn't we debate this?' Varro asked.

'Shut up, Varro!' Glabrio ordered, and the great debater fell silent.

Only Fabius Quintus saw it, a movement so fast and so subtle that no one else was aware. Paula's hand brushed quickly over Julia's cup on the table beside her and then pulled back, as fast as a dragonfly over a ruby pond. Julia was already standing, and the others joined her, raising their cups too.

'On pain of death, Julia?' Calidus had to hear her say it. It was tradition – what's fine, what's Roman.

She took the cup and turned to look at Fabius Quintus, silent by her side. Her eyes were dead; he looked into them, looking for just one spark of love, or loss, or sorrow. Then she turned back to the room. 'On pain of death,' she said.

Quintus held her arm and placed his hand over the cup. Again, he looked into her eyes and this time, saw just a distant star, far away, wink out and die. She smiled at him and shook her head. He took his hand away, and she drank deeply, emptying the contents and slamming down the cup.

'Well, that's that,' Poppaea said, sweeping past them all. 'Thank you, Flavia, for a most engaging evening. Calidus – could you unlock the doors? I …'

But she never finished her sentence. Julia clutched her throat, choking and gurgling. Quintus grabbed her and held her, but her convulsions were stronger than he was, and they ended up on the floor beyond the couches, Julia's body arching over his legs as he tried to cradle her. There were shrieks from the women, and Virinia Metella went down for the third time, ignored by everyone. Only Paula remained calm, crossing the room to where the prisoner lay dying, her eyes glazed, wine and blood oozing from the corner of her mouth. She had done the work of the Bacchantes too, tonight, the dark art that not only Locusta knew. And the tribune had let her do it.

Quintus looked up at her, hard, knowing.

'At least,' Paula said, 'she won't kill any more good men.' She looked at Calidus, still standing with Flavia across the room, 'And she won't cause others to be obsessed with her. Or with what she's done.' She turned on her heel and walked over to him. 'Is it over now, Cal?' she asked, tears in her eyes. 'Can old Gaius Lucius Nerva sleep peacefully in his tomb? Can you be Calidus again?'

He looked at her, wondering. He would always wonder. But he had hunted enough killers for one lifetime. It was time to move on, to bury the dead and wonder what future Rome had in the hands of Tiberius Claudius Drusus Germanicus Nero.

'Yes,' he said, in that room where a kind of justice had prevailed. 'Yes, I can.'

He looked across at old Numidius. *Someone*, Calidus had gambled, would know *something* sparked by reliving the night at Gellius' villa. He hadn't expected it to be the oldest man in the room and he hadn't expected that the evidence would point to Julia.

But this was Nero's Rome, a city crawling with the cruel, the licentious, the insane. Now, perhaps, at least at the Villa Nerva, there would be a time for peace.

Lightning Source UK Ltd.
Milton Keynes UK
UKHW040641201221
395966UK00001B/154

9 781839 011733